Beyond the Blonde

Beyond the Blonde

KATHLEEN FLYNN-HUI

WARNER BOOKS

NEW YORK   BOSTON

Warner Books

Time Warner Book Group
1271 Avenue of the Americas, New York, NY 10020
Visit our Web site at www.twbookmark.com.

Printed in the United States of America

First Edition: September 2005
10 9 8 7 6 5 4 3 2 1

Library of Congress Cataloging-in-Publication Data
Flynn-Hui, Kathleen.
    Beyond the blonde / Kathleen Flynn-Hui.— 1st ed.
      p. cm.
    Summary: "A young woman from rural New Hampshire is thrust into the world of New York's hottest hair salon, tending to socialites and actresses, models and moguls"—Provided by publisher.
    ISBN 0-446-50017-8
    1. Young women—Fiction. 2. New York (N.Y.)—Fiction. 3. Beauty operators—Fiction. I. Title.
    PS3606.L94B49 2005
    813'.6—dc22   2005010560

To Kao, Jade, and Cameron
You make my life worth living—I love you.

And Mom, thank you for always being there.

ACKNOWLEDGMENTS

I owe a debt of gratitude to the many people who have helped me along the path from beauty school to Madison Avenue.

To all the hairdressers, everywhere: You know we're the lucky ones!
Also, to Hubert, for keeping me blond.
To all my friends and colleagues for their support.
To my assistants who no longer need my assistance, thank you.
And to my current assistants—I could never get through a day without you.

To a very special friend and client, without whom this book would never have happened.

To Jennifer Rudolph Walsh, Sylvie Rabineau, Caryn Karmatz Rudy, and all the folks at Warner Books. You guys are a dream team.

And finally, to all of my clients, with whom I've shared laughs, tears, drinks, stories. Some I can tell—and some I'll never tell. It's just all been—and will always be—a great experience.

Beyond *the* Blonde

Why Pay Retail?
Or, A Hair-Raising Event

I would have to say that it all began—or, rather, it all began to end—the morning Faith Honeycomb passed out on the floor of the Salon Jean-Luc. Up until then it had been a busy day. As in *crazy* busy. I was thirty-four years old, but in nearly a decade as a senior colorist I had rarely seen the salon so completely insane. The frenzy was brought on by that crowning event in the New York City social season: the Pink and Purple Charity Ball. This particular ball spanned all age groups: Park Avenue dowagers bought their thousand-dollar tickets and invited their granddaughters, who took the afternoon off from Spence or Brearley or Dalton to get their hair done. Socialites arrived by chauffeured Mercedes sedans starting the moment the salon opened, and we were slightly understaffed because some of the stylists were out making house calls.

All up and down Fifth Avenue blow-dryers were being plugged into wall sockets and hair was being washed in bathroom sinks. Manicurists were spreading towels across laps and dipping bejeweled hands into bowls as telephones rang and little dogs scurried underfoot.

"Darling! Where are you?" Pause. "John Frieda? Really."

This "Really" would be a drawn-out sigh, a pity party for the poor dear who had to be ministered to in public.

"*Moi?* At home, darling. With the marvelous . . . What is your name, honey? Oh, never mind. A girl from Jean-Luc who is a *genius* with the blow-dry."

A house call from a junior stylist at Jean-Luc cost a minimum of five hundred dollars, and a senior stylist could run you a thousand. But some people will pay a lot for their privacy. Like, for example, if you've had a face lift, otherwise known as *having work done* or *taking a quick trip to Beverly Hills.* Some people will go to great lengths to make sure nobody sees the scars.

Anyway, back to poor Faith Honeycomb. What with all the ladies in for their preball primping, there was no indication—no *frisson* in the air (*frisson* being an expression that the ladies who frequented the salon loved to use, along with *chérie, pourquoi,* and *mon Dieu*)—that an ambulance would screech to the curb and a squad of EMS technicians with their equipment and squawking radios would invade the plush taupe-and-burgundy inner sanctum of Jean-Luc.

I was working on Mrs. H at my station. It was ten forty-five, and she was already my third head of the day: a double-process with a chestnut base and golden auburn highlights. Tiffany, my assistant, had wheeled a tray next to me, with tail combs and clips, cotton, extra gloves, and three pots of L'Oréal color, one of which I had a feeling was there by mistake, left over from Mrs. G's Scandinavian blond highlights.

"Tiff, could you check this?" I asked, pointing to the bowl

of thick white bleach that would—if I hadn't caught it—have turned Mrs. H into a punk rocker instead of the Park Avenue matron that she was. And that would have been a catastrophe.

Let me explain: There are all sorts of reasons why women pick one colorist over another. Some will go to you if you have the same kind of dog or because they like the way you look. Some will go only to a man, because they want to feel a man's hands on them. Then, of course, you have the editorial mongrels, who will go only to whoever is in this month's *Elle* or *Allure*. But no matter what brings them to you in the first place, they'll drop you cold if you're not a good colorist.

Which means no mistakes. Not ever. Brain surgeons are allowed more mistakes than hair colorists. Don't misunderstand me. I'm not saying that what I do is brain surgery or in any way important. Between you and me, it's just hair. But a certain kind of woman cares about her hair. A lot.

Anyway, that crisis was averted. Out of the corner of my eye, I watched Tiffany dump the bleach and mix Mrs. H's color. She had been out late the night before. It was the birthday of one of the assistants, and they had gone club hopping. I could see her hands shaking as she opened one of Mrs. H's foils. I made a mental note to talk to her. She was younger than me, and I could see all the pitfalls, the mess her life was going to be if she wasn't careful. Assistants came and assistants went. I mean, the pressure was on, and they made, like, *no* money. They lived on their tips, sometimes for years, hoping and praying that one day they'd hear that magic word: promotion. It was hard. All any of them dreamed of was one day having their name printed on a Jean-Luc announcement and placed by the vase of freesia by the front desk: *We are pleased to announce that* [insert name here] *has been promoted to junior stylist.* I should know. I had been one of those lowly assistants myself.

"Sorry, Georgia," Tiff whispered over Mrs. H's head. Not that Mrs. H would have noticed. She was deep into the latest issue of British *Vogue*. I peered over her shoulder and saw that she was reading about the new generation of skin creams.

"No problem," I said.

No, it wasn't easy being an assistant—especially being an assistant at Jean-Luc, the salon of the moment, the epicenter of beautification for all Manhattan women—or really all women of the tristate area. Come to think of it, geography was meaningless to the Jean-Luc customer—dozens of women flew to New York for the sole purpose of having Jean-Luc himself rake his elegant hands through their hair and pronounce: *This isn't working for me . . . it is too* [fill in the adjective] *fluffy. How you say . . . shaggy. You are a beautiful woman. Bee-you-tee-ful.* And with a blandishment of his famous scissors, a toss of his own long dark mane: *And now, we will create a new you . . . yes?*

I had three clients waiting on the banquette in their burgundy robes (burgundy for color, taupe for cuts and styling) and two others who had just checked in and were getting changed. Jean-Luc had instructed the front desk to book clients for me every fifteen minutes, and even by midmorning there was a bottleneck of waiting ladies. Ladies who weren't used to being kept waiting but waited nonetheless. Patiently. Sometimes for hours. Somewhere in the rules of etiquette it was written that one never, ever, got huffy with one's colorist or stylist. Doctors, lawyers, accountants, and stockbrokers could all be yelled at—and easily replaced—but we at Jean-Luc were golden. They *needed* us. Mrs. H's formula (and Mrs. P's, and Mrs. B's, and Ms. A's on the banquette) was my little secret, locked in my file box—a small metal box where every single client's formula was recorded on index cards. What each of them would have done for their formula! They would have gone six months without Botox. A year without self-tanner. *Please, Georgia,* they'd beg, *I'm going to be in Aspen all month. What will I do?* And part of me was tempted to give it to them. It didn't matter, really. I mean, I could write down their formula, but the minute they gave it to some Colorado hairdresser, it would just turn to shit. It was how the formula was applied that made all the difference.

I saw Mrs. P on the banquette check her gold Cartier watch. She definitely didn't have the primo appointment of the day. That would have been more like four o'clock. That way, there would have been plenty of time for all those beautifying-but-hair-mussing treatments: the Tracie Martyn electric current facial. A salt scrub at Bliss and then a massage from the divine Rebecca at Exhale Spa. And *then,* after the oils and the electric currents, the blow-dry.

Let me give you an idea of the perfect pre–charity ball day in the life of a Jean-Luc woman. For argument's sake, let's make her one of the youngish ones, who lives in a twelve-room apartment on East Seventy-something Street. First, she would require a very strong cup of espresso at Via Quadronno, the café on East Seventy-third that feels like a quick trip to Milan. This, of course, after dropping the children off at All Souls preschool or the 92nd Street Y. This drop-off is, in equal parts, guilt induced (the nanny does everything else for the rest of the day) and an important social networking opportunity. Where else do movie stars, wives of minimoguls, heiresses, and the occasional scruffy-but-successful artist dad all mingle together but in the halls of their children's school? After the espresso, back home for a two-hour private yoga session. A shower, hair left undone, then a quick dash to the shrink to discuss said guilt about neglecting children and the ongoing question: To Prozac or not to

Prozac? After the shrink, feeling that mental lightness unique to yoga, psychoanalysis, and an empty stomach, a quick stop at Barneys. Damage: three-hundred-dollar jeans, a six-hundred-dollar knitted poncho (so Bohemian!), and a pair of antique diamond earrings. Later, the guilt comes roaring back (will have to hide bill for earrings from husband), and she makes her way over to the Salon Jean-Luc. We are her church, her temple, the place where she will be undone, then done. Restored. Brought back to her perfect, radiant self.

Mrs. P was one of these. I called her "the Manhattan." I secretly classified all my clients this way. The Manhattan. The Greenwich. The Bedford. The Long Island. The New Jersey. Even the Boston and the California. But more on that later. I still had the back of Mrs. H's highlights to do, but I walked over to the banquette and paid quick respects to my waiting clients.

"Mrs. P!" Kiss, kiss. As if I had only that moment spotted her there. "Great lip color."

Mrs. P smiled delightedly. "Chanel," she said. "I just picked it up at Barneys." Then she held up a pale green leather bag with the small silver Prada triangle at its center.

"I just picked this up, too, to go with my suit," she whispered conspiratorially. "What do you think, Georgia?"

Seven hundred and ninety-five dollars, was what I was thinking. I couldn't imagine spending that kind of money on a bag, but then I hadn't paid retail in years. I can tell you the exact moment that I realized I didn't have to. It was back when I was a junior colorist at Jean-Luc and I had no money, but still I needed some nice stuff to wear. Clients respect you more if you have a pretty ring on or a good pair of shoes. It makes them feel more like you're one of them. So I was on the seventh floor of Barneys, standing on line, waiting to pay for a sweater—a little cashmere cardigan in a bright tangerine that would look

6

good peeking out from under my white smock. And all of a sudden, someone snatched the sweater out of my arms. I whirled around, and there was Kathryn, one of the other junior stylists.

"What are you doing?" she very nearly hissed.

"Um . . . buying a sweater?" I said, taking it back from her.

She pulled it away from me again. "We don't pay retail," she said. She checked the label on the sweater. It was by an up-and-coming designer. Not as big as Calvin or Ralph, and the sweater wasn't even that expensive.

"She's a client," Kathryn said about the designer. She folded the sweater and put it on the counter. "Let's go."

Back at the salon, I got my first lesson in the art and science of graciously accepting gifts from clients. Because they *wanted* to shower us with gifts. They really did. I watched and listened as Kathryn called the designer client and told her how much we had loved the little tangerine cardigan. Do I need to tell you what happened? You think the client sent over the sweater the next day, right? Wrong. She sent over two shoppings bags—one for me, one for Kathryn—full of sweaters. One in every single color. I'll tell you, it was a revelation.

Mrs. P was still waiting for my verdict on her brand-new Prada bag. It *was* a cute bag. I made a mental note to call my client at Prada.

"Perfect," I said. "I'll be with you in a few minutes."

Now, I know I mentioned the Manhattan a while back, and by this I do not mean the delicious cocktail, though often the Manhattan client can be equally tart, bracing, and sometimes even a bit bitter. But the Manhattan (which actually is split into two broad categories) is far from the only type of client who sits in my chair every day. I thought it might be helpful if I created a road map, a glossary if you will, of the various types of Jean-Luc women.

1. *The Manhattan (socialite):* I believe I covered her fairly extensively earlier. But oh, let me add this. I hate to generalize, but she tends to be a lousy tipper. In my experience, people who have never had to make their own money don't really think about how other people make theirs.

2. *The Manhattan (working woman):* Zips into the salon while on cell phone. Cell phone does not leave ear, even when head is in sink. Orders lunch from the Viand coffee shop on Madison and eats it while multitasking: hair, manicure, pedicure, business call. Only for her every-six-weeks-like-clockwork eyebrow wax does she close her eyes and stay still. This, the eyebrow wax, is the closest thing to a Zen moment that she ever has. The MWW is often married to (or divorced from) an equally type-A executive, whom she drags in on Saturday mornings for his haircut, manicure, and, for those unfortunately hairy ones—*eeeew alert!*—back wax. Kids? Rarely. Or you'd never know it. One of my MWW mother clients has shown me photographs of the house she just purchased in Litchfield County, but not of her children. Needless to say, the MWWs are fantastic tippers.

3. *The Bedford:* Think horses and everything that goes along with them. Rolling hills and stone walls, houses with names. These ladies don't have just street addresses. No. They have stationery printed with the names and sometimes elegant, lightly etched drawings of their homes: *Longmeadow Manor. Hilly*

Knoll Farm. The Bedford wears haute couture riding clothes when she drives into the city in her car (Range Rover, black) to have her hair done. These, of course, are not the clothes she'd actually ride in: a cashmere sweater set, pearl earrings, suede jodhpurs by Ralph. In the circles the Bedford runs (or rather rides) in, Ralph means only one man—he of the polo pony empire. Ralph actually has a home in Bedford, which makes the whole thing even more authentic. The Bedford wants to leave the salon looking as though she's had nothing done. Hair color must be beyond subtle. She must look like she's been born with it. Actually, she often brings in photos of her children, or even the children themselves, and asks me to copy their color exactly. Usually she wears no makeup. She has very good bones and a lanky figure from all that riding. You will never hear her use a swear word. She likes to say *gosh darn,* and *I'll be,* and *heavens to Betsy.* The Bedford is a reasonably good tipper, always leaving exactly twenty percent.

4. *The Greenwich:* Hard to believe, really, that Greenwich and Bedford are next to each other, geographically speaking. Because the Greenwich couldn't be more different from the Bedford and still be a rich white woman. Range Rover? No. Mercedes, yes, yes, yes. Preferably the 500-something sedan, but if the Greenwich has a large number of kids—often she has three, four, even five—the Hummer becomes the vehicle of choice. There's nothing quite like seeing the Greenwich, her makeup and hair already perfect before she enters the salon, stuck circling the block on Fifth Avenue because no parking garage wants to take her Hummer. I mean, she looks like a little kid pretending to drive her parents' car. I'd have to say that the Greenwich has the best fashion sense of all the suburban clients. In fact, she's so terrified of appearing suburban—she,

who left the city after her second kid was born and you just couldn't find anything decent for under three million—that she spends hours every day scouring the Barneys and Bergdorf catalogs, surfing the Internet for fashion Web sites like Net-a-Porter or Scoop.com, reading *W* and *Vogue* cover to cover, examining ads, dog-earing pages of interest, and calling her personal shopper so that she'll be sure to have just that season's Balenciaga bag or the hottest pair of designer jeans. She doesn't want to lose track. Seven for all Mankind is *so* over. Diesels aren't far behind. Which to acquire? Her California Closets are ready and waiting. Notify? Rogan? Each month *Vogue* anoints a new favorite. It's impossible to keep up, but still the Greenwich tries. Oh, how she tries! Her hair is perfection. Highlights every eight weeks, with root touch-ups in between. Layers or no layers, depending on what Jennifer Aniston is doing. Earth-toned makeup from Bobbi Brown in shades like brick, sand, and stone. She wears a huge men's chronograph on her skinny wrist and checks the time religiously, because she has to be home in time for pickup at her kids' schools. I guess if you took the MWW, but removed the big career and built her a faux Tudor mansion with a cathedral ceiling in the entranceway and huge leather sofas in the surround sound media room, you'd pretty much be left with the Greenwich. And as a tipper? Hmm. I don't like to bad-mouth my clients. *But,* I'd have to say she's a little worse than average. Sometimes she's in such a rush to beat the traffic that she just forgets.

5. *The Five Towns:* You'll know a lot of what you need to know about the client from Long Island if you understand that she lives in one of the five towns commonly known as, well, either "the five towns" or "the south shore": Lawrence, Cedarhurst, Inwood, Hewlett, and Woodmere. The FT is a lit-

tle . . . flashier than her northern Westchester and Connecticut counterparts. She favors the bling-bling designers, and in fact she uses the term *bling-bling* in regular conversation. As in, *I'm gonna take me to Fred Leighton later on and get me a little bling-bling.* Gucci, Vuitton, and Dolce & Gabbana are her gods. And she prefers these designers with their labels facing outward, if you know what I mean. She is not about subtle. It would not be unreasonable to expect the Five Towns to show up at the salon (her husband's driver waiting downstairs in their Lincoln Navigator, the windows tinted black) wearing half the alphabet on her back. A D&G gold belt buckle, the candy-colored bag embossed with dozens of LVs, loafers festooned with interlocking Gs. Don't get me wrong, though. The FT is a nice lady, and she knows exactly who she is. Her role model, her idol to end all idols, is—depending on her age—either Madonna or Britney Spears. And she wants *color.* She's not interested in natural. She's a lot of fun, this client, because she always wants to try something new. *Make me red this time, darling.* And she's almost never unhappy with the results. She has a heart of gold, the FT. A lot of clients, they sit in my chair month after month, year after year, and never ask me one single question. The FT knows about my whole life, and my assistant's life, and the shampoo lady's life. She may be rich as all get-out, but she's not a snob, and she remembers where she came from, which is usually the very tip of Long Island—the wrong tip, that is to say, Queens. And speaking of tips, she's the best, even better than the MWW.

6. *The Short Hills:* Think the New Jersey version of the Greenwich. In other words, the Greenwich with a serious inferiority complex, since it's just about impossible to live in New Jersey and not feel just a teensy bit bad about it. And to make up for feeling bad about it, and to avoid resentment of her hus-

band (whose Wall Street commute and only average-by-Wall-Street-standards bonus means a perfectly nice Colonial in Short Hills rather than, say, a mansion in Greenwich or a duplex on Park Avenue), she requires the best of everything, as dictated by that amazing place, Mecca for all Jean-Luc clients who reside in the state of New Jersey: the Short Hills Mall. It is there, at the mall, that the SH develops her aesthetic sensibility. Tiffany for her 4.2-carat diamond solitaire—upgraded from the 2.1-carat diamond that her husband, then a junior trader, had given her as an engagement ring. Cartier for the watch. And all those cute little departments at Neiman Marcus for everything else. Her style could be described as suburban chic, which, contrary to popular opinion, is not an oxymoron. Because unlike the Greenwich, she isn't trying to look as though she lives in the city. She wears head-to-toe Juicy Couture velour sweat suits and JP Tod's driving loafers, the ones with all the small rubber nubs in the soles. She will not be seen without her status handbag, also by Tod's. Her most fun accessory, though, is her cell phone, with all the latest bells and whistles, encrusted with pink rhinestones. The SH is fussy about her hair. After all, she could be getting it done closer to home—there's a perfectly decent place in Millburn—but her visits to Jean-Luc are part of her quest for the best of everything. And so, having driven her BMW convertible all the way into town, she wants exactly the highlights on the magazine pages that she unfolds from her purse. Before I even look at the clippings, I can almost always guess. For blondes, it's Meg Ryan or, lately, Jessica Simpson. For brunettes, it's Jennifer Aniston or, occasionally, Jennifer Lopez. Sometimes I have to laugh, because the celebrity whose hair they're showing me and asking me to copy is someone who has been seeing me forever. *Do you think you can do this?* the SH will ask. And I'll nod. I think I can.

7. *The Beverly Hills:* Oh, what a difference a coast makes! The BH has her choice of fabulous salons to pick from, just a fifteen-minute drive down Rodeo or Burton Way. She has Laurent D, Frederic Fekkai, even old José Eber is still around somewhere. Why, you might ask, would she fly all the way to New York to have her hair done at Jean-Luc? Because she *can,* darling. Because the grass is always greener and the blonde is always blonder. Because New York, to people who live in L.A., is the height of sophistication. I can always spot a BH a mile away. She's gorgeous, of course. Even the ones who aren't famous look as if they should be. And she's dressed in Fred Segal fabulousness—a kind of blend of faded denim, diamonds, bits of turquoise, and a perfectly cut, buttery shirt of some kind, showing off a glowing, not-too-brown tan. Those Beach Boys knew what they were singing about, I'll tell you. A California Girl stops traffic on Madison Avenue. I've seen it happen over and over again. But—not to diss my professional colleagues on the West Coast, and truly I'm not talking about anyone in particular—their hair is a fucking mess. The BH often comes to me with hair the color and texture of straw from being so overprocessed. *Honey, you've got so many chemicals in your hair, I'm surprised you didn't set off alarms at the airport,* I'll tell her. I mean, whoever decided that platinum blond was the answer to all that ails the BH woman? I spend hours doing corrective color. Weaving in bits of buttery highlights, hints of dark blond, giving them back the color they ought to have after hanging out on Malibu beach. Some of them are nervous when they come to see me, because their next stop is Letterman or a crack-of-dawn call for the *Today* show. The young starlets sit in my chair, quivering: This appearance is a make-or-break for them. At least I can give them great hair. It's amazing what great hair can do for a panic attack. Oh, and in terms of tipping? I

know this is going to seem unfair, but we don't charge a lot of the BHs—whether they're full-fledged stars or stars in the making. Even the ones who are just starting out get a discount. And they don't tip. Not a penny. Not at all. They feel entitled to be comped—after all, it's publicity that money can't buy when some magazine asks them who does their hair and they say, *Georgia at Jean-Luc in New York*—so who can blame them?

A fine mist of styling products and water being blown off damp hair hovered like a fog over the salon floor. The night of the Pink and Purple Ball happened to be a Tuesday—one of our busiest days, even in a normal week. Saturdays we got a lot of bridge-and-tunnel, but Tuesdays were the big days for those in the know and friends of those in the know. (If Thursday had, long ago, become the new Saturday, now Tuesday was the new Thursday.) Faith Honeycomb was at her usual station, next to the window, coloring the roots of an actress I recognized but couldn't quite place. Dark hair, angular cheekbones, a strong jaw I had seen on television, but where? Most of the actresses went to Faith. There were even some who flew in monthly from the West Coast or sent her a first-class plane ticket. She was the doyenne of hair colorists, the first who had actually become famous herself. Faith was somewhere north of sixty—no one knew for sure—and her own hair had never seen a chemical. It was snow white and cut into a sharp, shoulder-length bob. Her blue eyes flashed, and her head cocked to one side like a watchdog's as she listened to her actress-client.

On the other side of the salon, by the window, I saw T, the hot-shot publicist and a perfect example of an MWW, in Jean-Luc's chair. He stood behind her, his hands resting gently on her shoulders, dark eyes boring into hers in the mirror as she talked rapidly, gesturing to her raven pageboy. I wondered what they could possibly be talking about, given that T hadn't changed her hair in ten years. All women—even T—seemed to shrink as they sat in our chairs. The robes, the small towels around their necks, their sleek, wet heads, were great equalizers. Devoid of all their trappings (well, *most* of their trappings—the watches, rings, and handbags still remained), they lost their shine. But then, after their highlights, haircuts, waxing, blowouts, or updos, after they put on their elegant clothes once again, they came back to life: buffed, polished, confident, and ready to tackle the world.

"Fifteen minutes under the lamps," I said to Tiffany, turning Mrs. H over to her.

"It won't be too light, will it?" asked Mrs. H as she rolled up the British *Vogue* (the salon's copy) and stuffed it into her oversize handbag.

"Would I make you too light?"

She started to answer, *Of course not,* but I had already turned to Mrs. P. It was a rhetorical question, after all.

I had just asked Tiffany for a tube of 6 and a half of 6.1 when I heard the crash behind me.

"Oh, my *God!*" someone screamed.

I wheeled around just in time to see Faith Honeycomb crumple like a piece of discarded tissue to the floor, her sleek white bob fanning around her.

"Somebody do something!" Sweetie shouted. Sweetie was the salon's head receptionist, whose job over the years had morphed into being Faith Honeycomb's personal assistant. Sweetie knelt next to Faith, his long auburn curls hanging and his dress hiked up above his knees—knees that were truly the only giveaway that Sweetie was a man.

"Faith! Honey! Faith, can you hear me? Blink or something. Open your eyes!"

The salon had grown silent, the din of blow-dryers suddenly quiet. Horrible French pop music piped through the sound system. I heard someone in the next station talking to 911.

In the distance, through the thick double windows of the salon, an ambulance wailed. Was it coming for Faith, so soon? I pressed my face against the glass and peered down at Fifty-seventh Street. An ambulance roared by the entrance to our building and kept going. I wanted to run downstairs in my white smock and flag it, make it stop like a taxi.

All around me there was a steady murmur of voices. *Heart attack,* I heard someone say. *Stroke. Seizure. Allergy. Shock.* I looked down at Faith, who appeared to be sleeping peacefully on the floor, her lips curled up into a rare, small smile.

"Georgia?" The unmistakable accent, the fingers brushing my shoulders. Jean-Luc had suddenly appeared behind me. "You will need to . . . *handle* . . . Faith's clients," he whispered, gesturing to several women seated on Faith's special banquette. They all had a similar expression on their faces, and I tried to figure out what it was. Worried? No, that wasn't it. Disturbed? Agitated? No, and no. Then finally—as the EMS technicians burst through the doors of Jean-Luc and transferred Faith to a stretcher—I realized what it was: They were put out. It was, after all, the night of the Pink and Purple Ball.

"Faith! Darling! I'm coming with you," Sweetie wailed. Mascara was running down his cheeks in great black rivulets.

"I'm sorry . . . ma'am," said one of the technicians, looking mildly confused by the appellation. "No one's allowed in the ambulance."

"I don't think you understand," Sweetie said, drawing himself up to his full, towering height. "This is *Faith Honeycomb*." His glossy lips quivered over her name.

"I don't care if it's Jennifer fucking Lopez," snapped the technician. Sweetie was blocking their way. "Those are the rules. Now *move!*"

They carried Faith past Jean-Luc's station and through the reception area, nearly toppling the enormous vase of freesia and baby roses that was placed there each morning. Sweetie followed them, wailing like a widow in a funeral cortege. The salon doors swung silently shut behind them, and slowly the usual sounds resumed—sputtering at first, then catching like a car's engine, until within minutes the salon was back to its usual speed and roar.

Mrs. P looked at me in the mirror as I stood behind her, trying to breathe.

"Georgia?" she asked, wiping a nonexistent bit of smudge from beneath her eye. "My goodness. *That* was exciting." She said it in the droll, flat way that only a woman born in Darien and educated at Miss Porter's can get away with. As if life itself were ironic. Especially when it's happening to somebody else.

My fingers tightened around the handle of my tail comb, which I wanted to jab into her hard pink scalp. I looked around me as people resumed what they had been doing before Faith Honeycomb had had the poor taste to crash into the French tile floor. Two assistants were looking at a page from *Hampton's* magazine and giggling. T had moved from Jean-Luc's chair to the manicure station, her hair damp, freshly polished fingernails gingerly holding her cell phone to her ear. The woman in the seat in Faith's station—the one Faith had just started to work on—calmly ordered a seafood salad and iced tea from Nello's. She caught my eye and beckoned me over to her. I didn't know her name, but I had seen her around the salon. She was one of the ladies we called the OWs—Old WASPs—dressed in threadbare cashmere and baggy khakis, and possessor of one of the few decent face lifts around. She reminded me a tiny bit of my own mother, though I wasn't sure why. Lord knows it wasn't her social status. Her eyes crinkled in a way that seemed kind, and I bent toward her.

"I just want to remind you, sweetheart, that Faith always uses a gloss."

I took a few steps back. I didn't trust myself to speak, much less douse this woman's head in chemicals. I thought of poor Faith Honeycomb, alone in the back of an ambulance racing through the streets of Manhattan. Faith, with her meticulous *maquillage* and precision-cut hair, awakening (if indeed she were to awaken) in the dingy, frightening corridors of a city hospital. She wasn't married and had never had kids. We at the salon were the closest thing to a family that she had.

That will never be me.

"Georgia?" Mrs. P sounded impatient.

That will never, never, never be me.

I turned back to her, forcing myself to smile. "Yes, Mrs. P?"

"Not to rush you, darling. But I have a one o'clock appointment with the caterer for Kristen's wedding."

A Colorist's Humble Roots
(Get It?)

Sometimes in the middle of a busy day, when clients are sitting along the banquette waiting for me, and others are on the phone trying to book appointments months in advance, when socialites are showering me with gifts, when Hollywood agents are begging me for an hour of my time or are willing to fly me to Los Angeles first class, I just need to stop for a minute and remember who I really am. I take a few deep breaths just to check and make sure I'm the same person I always was—a girl who grew up dirt poor in Weekeepeemie, New Hampshire. I mean, my main ambition in life was to go to beauty school and get a job somewhere coloring women's hair.

Whenever I look at anybody in New York City, I always wonder where they really come from. Because nobody actually comes from New York. Think about it. How many real New Yorkers do you know? I make a game out of it, trying to find the inner hick in all the cool people walking up Madison Avenue or across Prince Street in SoHo. That skinny guy in old Levi's and a faded black T-shirt that looks old but I know cost him eighty-five dollars at the Helmut Lang store? I'd say Maryland. He grew up in Maryland, in a three-bedroom split-level. And that girl with the nose ring and lipstick the color of dried blood, dressed in head-to-toe black leather? She's got the suburbs written all over her. New Jersey, maybe. Or outside Philly. Her dad's probably a dermatologist or something, and her mom checks in ten times a day to make sure she hasn't been mugged. I don't know why, but I'm usually right about these things. It comes from a lot of years of people sitting in my chair and telling me their life stories. They can't help it. They tell me things they don't even tell their shrinks. I'm like the shrink of hair. I spend more time with my clients than shrinks do, and I can tell you this: When my clients leave me, they actually feel better.

From the time I was a little girl, I wanted to be a colorist. Back in Weekeepeemie, my mother had a hair salon—we called it a beauty parlor—that women came to from miles and miles away. Have you ever noticed the way the names of beauty parlors change the minute you get outside a major city? Here are a few of my personal favorites:

1. Hair to Stay
2. Shear Genius
3. The Mane Event
4. Dis-Tressed

I mean, what do puns and hair have in common? This is not a trick question. The answer is, nothing. So my mother's shop was just called Doreen's. Plain, simple, honest. Just like my mother. And that's where the women of Weekeepeemie went when they were looking for a little lift. I grew up thinking of the weekly beauty parlor appointment as a necessity. The visit to the grocery store or the dentist could wait. In fact, some of the ladies who frequented my mother's place had few, if any, of their own teeth, but their hair was perfect: teased and sprayed until it would have taken a hurricane to mess it up.

I was under my mother's feet in a bassinet that caught the snippings of wet hair on the floor of Doreen's before it was even, in fact, called Doreen's. It was owned by an old lady, Mabel Smith, who died when I was eleven, and her estate sold the beauty parlor to my mother for a fair price. One of the first things my mother did once she had signed the papers at the bank was to bring home a long piece of plywood, which she, my sister, Melodie, and I painted white.

"What should we call it?" my mother asked us.

"How about *Folly*?" asked Melodie.

We looked at her blankly.

"You know, for *follicle,*" she said, cracking up, her high voice in a loud hiccup.

"What's follicle?" I asked.

Melodie was a year younger than me but had already been placed out of fifth grade and was reading and doing math on a high school level.

"Never mind, Georgia," my mother said. She was still young and pretty then, her long dirty-blond hair caught in a ponytail, her face free of makeup.

"What would Dad think?" Melodie asked, her eyes glinting the way they did when she was saying something she knew she wasn't supposed to say.

"Well, it doesn't really matter what your father would think," my mother said softly. "Since it isn't any of his business."

"I know," I said quickly, speaking in the hopes of avoiding the sad, lost look that often came over my mother when one of us mentioned our father. He had walked out when I was eight and Mel was seven, and he hardly bothered to send us any money. Once, I had called him a bastard, and Doreen slapped me. *Your father may have left us,* she said angrily, *but that doesn't give you the right to talk like nobody raised you right.* Saying somebody wasn't raised right was the worst thing my mother could say about anybody. I shut up after that and pretty much never mentioned my father again.

"Let's name the salon after you!" I said, hoping to cheer my mother up.

"Oh, I don't know . . ." She trailed off.

"Everybody only comes there to see you, anyway," I said.

"Doreen's Beauty Parlor." My mother tried it on for size.

"Doreen's Hair Emporium," said Melodie.

"How about just 'Doreen's'?" I asked.

Our mother paused and thought about it for a minute. Then her face broke into the first grin I had seen in ages. "How *about* 'Doreen's'?" she said, spreading her arms wide. "Our motto is: 'We curl up and dye for you.'"

We looked at her blankly.

"Get it?" she said. "We *curl* up and—"

"We got it," Mel said solemnly.

"We just hope you don't try that one out on anyone else," I said.

It was one of the rare times that my sister and I were in complete agreement.

We—my mother, sister, and I—set to work with the white-painted plywood, hot pink paint, and stencils she had bought from a catalog. The three of us worked for hours, getting it just right, and when we had finished we added a small flowering vine around the D for Doreen. It was the happiest I could re-member any of us being since the bastard had left.

During the years my mother was getting her business off the ground, she did all her experimenting on me, since Melodie wouldn't let her go near her. I started out with long white-blond hair almost to my waist, but through my high school years I modeled all the haircuts of the moment. The Dorothy Hamill—a wedge that fell like a perfectly inverted triangle. The Toni Tennille—an unfortunate, curled-under bob with curled-under bangs. And finally, the greatest of them all: the Farrah. My junior year in high school, I had big fluffy layers and wings, enhanced by the Farrah Fawcett shampoo that I made my mother buy me at the drugstore.

"How can you let her do that to you?" Melodie asked me sometimes. "You look like a freak."

"I like it," I'd say, stung. I fought the urge to retaliate, to tell my sister that she was the one who was a freak. It was too close to the truth. She had brown hair that never saw a comb and Coke-bottle glasses with the ugliest frames you could buy north of Boston. I may have looked a little different by Wee-keepeemie standards, but I knew if I lived in New York or Los Angeles, I'd fit right in.

Anyway, I didn't tell Melodie that I was never happier than when I was being worked on by my mother. It didn't really mat-ter what she did to my hair. What mattered was her attention. I loved to sit in her chair, watching her squint and assess me, cocking her head to the side. Sometimes she cut my hair, other times she did highlights. At a time when every other beauty parlor was using those caps with holes in them to do color, my mother used foils. She called it "angel tipping"—taking small sections of my already blond hair and artfully placing bits of golden color.

My mother charged twenty dollars for a wash and style, twenty-five dollars for a haircut, and sixty dollars for color—steep prices for her clients—but even when she raised her rates, people kept coming. She worked from eight in the morning until nine at night, accommodating the ladies who worked in the factories and mills nearby. At one point she hired a manicurist, but that poor woman sat there at her little table, alone with her dozens of bottles of candy-colored polish. It seemed that fine-looking fingernails were not a priority, not when those same fingers would be snapping heads onto the necks of dolls on an assembly line.

Everybody always wanted Doreen—Doreen and only Doreen. It wasn't so much that my mother was good at what she did, though certainly she was. She had "the touch." I understood this from early on: You could be a perfectly okay colorist, but if you didn't know how to touch people, you were out of business. My mother had hands that made you feel things. Sympathetic hands that made you want to tell her your life story. So in a town with no psychologists or psychiatrists, no head shrinkers at all, Doreen's was the place people went to get a load off their minds.

Sometimes, when my mother came home at night, I could tell that she was sinking under the weight of an entire town's secrets and problems. Judy Johnston's daughter, pregnant at fifteen. Marcie Appleby's husband's exploratory surgery. Doreen had pale blue shadows under her eyes, and her skin was so thin, so translucent, that I could see the threads of delicate veins in her temples and along her jaw.

Melodie and I would have been home from school for hours—we were in high school by then—and most nights I made us dinner, keeping my mother's dish warm in the oven until she got home. Our kitchen was my favorite room in the house. It had a checkered Formica floor, and we had a big old farm table that we'd found at a garage sale and painted sky blue. No matter how broke we were, Doreen always made sure there was a bowl of fresh fruit on the table. Canned fruit was what people who weren't raised right ate.

My mother came in the door smelling so sweet that it stung the insides of my nostrils.

"Poor Mrs. McCormick," she said, shaking out her pony-tail, her hair spilling over her shoulders in a blond cascade.

"What's wrong with Mrs. McCormick?" I asked, even though I knew better. My mother never gossiped.

She sighed, shrugged off her coat, then took her supper from the oven. "Some people have it rough, Georgia-pie," she said to me. It was one of my mother's great gifts that she didn't see her own life as rough. Despite the fact that she was a single mother raising her two kids without any help, she saw herself as blessed.

"Where's your sister?" she asked.

I pointed to the ceiling. "Upstairs, finishing her home-work," I said, though in all likelihood it had taken Melodie ten minutes to breeze through geometry problems that she could have solved when she was eight. I knew my mother worried about Melodie. She was too smart for her own good—*scary* smart. Where had all those brains come from? It seemed to me that with her head stuffed so full of brain cells, she had no room for the other stuff—the stuff that was all-important in high school. Melodie had no friends, and she didn't seem to care. She spent all her free time in the library or in her room with the door shut, reading books that I didn't understand.

My reading material involved pictures. Each week I de-voured the previous week's copy of *People* that my mother brought home from the salon. I studied celebrities, paying particular attention to the young Hollywood starlets: what they wore, how they put on their makeup, the precise cut and color of their hair. My favorite book was by the socialite Cornelia Guest. *The Debutante's Guide to Life* was my bible. I had seen a picture of Cornelia Guest dancing the night away at Studio 54 with Sylvester Stallone. Even though I had never been to New York, I just knew that those New York City girls who grew up in palaces on Fifth Avenue had never been worried for a single second their whole lives. All they thought about was where to have lunch or whether to paint their toenails pale pink or dark red. It was all about money. Money was the key to opening all sorts of magic doors. I didn't know what these doors looked like, or what it would feel like to walk through them, but I knew they were there.

"There's something I want to talk to you about, Georgia," my mother said as she tucked into the mac-and-cheese I had prepared. She blinked her tired eyes at me, a furrow in her brow. "About next year."

Next year meant only one thing to me. I was going to beauty school, which would be the beginning of my real life. All I wanted in the whole world was to get my license and start working at Doreen's. I knew that this wasn't what Doreen really wanted for me, but I figured she'd come around in time. My mother wanted me to get what she referred to as "a real education." She wanted me to become a professional of some sort: a nurse, maybe. Or an accountant like Mrs. Peabody in town, who had a shingle outside her house on Main Street. I wasn't born to be a nurse or an accountant. Not that there's anything wrong with either of those occupations. But they weren't for me. Frankly, the thought made me want to stick my head in the toilet and flush.

"I've changed my mind about beauty school," said my

mother. She spoke slowly, as if each word made her more tired. "I don't want you to go."

"Why?" I asked, stunned. "What happened?"

"I do not want you spending your life working in a hair salon in Weekeepeemie," my mother said fiercely. She was looking out the window at the sliver of Weekeepeemie Lake that we could see behind a thicket of autumn leaves. "That is not going to happen to you. Period. End of story."

"But I like it here," I said. I was trying not to cry. "I love the salon."

"Georgia, you have to give the rest of life a try," my mother said. Then she leaned over and dug around in her handbag.

"What happened?" I repeated. "Something must have happened."

"Nothing happened," my mother said.

I knew there was no way that was true. Something must have made the blue shadows beneath her eyes even darker than usual. If I had really thought about it, I probably could have figured out that it had something to do with money, and with my father, who hadn't sent a check in a good long while, despite the letters from my mother's legal aid lawyer. My mother didn't want me to grow up and be her. How could I have explained to her that she was my hero and that the biggest compliment in the world, to me, was when somebody told me I was just like my mother?

"Here," my mother was saying. "Happy Early Birthday." She handed me an envelope. "I knew how disappointed you'd be, and I thought maybe this . . ."

I fumbled open the envelope. My legs felt like lead, my insides numb. How could she do this to me?

I pulled out a round-trip bus ticket to New York City and looked up at my mother questioningly.

"To visit Ursula," she said. "I thought maybe if you saw—"

"Wow," I said. "New York?"

My mother nodded. So the most exciting thing and the most disappointing thing that had happened to me in years happened all at once.

URSULA WAS THE only person I had ever known who lived in New York. And technically she didn't even live in the city (she lived in Queens), but my teenage mind smoothed over these technicalities to the point where they were erased completely. When I was a kid, Ursula was in our house all the time. She baby-sat Melodie and me, and she worked for Doreen whenever Doreen needed extra help. She was my all-time favorite person as I grew up, until she broke my heart by leaving Weekeepeemie when I was ten to go to a two-year secretarial school outside Boston.

In preparation for my trip, I tore pages out of magazines, scribbled down the names of Broadway shows. I wanted to see *Cats, La Cage aux Folles, A Chorus Line.* I wanted to ride the subway and go to Bloomingdale's. I went shopping with my mother before I left. We went to an outlet mall an hour from home, where, amid the plaid jackets and discarded cashmere sweaters, I spied complete and total fabulousness: a red leather jumpsuit marked down from six hundred dollars to one hundred. It was so far out of our price range that I could barely stand to look at it, but my mother pulled it off the rack anyway.

"Try it," she said, handing it to me.

"But it's so expensive!"

A dreamy look came over my mother's face. "You're only young once," she said.

In the dressing room, I yanked off my Danskin top, untied my wraparound skirt. (I had a rainbow of these—they were my uniform. One in every color.) The red leather clung to my body like the second skin it was, transforming me from New Hampshire high school girl to someone who really ought to be in a Michael Jackson video.

"We're buying it," said my mother, looking at me in the community dressing room mirror.

"But, Mom . . ." I didn't want to protest too loudly. I couldn't believe she was going to buy it for me. I was torn— I didn't want to be selfish, but looking at myself in the mirror, I saw a new Georgia Watkins, as if a red leather jumpsuit could change everything.

"No buts," she said firmly. "It's your birthday present."

"But the trip to New York—"

"Never mind." My mother smiled. "You have to have it."

ON THE BONANZA bus from Weekeepeemie to New York, I wore my new outfit. Peeking out from the zippered top of the jumpsuit was my lavender scoop-necked Danskin top, and my eye shadow matched the Danskin top perfectly. I wore clear lip gloss with just a hint of pink, because I had read in all the magazines that if you emphasize one feature, you need to keep the others subtle. Strong eyes, subtle lips. Strong lips, subtle eyes. And so forth.

I couldn't help but notice that people were looking at me funny, but I didn't care. With my Farrah-esque waves and that jumpsuit, I felt like a million bucks. What did *they* know? In the land of L.L.Bean boots and flannel shirts, I saw myself as a strange, exotic flower. Everybody fabulous had started someplace else, some small, dead-end town where people didn't understand them.

I held my head high, put on my dark glasses, and pretended to be a movie star. Never mind that a movie star would never find herself in the Danbury, Connecticut, bus terminal, switching buses, with her black LeSportsac overnight bag slung over her shoulder.

We were due to arrive at Port Authority in New York at five in the afternoon. I was sitting in the second to last row of the bus, because it was the only window seat available and I wanted to see our approach to New York. I hadn't considered just how close the second to last row was to the bus's bathroom, and by the end of the trip I was faint from trying to hold my breath. But then we rounded a bend on the highway and there was the George Washington Bridge, strung across the Hudson River, looking huge and majestic, just as it did in pictures. We crossed the bridge, then headed south into Manhattan. The bus lumbered down Columbus Avenue from 110th Street, and through the window all I could see were boarded-up buildings and abandoned storefronts, empty streets. Where were we? What New York was this?

The bus made a series of turns and then everything became dark and gray as we entered Port Authority. It never ceases to amaze me that people who visit New York for the first time don't turn around and run back to whatever little corner of the world they come from. I mean, Port Authority? The place is— and was—and probably always will be a dump. It was even smellier and grosser than the second to last seat on the Bonanza bus. But was this what I noticed, at sixteen, climbing down the steps and onto the platform?

Not hardly.

There was Ursula, waiting for me on the platform. She was

a big-boned woman, easy to spot in a crowd with her thick, long, wavy brown hair and her smart city suit. Even though she was on the tall side, Ursula always wore heels. In a sea of commuters, dowdy women who wore sneakers with their business attire, Ursula was perfectly turned out. She never would have been caught dead in a pair of Reeboks.

"Georgia!" She waved as I climbed down the stairs of the bus. "Over here!"

I slung my bag over my shoulder and walked over to her. I felt suddenly self-conscious in my red leather jumpsuit because, I realized, I did care what Ursula thought. She was a goddess. An urban goddess of chic.

"My God, let me take a look at you!" Her voice was low and booming, to go along with the rest of her commanding presence, and people turned and looked at me along with her.

"You're gorgeous," she exclaimed. It sounded funny when she said it: *gaw-jus*. She engulfed me in a hug and I breathed in her scent, which I knew was Jean Naté. I had started to use Jean Naté myself. That bright yellow-and-white bottle cheered me on every morning, and the song they played on the television commercial for the perfume—"Jean Na-tay, Jean Na-tay"— often ran through my head while I sat in math class, willing the minutes away.

Ursula linked her arm through mine and we strode through the dingy Port Authority terminal like actresses walking the red carpet at the Academy Awards. It was five-thirty—the middle of the evening rush—and buses and taxis were blaring their horns on Eighth Avenue. The pretzel vendor on the corner of Eighth Avenue, the heavyset policewoman directing traffic with a whistle in her mouth, the man on the motorcycle stopped at a red light—I tried to take it all in, but it was too much for me. I could barely breathe from so much excitement.

"Did you have to leave work early on my account?" I asked Ursula.

"Just a few minutes." Ursula steered me toward a subway entrance. "My boss was a pain about it. Old coot. You'd think I was asking him for a key to the vault."

Ursula worked in a midtown bank. I thought that meant she was a banker, but actually she was a bank teller, on the receiving end, all day long, of an angry, disgruntled public that was tired of waiting. She was only twenty-eight, but I saw her as aeons older than me—those twelve years between us were a lifetime.

The train pulled into the subway station in a pastel blur of steel and graffiti. Ursula shoved me and then herself through the sliding doors. I smelled food, something oniony mixed with newsprint and sweat. For a minute I was hit by a wave of something like seasickness. There were so many people, and they all looked as if they had to get somewhere fast. Nobody looked me in the eye and smiled, the way they did in Weekeepeemie. My whole life, I had never been anyplace where people didn't know me. That's what it's like to grow up in a small town. Wherever you go—the grocery, the cleaners, the Laundromat—people say, *Hey there, Georgia. How's life treating you? How's that beautiful mother of yours?* You buy some Tylenol at the drugstore, and the next day somebody asks you if you still have that headache.

"This is great." Ursula fingered the leather sleeve of my jumpsuit.

"I got it at the mall with my mom." I spoke loudly, over the subway's roar.

"Your mother got this for you?" Ursula raised an eyebrow.

I nodded.

"Well, baby, do you know where I'm going to take you tomorrow?" Ursula asked.

I waited, watching her like a puppy. I was taking in everything about her: her pretty rhinestone earrings, the delicate chain with a cross that she wore around her neck.

"Fiorucci," she said.

"No shit!" I clamped a hand over my mouth. My panic went away with one single word. Fiorucci! It was the place where Cornelia Guest got her jeans, where in old issues of *Vogue* there were photos of models and actresses shopping. It *was* New York.

I HARDLY SLEPT that night. Visions of Fiorucci danced through my head. I loved the sound of it. *Fee-o-roo-chi.* It was sexy and cosmopolitan, mysterious, foreign. I had brought all my babysitting money with me to New York. A year's worth of hard-earned cash was stuffed into an envelope in my overnight bag, in a wad of singles, tens, and twenties. I had exactly two hundred and eighty-six dollars, which I had been saving for beauty school, but now my mother wasn't going to let me go—so what was I saving it for, anyway? I mean, life was happening right then and there. I was young, I was in New York, and I needed a wardrobe.

The next morning was clear and sunny; the previous night's rain had washed the city streets clean. Ursula's tiny garden studio in Forest Hills sparkled in the sunlight. Her secondhand furniture, including the lumpy sofa on which I had spent the night, seemed as elegant as the Ritz. I put on my Danskin top and wraparound skirt in my favorite color—pink—and carefully made up my face, with pale pink eye shadow to match.

I tried to act cool. No matter what, I couldn't let myself come off like a hick from New Hampshire. In New York, nothing made anybody blink, ever. The most famous movie star could walk by, and people would studiously avert their gaze. In later years I came to see this as an art form, the degree to which people would go to look blasé—and I understood this intuitively. As Ursula and I strode through the first floor of Fiorucci, I made sure that my pounding heart, the shriek of joy inside my head, were not even slightly visible on the surface. I saw a rack of jeans in the back of the store and made my way over there as if it were something I did every day.

Donna Summer was blaring on the stereo system: "Someone left the cake out in the rain . . ." I felt as if I were in a movie as I riffled through the rack of indigo denim with the distinctive, swirly Fiorucci stitching on the back pockets.

"Can I help you?" A salesgirl sidled up to me. She had long curly black hair and eyes outlined in cobalt blue.

"She'll try these on," said Ursula, who I hadn't even realized was standing next to me.

"What size?"

"Six," Ursula said confidently. I was glad she said something, because I was tongue-tied. This salesgirl was so amazing-looking, wearing head to toe Fiorucci: a red-and-white-striped nylon shirt, high-waisted jeans, a rhinestone belt, and Candies platform shoes.

"Try this, too." The salesgirl handed me a halter top made of heavy gold lamé that was so skimpy, it just tied in the back with a black string. I tried not to think about what my mother would think as I took it from the salesgirl and headed into the dressing room.

"I'll be out here," Ursula called to me. "Come and let me see you when you're ready!"

In the next dressing room, I heard two women talking as I wriggled the jeans up around my thighs. To get them over my hips, I had to lie flat on the floor and pull them up with the hook of a hanger. They were supposed to be skintight. I sucked in my belly and buttoned them. I could hardly breathe.

"Do you want to go to Halston after?" one female voice asked another. "I saw a dress I want to wear tonight."

"Are you going to 54?"

"Yeah. My guy's at the door tonight."

I reached behind me and tied the lamé halter in an awkward bow. The thing must have weighed five pounds, but even I knew that it looked amazing. I had a sixteen-year-old body— the body that was meant to wear high fashion, even though usually it was women twice or three times my age who actually bought it. I couldn't believe I was in a place where people were talking about Studio 54—that I was breathing the same air as these women who talked about it in bored, sophisticated tones. *My guy's at the door.* What did that even mean?

I pushed apart the dressing room curtains and walked back out into the neon-bright room where Ursula was sitting on a pink plastic blowup couch, her legs crossed primly as if she were in a doctor's waiting room.

"Jesus H. Christ," Ursula said. "Your mother will kill me."

I wasn't sure if I should even buy the top. It was more than half of my baby-sitting money, and I'd never be able to wear it in Weekeepeemie. It made the red leather jumpsuit look as tame as an old cardigan.

"You need shoes," the salesgirl piped up. She sized up my feet, then hurried back with a pair of black-and-gold platforms that picked up on the gold of the halter.

"You look like a model," said Ursula. "Like that girl—what's her name? The one who's dating Rod Stewart."

"Kelly Emberg?" the salesgirl asked helpfully.

"That's the one."

Well, that did it. If this outfit could inspire a comparison to Kelly Emberg, whom I stared at and studied each month in every magazine from *Mademoiselle* to *Vogue,* then I was going to have to buy it—all of it. The jeans, the halter, the shoes. Kelly Emberg was a gorgeous, feline creature with almond-shaped green eyes, sandy blond hair, and cheekbones that looked cut from glass. I looked at myself in the mirror. I was still plain old Georgia Watkins from Weekeepeemie inside—but maybe if my outsides looked different, my insides would catch up.

"Are you going to try anything on?" I asked Ursula. I felt bad that she was just sitting there, waiting for me.

"No, I'm good," she said. "This place is perfect for you, hon—but it isn't really my style."

I sort of understood what Ursula meant by that. She wore classic separates that she bought on sale at Macy's—and God knows, Fiorucci was anything but classic.

"I'm treating you to the shoes," Ursula said.

"Ursula! You shouldn't—"

"No. I want to," she responded. Which turned out to be a good thing, because just the jeans and halter made my pile of baby-sitting money dwindle down to next to nothing.

I DON'T KNOW where I got the guts to ask Ursula what I asked her next. I mean, she was already like my fairy godmother, bestowing upon me a shower of gifts: the gift of a weekend in the city, the gift of her own city sophistication, and, of course, the shoes. But I did. As we walked west on Fifty-eighth Street toward Central Park, I summoned up my nerve and asked:

"Ursula?" My voice was tiny because I knew my request was big.

"What, hon?"

"Could we go to Studio 54?"

"What?" She stopped in her tracks. "You mean, like, walk by it? We could do that. It isn't far from here."

"No, I mean—could we go? Try to get in? Maybe—tonight?"

"Wow . . ." Ursula shook her head as we resumed walking. "I don't know, George. It's not like the two of us can just waltz in there."

"We can *try,*" I said.

"They have doormen and stuff. Bouncers."

I thought of the two women I overheard at Fiorucci. *My guy's at the door.* Maybe that's what they meant.

"I was going to take you to the movies," Ursula said as we stopped at the hot dog vendor near the entrance to the park.

Now that was a tough one. I loved going to the movies—but the thing was, I could do that any old time in Weekeepeemie. Everything came to the movie theater at the mall sooner or later.

"Please? It'll be fun. It'll be an *adventure.*"

Ursula rolled her eyes. "Okay," she said with a smile.

My heart somersaulted. My whole body did a little dance.

"Really? Oh, my *God.*"

"It's going to be our little secret," Ursula said. "You can't tell Doreen. She'll have a heart attack."

"I won't tell her. I promise."

IT TOOK US the entire afternoon to get dressed and ready for our big night out. After a quick walk through Central Park and two hot dogs for each of us, we rode the subway back to Queens and walked to the small complex of two-story attached houses where Ursula lived. She was being really quiet, and I felt a little bad about it—I mean, I was pushing her to do something she didn't want to do—but I didn't feel bad enough to say, Let's forget it. I just couldn't. It felt like the chance of a lifetime, the only possibility I'd ever have of going to Studio 54.

My mother called to check in while Ursula and I were getting ready. It was the middle of Saturday afternoon, and I was surprised to hear from her; that was usually her busiest time of the week.

Ursula answered and very quickly put me on the phone: *Oh, hey, Doreen—let me get Georgia for you.* I think it was because she was trying to avoid out-and-out lying to my mother. Ursula knew that no matter how hip my mother pretended to be, there was no way our little expedition was going to be okay with her—and that, in fact, if she had seen me in my full disco regalia, she would have flown down to New York on her broomstick, screeching like the Wicked Witch of the West.

"Hi, Mom." Through the phone line, I could hear the drone of a blow-dryer, a few scattered voices. "What's up?"

"Nothing's up. I just miss my girl." My mother paused. "Can't I just miss my girl?"

"Yeah, sure. I miss you, too," I mumbled, embarrassed. The fact was, I hadn't given my mother two seconds' thought since I got on the bus from Weekeepeemie. I had a sudden flurry of uncomfortable feelings: guilt, remorse, and worst of all, an aching sense of sorrow for my mom. She had nobody, really, except Melodie and me—and with me away, Melodie was probably even more difficult to handle.

"So what are you guys doing?" she asked.

"Nothing much." I was trying not to tell an actual lie. It was technically true, at that moment, that we weren't doing much.

"Well, we're a little slow today. Elsa McNaughton booked a double-process and haircut, then canceled an hour before."

"You're gonna charge her, right?"

"I can't, Georgia. She'll get so huffy that I'll wind up losing a valuable client."

"It shouldn't work that way."

It made me so mad that rich women like Elsa McNaughton could live by their own set of rules. It wasn't fair. Didn't they realize that my mother was trying to make a living?

"Oh, here comes Mrs. Klemm," said my mother. "I'd better run." She blew kisses into the phone. "You be good. I'll see you tomorrow—I'll be waiting for you when you get off the bus." She paused, as if trying to stop herself, and then said: "So Ursula has a pretty great life there in New York, doesn't she? You know, I hope you talk to her about that secretarial school she went to."

"Okay."

"Okay-stop-bugging-me-Mom? Or, Okay-I'll-talk-to-Ursula?"

"Just okay," I said softly. "Go take care of the clients."

I placed the phone back in its cradle, grateful that Ursula had made herself scarce, taking a shower during our conversation. I sat back down at the makeup mirror and finished applying my false eyelashes. I blinked a few times to make sure the glue had set, then brushed the rest of my eye makeup with loose powder, just like I'd read about in *Glamour.*

Ursula came out of the steamy bathroom, her hair wrapped in a thick towel.

"You didn't tell her, did you?" she asked.

"No."

"Maybe we shouldn't do this, George. Your mother trusts me to take care of you."

We *had* to go. We just had to.

Ursula looked at me for a long minute, and I wondered what she was seeing. Something crossed her face, some unreadable expression.

"What?"

She shook her head. "Nothing."

"No, what?"

"It's just . . . Your mother has big dreams for you, George. She wants you to—"

"I know what she wants," I blurted out, interrupting. "She wants me to go to school and become some . . ."

I trailed off, realizing I was coming dangerously close to insulting Ursula.

"Become what?" she prodded.

"I don't know." Suddenly I felt like crying. "I just want to do hair. Is that so terrible?"

THE LOCAL QUEENS car service was due to arrive at Ursula's door at nine in the evening. We didn't know what to do with ourselves in the intervening hours, so we sat there on her sofa, watching TV and eating Jiffy Pop popcorn in our dress-up clothes. We knew enough not to show up at Studio 54 until the night was well under way. As we sat and sat, watching *Wheel of Fortune* and *Jeopardy!,* I felt my energy plummet. This was a crazy idea; I was sorry I had come up with it. We should just change into our jeans and go see a movie.

"They're never gonna let us in," I moaned after a while.

What had I even been thinking? I probably had HIGH SCHOOL KID FROM NEW HAMPSHIRE in neon lights above my head.

"You have to have the attitude that you can just walk right in there," Ursula said. "Like you deserve to be there."

She hopped off the bed and demonstrated her haughty, velvet-rope walk: eyes focused slightly higher than any bouncer's gaze, mouth slack, relaxed, limbs loose and swinging.

"How do you know how to do that?" I asked her. I was amazed.

"Oh, I've seen it on TV," Ursula said. "It's easy, if you just watch the actresses."

"I watch them all the time," I said.

A horn beeped outside.

"There's our car," said Ursula. She paused. "You know, we can still change our minds."

"No! I want to!" I felt as though I had to make myself do it. It was a test, a mountain I had to climb or I'd never forgive myself.

Ursula grabbed her coat—a grayish brown trench—and my heart sank. The coat transformed her from disco chick to uncool in a single sweep of vinyl.

"You can't wear that!"

She stopped and stared at me. "It's chilly out," she said. She handed me a navy blue cardigan sweater to put over my gold lamé halter. I would rather have frozen to death than put that thing on. But Ursula's cheeks were bright pink, and I sensed that she was wishing she had never agreed to go. I grabbed the sweater, figuring I'd find a way to ditch it before we got into Manhattan.

A beat-up old station wagon was waiting at the curb, its engine rattling. A sign—FOREST HILLS LIVERY—was propped in the back window.

"Jeez," said Ursula.

"That's our car?"

"Jeez," she repeated. And then, "Don't worry. When we get there, we'll get out at the end of the block and walk."

We slid into the back of the wagon, the cracked-leather seats creaking and groaning beneath us. An air freshener shaped like a pine tree dangled from the rearview mirror; it didn't do much to get rid of the stale cigarette stench. I looked out the dirty window and imagined that we were seated in the back of a sleek black limousine and the driver—instead of this guy with his shirt riding over his gray, hairy belly—was a uniformed, dapper gentleman who would open the door for us when we arrived at Studio 54.

As we sped across the Fifty-ninth Street Bridge and down Second Avenue, I thought about all the people living in those tall buildings and wondered about their lives. Who were they? How had they gotten there? Was there a secret password, a key, that allowed some people in and kept others with their noses pressed against the glass?

"You can have one cocktail," Ursula said as we idled in Saturday night traffic. "Just one, Georgia—I'm not kidding. You're underage."

"Fine." I shrugged, but my heart did another little secret dance. I hadn't expected Ursula to let me have even one drink. But more than that, I realized that what she was saying meant that she thought we'd get in.

"And we're only staying until midnight," she warned. "Not a minute later or you'll turn into a pumpkin."

"Okay." I reached over and gave her hand a squeeze. "Ursula, I'm so excited. Thanks for doing this!"

Traffic eased up a bit, and finally we were on Fifty-fourth Street. It seemed to me that everywhere I looked was straight out of a movie. It wouldn't even be bad to be poor in New York City. It would be romantic, sort of. Not like Weekeepeemie, where poor people had baggy, wrinkled faces and lived in lean-tos with outhouses in the backyard.

"What are you thinking?" asked Ursula. "You look so dreamy."

I had been thinking, at that moment, of Audrey Hepburn in *Breakfast at Tiffany's*, but I didn't want to say so.

"Just about moving here," I said.

"It isn't easy, you know."

"I know that."

She looked at me sideways.

I nodded.

"Well, when you come you can stay on my sofa," she said. "Maybe we can even get you a studio with a roommate in Forest Hills Gardens."

I thought about what it would be like to live in New York with Ursula. We'd go out all the time, drink cocktails out of fancy glasses, get rides in the backs of stretch limos. But Forest Hill Gardens? I had never heard of one famous person who lived in the outer boroughs. Though of course Ursula was the only actual person I knew who lived anywhere in New York City.

"Where do you ladies want me to drop you off?" the driver asked.

Down the block, halfway down Fifty-fourth Street, I saw the pink glow of a neon "54."

"Here's good," Ursula said. She handed the driver a twenty and we got out of the wagon.

"Oh, my *God*," she breathed as we teetered on the uneven sidewalk. "Look at that crowd of people."

There were hundreds, swarming, crushed between the

street and the velvet ropes in front of the club. I couldn't quite make out their faces, but I could see the pile of bodies as we approached, and the hair—every color under the rainbow. Dyed hot pink, turquoise, black-and-white streaks like a skunk.

"We're never going to get in," I moaned.

"Put on your party face," said Ursula. "Come on!" I recognized her expression: She was determined. We joined the crowd, pulled into its outer edges. A floodlight moved over us as if we were prisoners in a prison yard. A big guy with long streaked hair and the darkest sunglasses stood by the velvet rope, scanning the crowd. I heard all sorts of accents floating around us: the New Jersey twang, the distinctive Long Island whine. These people looked cold. As if they had been waiting for hours. Two platinum blondes with stick-straight hair wrapped their coats around themselves.

"Let's just go someplace else," I heard one of them say. "We're never getting in here."

"What time is it?"

"Ten-thirty."

In my platforms I was taller than a lot of the women and some of the men. Who cared if I could barely walk? Ursula and I started to make our way around the edge of the crowd. There were fancy cars lined up by the curb, big and small limos, some smaller, expensive-looking cars with drivers sitting inside, engines running.

A big black car pulled up, and when the door opened a low hum went through the crowd, a murmur that seemed to unite everyone. A small, very pale man with a shock of snow white hair, skinny in black jeans and a black jacket, slid through the throng with no apparent effort, and the bouncer unhooked the velvet rope as he approached. The man disappeared into the doors of the club like a ghost.

"Who was *that*?" I asked Ursula. It was cold enough for steam to be coming out of my mouth.

"I'm trying to remember his name," she said. "Somebody famous. Some big-deal designer or something."

I was watching the spot where the man had just been when I realized that I had caught the bouncer's eye. I couldn't actually *see* his eyes behind those dark glasses, but he was pointing a finger, crooking it like a gun, right at me. I turned around to see if he was pointing to someone behind me, but there was nobody behind me. We were as far on the edge of the crowd as we could be.

"*Me?*" I pointed at my own chest.

A brief, almost imperceptible nod.

"We're going in." I grabbed Ursula's arm, and we started to force our way through the pile of bodies.

"Excuse me!" Ursula sang out. "Coming through!"

I could barely breathe, assaulted by all the different smells: perfume, sweat, cigarette smoke, and marijuana. People had joints lit up, right out in the open where anybody could see them.

"Coming through!" Ursula sang again. "Holy cow, Georgia—he was actually pointing to *us*." Her breath hit my ear.

Finally we reached the front—the velvet rope close enough to touch. The bouncer had arms the size of my waist, and his teeth were impossibly white. He had a two-way radio in one hand. Even a foot away, I couldn't see his eyes. The lenses of his glasses were mirrored, and I saw myself: a convex blond blur.

"You." He pointed to me.

Ursula and I started to move through the barricade.

"You." He put a hand on my arm. "*Just* you." He didn't even turn to address Ursula. "Not you."

Someone behind me was whistling—a loud, piercing

sound. A horn blasted. In the distance, the siren of a fire truck wailed. Everything seemed to slow down; the air felt thick and wavery.

I forced myself to turn and look Ursula in the eye. I was afraid of exactly what I saw there: hurt, confusion, a cloud of pained disbelief. Her brow furrowed, crumpled. She looked ten years older in an instant.

"You going in?" the bouncer asked. I thought I detected a smirk.

"You go in," Ursula said in a small voice. "I'll pick you up at midnight."

What was she even saying?

"I'm not going without you." I shot the bouncer a pleading look. How could he be so heartless? He shook his head.

"It's only right that you go in," Ursula said again.

"I can't believe this is happening," I muttered. Of course, there was a part of me—a pretty big part—that wanted to glide past the bouncer and into the club, where the disco beat was so loud that I could hear it through the thick concrete walls. It was my big chance, and I knew it might never happen again. How many chances did anyone get in one small lifetime?

I looked at Ursula again. I had known her since I was born. She'd baby-sat me since I was a toddler, and my whole life I had admired her. She had made something of herself, something bigger than all the trapped worlds of the women of Wee-keepeemie. And now here she was, shivering in front of me in the chilly Manhattan night, her whole face fallen. I felt so many things, a swirl of competing emotions. I wanted to punch the bouncer, pummel his chest for hurting one of my favorite people in the world. At the same time, I felt a strange, uncomfortable satisfaction. Hard as it was to admit, there was a sliver of hard-edged joy that the bouncer had singled me out—that

somehow I was deemed hipper, prettier, cooler, whatever—
than the woman I had looked up to all my life.

"Get in there," Ursula urged. She winked at me. Her eyes
were in danger of spilling over. "Don't be an idiot."

"Let's go home," I said. I pulled her by the arm and fought
my way back through the mob. I wanted to get as far away from
the velvet ropes of Studio 54 as possible. If I could have blinked
us both back to New Hampshire, where people weren't dressed
in gold lamé and Fiorucci jeans—but also knew how to be kind
and solicitous of one another—I would have done it in a
minute.

We walked in silence over to the avenue, where taxis
whizzed by us in a yellow blur and the lights of Times Square
in the distance looked like a country fair. I held on to the sleeve
of Ursula's trench coat, feeling the tenseness of her arm beneath
the vinyl.

"I'm sorry," I finally said. We walked south to the subway
station.

"Don't be silly." She didn't look at me.

"No really—I never should have—"

"Just stop," she said softly.

But I was sixteen years old, and I didn't know when to be
quiet. It didn't occur to me that by apologizing profusely to Ursula, I was actually only trying to make myself feel better—and
it was making her feel worse.

"I'm sure that guy was making a mistake," I went on. "I
mean, why would he—"

"*Please.*" Ursula grabbed my hand and squeezed it tightly.
"Georgia. Just shut up."

We climbed down the stairs of the subway station, with
each step descending farther and farther away from anything
resembling glamour. On the fluorescently lit, urine-soaked

47

platform, no one even took notice of us: two young women in our evening finery, our makeup already rubbed off our faces. My eyes were stinging. One of my false eyelashes was starting to come off.

The train screeched into the station, and the doors opened. We walked carefully inside in our high heels, then settled onto a hard bench. Ursula wrapped her coat tightly around herself, shivering. We must have been halfway home before she said anything, and when she did, it was with a sigh. "You got in," she said, leaning over and kissing me on the cheek. "Just remember that, when you're back home. You got in."

Beauty School

"I am Mrs. Bosco."

The small, round woman standing behind her desk in the classroom of the Wilfred Academy of Beauty spoke her own name with reverence, as if the fourteen students around the U-shaped table should have heard of her.

It was my first day. I had poked and prodded, whined and moaned, wept—and then, finally, had simply refused to take no for an answer from Doreen. My mother loved me a lot, bottom line. She just wanted me to be happy. So here I was. I looked around me. Why had I pushed so hard . . . for this? We were supposed to spend four hundred hours learning theory before we turned to practice. I *knew* theory. I knew practice, for that matter. Already I was having a hard time listening. I focused instead on Mrs. Bosco herself, who was wearing a red skirt with gold flecks and a red-and-black sweater that was so tight, the fleshy part of her back bulged over her bra straps when she turned and began writing on the chalkboard behind her.

"Chemical relaxer," she wrote. Then, "Protective gel."

She turned to face the class once more. Her skin was paper white, and her hair was the kind of jet black that no one is born with. She had amazing eyes—they were actually violet—and I realized that she looked shockingly like Elizabeth Taylor. Not the pretty young Elizabeth Taylor of *National Velvet*. Not the gorgeous grown-up Elizabeth Taylor of *Cleopatra*. No, this woman bore an uncanny and unfortunate resemblance to the present-day Elizabeth Taylor as portrayed by John Belushi on *Saturday Night Live*.

"Can anyone tell me how these two products are connected?" she asked in a whispery voice, tapping one shiny coral fingernail on her desk.

She looked around the table, and I followed her gaze. Of the fourteen of us, there were twelve women and two men. One of the men wore the thick flannel shirt and heavy work pants that were considered a uniform by most of the men and boys I knew. He struck me as someone who should be out chopping wood or tearing down a diesel engine, until I noticed one small detail: On his large, square hands grew a single four-inch fingernail painted a deep shade of red. The other man, seated at the small end of the U, was simply the most beautiful man I had ever seen. He had dark hair that fell over his forehead, brown eyes framed by long, thick lashes, a strong nose, and full, pillowy lips that *forced* you to think about kissing him. He angled his face as he listened to Mrs. Bosco, and the light caught the long, jagged line of a scar running from the corner of his eye and down his cheek, ending near his mouth. Instead of marring his face, if anything the scar only enhanced his beauty. I was staring at him, imagining tracing my finger along the line of that scar, when Mrs. Bosco's voice broke into my daydream.

"Excuse me," she was saying. "Hello? The blonde over there?"

A quick look around made it clear she must be talking to me, unless she meant the girl with a peroxide crew cut to my left.

Reluctantly, I looked up. Mrs. Bosco's violet eyes were indeed trained on me.

"What's your name?" she asked.

"Georgia Watkins, ma'am."

She raised a perfectly groomed eyebrow. "Doreen's daughter?"

I nodded, my cheeks burning. Why hadn't my mother told me she knew my teacher?

"Well. Surely Doreen Watkins's daughter knows the answer to such a basic question."

I took a deep breath. "I'm sorry, ma'am. What was the question?"

"Stop calling me 'ma'am'!"

Out of the corner of my eye, I saw the beautiful, scarred boy tentatively raise his hand.

"Yes?"

"You put the protective gel on the scalp before applying the chemical relaxer," he said. His voice was as pretty as he was— low and musical.

"I'm glad *somebody* is paying attention. And what is your name?"

"Patrick," he said. "Patrick Shaw."

WILFRED ACADEMY WAS in a small strip mall just off the highway. There was a Chinese restaurant called Ming Dynasty, a bakery, a video rental store, a dry cleaner, and Joey's Grocery. That first morning, at coffee break, a bunch of us drifted over to Joey's. I didn't know anybody's name (except Patrick and the girl with the peroxide crew cut, who wore a gold necklace with a rhinestone *Janet* emblazoned in a swirling script).

"Do you want to get some coffee?" Patrick fell into step next to me.

"I don't drink coffee. It makes your pores big."

Oh, my God. My cheeks burned, and I wished I could stuff the words back into my mouth. Here was the most gorgeous guy I had ever seen, and I was talking about my *pores*? What was my problem?

But wait. Actually, he seemed interested.

"Really?"

"Yeah. I read about it in a magazine."

"You know, there's this product I heard about—"

"The Body Shop pore reducer!"

"That's the one!"

I had never been able to connect to the boys at Weekeepeemie High. All they wanted to do was drink Boone's Farm strawberry wine and go dirt bike racing after school. I had watched carefully what happened to the kids who graduated from Weekeepeemie, particularly the most popular kids. It seemed to me that being popular in high school led to a future (for girls) of three kids and a sweat suit by age twenty-five and pumping gas (for guys) at the Texaco Station on Route 109.

But here was a guy who knew things.

Check that. A *gorgeous* guy who knew things.

"So Mrs. Bosco knows your mom?" he asked, holding the

door open for me. The light caught his scar again; I tried not to stare at it.

"Yeah. My mom has a salon," I said. "In Weekeepeemie."

"Your mom is *Doreen*? Doreen of Doreen's?"

I nodded.

"She *rocks*, your mother. I mean, Doreen's is the only place up here I ever wanted to work."

We ordered a sandwich and got two cans of Diet Coke from the refrigerated case. The guy in the flannel shirt behind the counter hardly even glanced up when we paid him. I could tell he was used to the Wilfred Academy crowd—all of us weird-looking by local standards.

"I'll introduce you to my mom," I said. "I'm working there on Saturdays."

"Well, actually—"

"Really—it's no big deal."

"It's not that," said Patrick. "It's just that I've already got a gig lined up for when I get my license."

"Yeah? Where?"

At that moment, a girl with dyed red hair and hoop earrings sidled up to us. She was holding a big, steaming cup of coffee, and I noticed with some satisfaction that she did indeed have big pores.

"Hi, I'm Violet," she said. A wad of pink bubble gum was visible when she opened her mouth.

"Hi," we both echoed faintly. Violet was one of those people—I felt it instantly—who just made you want to take a big step back.

"So what do you guys want to do when you get your license?" she asked, taking a sip of coffee. How could she drink that stuff with gum in her mouth? "Like, what do you want to *be*?"

"A colorist," I said.

"A stylist," said Patrick.

"Oooh, a *stylist*. How *fancy*," said Violet.

"It's what they're called," he said mildly.

"How'd you get that scar on your face?" she asked abruptly.

I inhaled, appalled and amazed. Patrick lifted a hand—it seemed reflexive, involuntary—to his cheek.

"Do you always say whatever pops into your head?" he asked.

"*Sorry*. Was that rude?"

The question didn't seem to deserve an answer. But still she stood there, watching us. I realized she was waiting for Patrick to tell her about his scar.

I turned to him. "I'm going to walk back," I said. "Want to come?"

We zigzagged across the parking lot instead of walking the long way around. I felt like apologizing for Violet, even though I had never laid eyes on her until five minutes before. Patrick had a softness to his face, a gentleness that made you want to protect him.

"So where's the job you have lined up after you graduate?" I tried to change the subject.

"It's in New York City," he said. "There's a new salon opening this winter that a friend told me about. It's going to be *so* hot. I mean, I know I'm going to have to start out sweeping hair off the floor and getting coffee for the clients—but still, it's a foot in the door."

"What's it called?"

"Jean-Luc."

ON WEEKENDS, DURING the months I was in beauty school, I worked at Doreen's. I did a little bit of everything: single- and double-process, highlights, perms (though only when customers insisted), haircuts, and blow-drys. I was pleased each time a customer asked for something new, as I was eager to pick up as much experience as possible. Meanwhile, at school, one of the main things Mrs. Bosco was focused on was the state board roller set. It was a style that involved all the necessary skills: a combination of finger-waving, pin curls, and rollers, the end result of which was a hairdo that looked just like the picture of "Dear Abby" that ran in the newspaper over her column. Fortunately, it was a style preferred by many of my mother's older customers, so I got plenty of practice. Way before I had completed my eight hundred hours, I could have performed the state board roller set in my sleep.

My mom needed all the help she could get from me at Doreen's. Some nights I even went in after school to do a few late customers. Mrs. Smith liked the way I did her blue rinse, and then there was Mrs. Matthews, who came in for a roller set every other week and did not wash her hair in between appointments.

"Georgia, I'm going to need you to open the salon for me on Monday," my mother said as we drove home at the end of a long, busy winter Saturday.

"But I have school! Mrs. Bosco will never—"

"I'll talk to Edna Bosco," my mother said. "Don't you worry about that."

"What's going on?"

"Your sister has an interview."

"What kind of interview? For a *MAD* magazine contest?"

"That's not nice, Georgia." She paused. "It's for college."

It was raining—a hard, sleety rain—and her hands gripped

the steering wheel tightly. She had always been a nervous driver.

"What do you mean, college? She's *sixteen*!"

"Boston University has offered your sister a full scholarship."

"How did she—"

"Apparently she just went ahead and did it," my mother said. "Took her SATs, got her recommendations, sent in the application."

My mother flipped on the directional and turned off the highway at our exit. A tractor-trailer was in front of us, spitting up slush.

"Why do you need to go with her?"

A muscle worked in my mother's jaw. "Do you really need me to answer that question?"

"No. I'm sorry."

It was obvious that my mother needed to go with Melodie. For starters, she had failed her driving test three times.

"I guess I'm just really surprised," I said.

"Yeah. Me too."

"Is this a good thing?"

She sighed. "I think so. I've done some reading—I think BU might be the perfect place for her. They'll . . . appreciate her. The kids in Weekeepeemie . . ." She trailed off.

I didn't need her to finish the sentence. I knew. The kids in Weekeepeemie thought Melodie was a freak. They thought I was a freak, too, but I didn't care. We were completely different kinds of freaks, Melodie and me. She lived her life in some other universe—a universe where it was apparently okay not to wash her face or straighten her skirt. She never looked people in the eye, and she shuffled down the halls of Weekeepeemie High muttering to herself. Kids didn't even make fun of her—

at least not to her face or mine—they just steered clear. While I—with my angel-tipped Farrah hair and my matching Danskin outfits—was just asking for it. My last year at Weekeepeemie High, they started to call me all sorts of names. The girls thought I was a slut because of the way I dressed, and the boys were bummed out that I wasn't. I tried not to pay attention. They said dirty things, mean things. But I held my head high. I figured they'd be pumping my gas someday.

"What time do you need to be in Boston?"

"Her appointment is at ten."

"I'll open the salon. No problem."

We pulled up in front of our house. It was already dark out, but no outdoor lights were on, not even the spotlight over the back door. A week's worth of free newspapers were scattered haphazardly along the back stoop; patches of snow and ice made the driveway treacherous.

"Careful." I held my mother's arm. Sometimes I lay awake at night and worried about what would happen if suddenly she couldn't work. We didn't have anything to fall back on, and our health insurance lapsed from time to time. We lived so close to the bone that it scared me.

Inside, the only light came from Melodie's room. I had a flash of intense love for my little sister. In so many ways, she couldn't take care of herself. Her vision was poor (which partially accounted for failing the driving test), and she wore those thick glasses that were almost always crooked on her face. She forgot to eat and needed to be reminded to go to the bathroom before long car trips, just like a little kid. But she had figured out a way to get out—to get herself where she needed to be. I just knew she was going to do great, big things, if she was only given half a chance.

"Melodie!" I hollered up the stairs. "Get down here, you nut-job!"

Her door at the top of the stairs cracked open, and her disheveled head popped out. As usual, Melodie looked as if she had just awakened from a long and fitful sleep.

"What do you want?" She yawned and rubbed her eyes.

"Why didn't you tell me?"

I climbed halfway up the stairs.

"Tell you what?"

"Come on. Don't play games. Mom told me—about college. That's amazing."

"I didn't think you'd care."

"How can you say that?"

"I don't know . . ." She sat on the top step. "I mean, you're more interested in other stuff."

"Like hair," I said flatly. I knew it. She thought I was stupid and silly and that what my mother and I did just didn't matter.

"Well, yeah."

"You're wrong."

"Okay."

"Don't humor me."

"Girls—stop," said my mother. She hung her down jacket on a hook by the door. "Just stop. You're all each other has."

It was a favorite expression of hers. I knew she really believed it, too. Family was it. Blood was everything. Anybody else was—in the end—not to be trusted.

"Freak," I muttered. I punched her pale, skinny arm.

"Freak." She gave me a rare grin, punching me back.

PATRICK SHAW BECAME my best friend faster than you could say "Access Hollywood." I wanted to be more than best friends with him, but I figured that we were colleagues now and anything beyond friendship could wait until after our eight hundred hours of beauty school were over. We recognized each other in the group of Wilfred students as the only ones who were not going to end up at Hair Today, Gone Tomorrow or at the Supercuts at the mall. Not that there was anything wrong with that. It was a style thing, mostly. While we were busy reading French *Vogue* and German *Elle,* the others perused hairstyle magazines that showed pictures of overly made-up models with spiky, streaky hair.

Patrick started counting down the hours during our second week of beauty school. We walked across the parking lot from Joey's into the dim lobby of the office building that housed Wilfred Academy, carrying our Diet Cokes and half-eaten Danish. "Six hundred and fifty-two hours," he said under his breath.

"That's not so many," I said.

He rolled his eyes. "Honey, I don't know about you, but I'm tired of biding my time."

I knew what he meant. If Patrick and I had one thing in common, it was that our desire to get out was greater than our need to fit in. It had been hard being seen as weird and different for all these years—and if it had been hard for me, I could only imagine what it must have been like for Patrick. He wasn't like the other guys in Weekeepeemie. He wasn't a jock, and he wasn't a dirt bike racer, and he wasn't working on a premature beer belly. How was he supposed to fit in? It seemed to me that he just never even tried.

As we were walking and talking, a car pulled up alongside us—I hadn't even heard it coming—and the driver lowered his window. I recognized Bud Knauer, one of the biggest assholes at Weekeepeemie High, which was really saying something. What did Bud want?

"Hey, Cher!" Bud called out the window.

Shit. That was another thing they called me at Weekeepeemie High.

Patrick looked over at the car. "Is that guy talking to us?"

"Ignore him," I said, walking faster.

"Cher!" Bud yelled again.

I found myself wishing I had worn something tamer that day. I had on a miniskirt, which all of a sudden made me feel like I was wearing underwear in public.

Next to Bud was another Weekeepeemie High guy whose name I didn't know. He had the smooshed-up face of a wrestler.

"Is that Sonny with you?" yelled the smooshed-up guy.

The two of them laughed as if they had said something hysterical.

"What's their problem?" asked Patrick. "Do you know them?"

"They went to my high school."

"Show me that cute little ass, Cher!"

I saw Patrick's face grow red. This was all making me nervous. No one else was around—where was everybody? I figured we had another fifty paces before we were back at Wilfred Academy.

"Leave her alone!" Patrick shouted. Then he stopped dead in his tracks and crossed his arms over his chest.

"Who are you talking to, pretty boy?" Bud asked.

"Fuck you. You just keep on driving, butt-face."

Bud hit the gas of his Mustang, scaring the shit out of me, but Patrick didn't budge. Then Bud threw the car into drive and it screeched down the road, and as if it were all happening in slow motion, the car turned and headed straight at us.

"Run!" I screamed at Patrick. We were almost at the building.

Patrick grabbed my hand and I practically flew through the air. It must have been less than ten seconds, but it was the scariest ten seconds of my life, I'll tell you. No one had ever called Bud Knauer "butt-face" before. The car squealed away, leaving a trail of dust in its wake, just as Patrick and I burst through the doors and into the stairwell. We collapsed on the first step, both of us out of breath.

"You shouldn't have done that," I panted.

"Are you kidding me? Do you think I was going to let him talk to you like that?"

We just sat there, listening to the sound of each other's breath. If I had to give you a precise moment when I fell hopelessly in love with Patrick Shaw, that would have been it. The man was a prince.

"Patrick," I said suddenly as we finally climbed the stairs to the second floor. "Listen—of course you don't have to tell me, but if you ever want to talk about it . . ."

I put a hand up to my own face, to the spot where Patrick's scar began.

Patrick stopped and shook his head. "I'm sorry," he said. "It's still not that long ago, and I can't really—"

"Somebody did this to you because you're so handsome," I said slowly. Even though "handsome" wasn't the right word. I don't know how I knew it—I just knew.

The color rose in Patrick's cheeks. "Afterward, they said they wanted to ruin my face," he said.

We had reached the top of the stairs and were standing outside the glass door of Wilfred.

"Well, they didn't," I said, reaching up on tiptoes to give him a kiss.

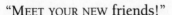

"MEET YOUR NEW friends!"

Mrs. Bosco swung open the huge closet in the Wilfred hall-way with a flourish, like Carol Merrill opening a curtain on *Let's Make a Deal*. Inside the closet, lined up on metal shelves, were dozens of mannequin heads, all covered by long, luxuriant brown hair.

"Okay, everybody—pick your heads. They're going to be with you for a while."

We all stood, crowded in the doorway. Patrick was behind me, nudging me in the back.

"It's real," said Mrs. Bosco. "That is to say *human*. All six-teen inches of it."

"Jeez," said Janet, behind me.

"Go on," said Mrs. Bosco. "They don't bite."

She turned to me. "You—Georgia Watkins. Go ahead and take one."

I scanned the shelves, wondering which one of the identi-cal heads to pick—which one would bring me luck. Finally, I chose the third one from the left. Her hair was just like the oth-ers—long, brown, and straight—but her plastic lips seemed to be smiling.

"Give her a name," said Mrs. Bosco.

"I'm sorry?" As always, I fought the urge to call her "ma'am."

"A name. You will all name your heads." She held out a fist-ful of Magic Markers as, slowly, everyone else filed into the closet and picked a head. I took a Magic Marker from Mrs. Bosco and walked back to the table in the center of the room.

When I uncapped it, it had the sweetish, chemical smell of wet ink.

I began writing across the neck of my mannequin in thick, bold letters: "**ETHEL.**"

Patrick peered over my shoulder. "Ethel?" he asked. "What the hell kind of name is that?"

"My grandmother's." I shrugged. "She wears a wig."

"Oh." His pen hovered for a moment above the neck of his mannequin. Then he wrote, *"Miranda,"* in strong, slanted script.

MIRANDA AND ETHEL accompanied Patrick and me wherever we went. We were all together, all the time. I didn't have a car, so Patrick drove me everywhere, picking me up most mornings in his light blue Chevy Impala.

"Two hundred and sixteen hours," he'd announce.

"One hundred eighty-eight."

"One hundred and twelve."

The state of our mannequins was a pretty good indication of how many hours we had spent practicing. Ethel was a sorry mess. Her eyes were smudged with caked liner and mascara that no amount of cold cream would remove. Her lips were the blurred, swollen shape of a woman's lipstick applied late at night, drunk, without the benefit of a mirror. And her hair . . . her hair! What was left of it was a peroxide, cotton-candy bit of frippery. We had permed and relaxed, curled and set, blow-dried and flat-ironed that original glossy brown hair until it resembled every hairdresser's worst nightmare: It was truly beyond repair, and it wasn't growing back.

On Saturdays we went together to Doreen's, where in just a

few months Patrick had already developed a following. He pulled the Impala sharply into a parking space next to the salon; Ethel and Miranda rolled across the backseat.

"Better not let the ladies see *these* ladies," Patrick said as he slammed the car door. "Or else they'll never let us touch a hair on their heads."

"I don't know," I said. "Maybe we could convince them that the bleached, frizzy look is the next big thing."

"Not that we'd ever do something like that," said Patrick.

Inside, my mother had Mrs. Stolley, the local real estate broker, in the first chair.

"Hi, honey!" she called out.

"Are you talking to him or to me?" I asked. My mother adored Patrick. When he wasn't at our house for supper, she made sure that I brought him a Tupperware container of food the next day, even if it was just a TV dinner. *Now there's a young man who's going places,* she said. *A nice, nice boy.* She never out-and-out asked if Patrick was my boyfriend. And I didn't tell her anything, because . . . well . . . there wasn't anything to tell.

"Patrick, Mrs. Carter is in the sink," my mother said. "I asked Karen to go ahead and shampoo her—she's in a hurry."

"No problem."

My mother was giving Mrs. Stolley a simple, layered short cut—the same cut she'd been giving her for a decade. The women of Weekeepeemie weren't big on change. Once they found something that worked for them—whether it was a no-nonsense wash and style or a weekly appointment for a roller set—they stuck with it.

"So how's business, Doreen?" I overheard Mrs. Stolley ask my mother as I walked around back to slip on my white smock.

The answer was muted. I strained to hear but couldn't make out what my mother was saying over the drone of hair dryers.

But Sharon Stolley had a voice that could cut through anything—high and piercing, always threatening to spill over into utter hysteria—and I could hear her response loud and clear.

"Well, you just march over to the bank and tell Tim Cornell that you're an old customer and he simply needs to give you more time!"

Again, my mother's voice was inaudible. My fingers fumbled over the buttons of my smock. I wondered, if we were really in trouble—*real* trouble as opposed to our monthly balancing act—whether or not my mother would tell me.

"Well, for goodness' sake, that's what second mortgages are for!" Mrs. Stolley's voice broadcast to the entire salon. I could picture her thin, birdlike arms waving in the air to punctuate her point, her small head darting beneath my mother's scissors.

"What's going on, Ma?" I came out in my smock. I probably should have waited until later, but I found the whole thing too disturbing to sit with for the whole day.

"Nothing you need to worry about, sweetheart." Her fingers, curved around the scissors' handles, were unusually tense, knuckles white from gripping too hard.

"Don't say that," I said. "Please."

Patrick ushered Mrs. Carter to the chair next to my mother's station, all the while keeping his gaze averted. Did he know something I didn't know?

"What's going on?" I repeated.

"I don't want to talk about it."

"Your mother had something called a balloon mortgage on the beauty parlor," said Mrs. Stolley. "And it just came due."

I pictured a hot-air balloon floating above Weekeepeemie and the small building that housed Doreen's dangling from its delicate strings. "What does that mean?" I asked.

"It means I owe the bank a lot of money," my mother said

softly. The other customers—all long-timers at Doreen's—were listening in while pretending to flip through *People* or *Entertainment Weekly*.

"How much?"

"Georgia, could we just drop it?"

"I need to know." I felt that if I had all the information, I could somehow fix things, perform a magic trick and make it all better, the way as a kid I'd thought that a kiss would take any kind of pain away.

"Fifty-three thousand dollars," my mother said. Her eyes met mine in the mirror above Mrs. Stolley's head. It was an impossible sum—I couldn't even compute it. That was more money than my mother made in a year—sometimes in two years. I could feel the eyes of all the customers on me, and in my ears buzzed a faint click and snip of scissors, but otherwise I was numb. Patrick, steady, dependable Patrick, put his hand on my shoulder, but I was afraid to look at him or at anyone else. I didn't know what to do.

"THERE'S ONLY ONE answer," Patrick said as he drove me home at the end of the day. I didn't think I'd make it through the eight double-processes and four highlights I had scheduled, but somehow—shaky hands and all—I had gotten the job done. Now we were stopped at a traffic light by the minimart. The engine of Patrick's Impala was banging in a worrisome way.

"There's no answer," I said. I trained my gaze on the light, willing it to turn green. I just wanted to go home. I wanted to climb into bed, get under the covers with *The Debutante's Guide to Life*. Reading it always made me feel better.

"Sure there is. Come to New York with me," said Patrick.

I shook my head. Even thinking about it was a cruel joke.

"I can't leave—especially now."

"Your mother needs money, right?"

"Right."

"Well, you can't help her that much staying here."

"But that was our deal. I'd get my license and work at Doreen's for a while."

"Georgia . . ." Patrick reached over and squeezed my knee. "How much money do you bring in at the salon?"

The light turned green, and we lurched forward.

"A few hundred bucks," I said. I instantly regretted saying "bucks." Cornelia Guest would never say "bucks."

"A day?" asked Patrick.

"A week."

"Oh."

We drove on in silence, except for the banging motor. We passed Mr. Shaw's nursery; all the flowers and plants were indoors for the winter season—and in New Hampshire, winter often lasted until the middle of April. It was brown and scrubby, the ground covered by mud and patches of melting snow. Then we drove by the big brick building of Weekeepeemie High. I looked out the window at the empty parking lot, the school quiet on a late Saturday afternoon, and thought about how, the whole time I was there, every single moment of every single day, all I wanted was to escape.

"Let me tell you something," said Patrick. "You and me . . . we're working-class people, right?"

I nodded.

"You know, there's only a couple of ways that we can make a lot of money. A whole lot of money," said Patrick. "One of them is becoming a contractor, or a builder. And we're not about to do *that*."

I laughed in spite of myself, imagining Patrick holding a chain saw.

"Another way is to go to New York and become hugely successful hairstylists," said Patrick. "And you know we can do it."

"What makes you think I could get a job in New York?" I asked him.

"I'll get you a job," he said. We turned onto my street—one identical split-level house after another.

"Patrick, that's so sweet of you, but you can't just—"

"You don't think I have the pull?"

"I don't know—I mean, this new salon—"

"Jean-Luc," he interrupted.

"Yeah, Jean-Luc. Do we even know if it's going to be successful? A million salons must open in New York every year."

Patrick pulled the Impala into my driveway and cut the engine, which gave one last bang. "Trust me," he said.

I looked up at the yellow light glowing in Melodie's window in the dusk. She was going to BU in the fall, and even though they were giving her full tuition, there was still room and board to consider. In fact, I had been doing little other than considering it for the last few months.

I turned to Patrick. His dark eyes were shining. And I realized that—of course. Of course I was going to New York with him to live and work at the Jean-Luc Salon. Of course Patrick and I were going to find an apartment together—maybe Ursula would be able to help us—and we were going to finally be in a place that made sense. Maybe Patrick and I would get married someday. And of course I'd make more money, mountains of money, enough to save Doreen's and put Melodie through school.

"Okay," I said. I leaned my head on Patrick's shoulder. "Okay."

The Hottest Salon in the World

Fourteen clients were lined up on the banquette—an entirely unreasonable number. Even Jean-Luc himself seemed slightly ruffled by the volume of it all, though a stranger wouldn't have known it to look at him. A single lock of brilliantined hair had fallen over his forehead in a comma, and there was a small but constant twitch at the corner of his mouth.

The salon had been open for three months, and in that short span of time it had become, no exaggeration, the hottest salon in the world. Jean-Luc was the envy of stylists from New York to Paris to Tokyo. There wasn't a magazine editor who did not—after receiving her complimentary haircut, highlights, blow-dry, and, in the case of a select few, a visit into Jean-Luc's *privée* inner sanctum—trot back to her magazine, her sleek head shining in the Manhattan afternoon sun, and commission an article about Jean-Luc. Here, Jean-Luc standing in front of the fountain of the Plaza hotel, dapper in his trademark black leather jacket. There, a photo taken inside the salon, of Jean-Luc styling the hair of the anchorwoman for the six o'clock news. His pronouncements were everywhere, quoted in *Vogue*, *Harper's Bazaar, Women's Wear Daily*: If Jean-Luc suggested that short was the new long, or blond the new red, or curls were over, ten thousand women followed suit. It had taken no time at all for women at Upper East Side cocktail parties and bene-fits to turn to one another with small, knowing smiles. *Jean-Luc?* one might ask the other. *But of course!*

I was assisting Richard, one of the senior colorists. Richard—who pronounced his name *Ree-shard*—was really named Ricky and was from somewhere in northern New Jer-sey—a fact that only I knew and had locked away like the valu-able secret it was. I had told only Patrick.

"Guess who called Richard today?"

"Who?"

"Richard's mom."

"Really? From Paris?"

"Um . . . no."

"Come on."

"Let's put it this way." I spoke in my best New Jersey accent. "Hiya, is Ricky there?"

Patrick clamped a hand over his mouth. *"Ricky?"*

"You can't tell anyone."

"Of course not."

"It's too good."

We both hated Richard, and we were in good company. But the clients loved him, and the clients were who mattered. Richard wore his long platinum hair pulled back in a ponytail and had a small diamond stud in his ear. He wore only Hermès from head to toe: our uniforms of black bottoms and white tops taken to the extreme, or at least the extremely expensive, which the clients knew and appreciated. His trademark—in case any-one could have missed it—was a black alligator belt with a gold H buckle.

"Darling, how's your little country place in—where is it again?" asked Mrs. L.

"New Hope," said Richard. He ran the long end of his tail comb through a section of her hair, then handed me the sec-tion. Richard didn't believe in hair clips or clamps, so to be his assistant was to be, in fact, a human hair clip. And being Richard's human hair clip was a promotion, actually, consider-ing where I had started. When Jean-Luc first hired me, I was sweeping the clients' hair from the marble floor. Blond, brunette, auburn, gray, and every shade in between were swept up and out of the way. By the end of the day, garbage bags were so full of hair that it looked as though we were dumping large fluffy animals into the trash.

For the moment I was happy—well, happy is maybe too strong a word, so let's say hopeful—assisting Richard. I kept sending him positive energy, the way I had read in magazines. Every time he said or did something nasty, I pictured him bathed in a sea of white, healing light.

"New Hope is *magnifique*—it is my little secret," Richard said.

Mrs. L sat pin straight in her chair. Her handbag, perched in front of her on its own built-in shelf, was encased in plastic. Most clients at the salon were given plastic Ziploc-type bags to protect their purses from the remote possibility of spilled con-ditioner or splattered bleach. This was an innovation of Jean-Luc's, after, in another salon, a client sued because of a ruined Hermès Kelly bag.

"I just had my window boxes done," said Richard. "On the second-floor balcony of my house. The flowers"—he waved his

hand in the air, narrowly missing my eye with his tail comb—
"they kept *dying*. Just withering and *dying*."

Mrs. L nodded sympathetically as I held another section of
her mouse-brown hair flecked with Richard's golden highlights.

"So do you know what I did?" Richard leaned forward and
dropped his voice to a whisper. "Silk."

"Silk?"

"The flowers," he said in his heavy French accent. "They
are silk."

"Brilliant," breathed Mrs. L.

Mrs. P, Richard's previous client, was at the sink, with a
gloss setting on her head. Her timer had gone off during
Richard's rhapsody about his window boxes, and I was not at
all sure he had heard it. It was my job to rinse the gloss, but it
was also my job to hold the sections of Mrs. L's hair, so I wasn't
sure what to do. There seemed to be no possibility of breaking
into their conversation.

"Do you think I could call your window box designer?"
asked Mrs. L. "My house in East Hampton needs help. There's
just simply too much sunshine."

"Of course—he's marvelous," said Richard. "He does have a
waiting list, but use my name."

Standing by Richard and doing nothing more than holding
hunks of hair gave me ample opportunity to check out the action in the salon. Richard may have had no idea that fourteen
clients were waiting on the banquette, but I did. I caught a
glimpse of Patrick, who had quickly gained a reputation for
giving a fabulous blow-dry. The clients always asked for him,
and even though he wasn't officially supposed to be taking his
own appointments, Jean-Luc had made an exception. Patrick
looked tense, and I saw that he was backed up, too.

"This place is a factory," I heard one of the clients complain as Jean-Luc passed by. Slowly he turned, step by step, inch by inch, and faced down the client.

"Madame," he said, drawing himself up to his full five feet seven inches. "Zees is not a factory. Zees"—he motioned to the bustling salon—"is poetry in motion. Zees is a thing of beauty."

He turned, snapping his fingers at one of the Romanian ladies. We had half a dozen such ladies who did manicures, pedicures, and waxing. Back home in Bucharest, the lady who came running when Jean-Luc snapped his fingers had been a chemistry teacher. "Please—a complimentary manicure," he said.

"Oh, thank you, Jean-Luc," the client said, tossing her wet head coquettishly.

Mostly, as I assisted Richard, I studied Faith Honeycomb. Her station was behind us, in its own private area—it even had its own special banquette for Faith's clients. If I looked in Richard's mirror, I could appear to be watching his client, but in fact I was focused entirely on Faith. She was her own little island of calm in the frenzy of the Jean-Luc Salon. No matter how backed up she got—and even this was an infrequent occurrence, since she ran her operation like an army general—she seemed unfrazzled. At peace, even. People whispered about Faith all the time. Was she a Zen Buddhist? Was she on Valium? But I thought I knew the secret to Faith's tranquillity: She was *focused*. While all the other colorists and stylists were busy swiveling their heads to see which movie star, which famous politician's girlfriend, had just walked through the door, Faith maintained her attention on her client, and consequently her work was always nothing less than remarkable. In many ways, she reminded me of my mother.

I watched as she did *baliage* on a blonde in her chair, painting carefully chosen strands of hair with the precision and concentration of a surgeon.

Not so Richard. It had now been at least five minutes since Mrs. P's timer had gone off, and Richard still hadn't noticed. He and Mrs. L had discovered that they shared the same personal trainer, and this had sent Richard into a fit of euphoria.

"I cannot believe!" he screeched. "Duncan, he is the best! Does he make you do those—how you call them—those crunchy things?"

"Oh, my God," moaned Mrs. L. "And what about that neck massage he gives you at the end? He calls it an adjustment, but—"

"Excuse me, Richard?" Mrs. P sidled up behind him.

"Yes, what is it, darling?"

"My—I think my timer may have gone off," said Mrs. P.

"Impossible!"

"No, really, I'm quite sure—"

Richard then finally glanced at Mrs. P's hair. The gloss had clearly been left on too long and had turned it, beneath the gel, a darker shade of red than she was going to be happy with. I watched as his nostrils flared.

"Georgia," he said in the softest, sweetest of tones, "would you be so kind as to accompany Mrs. P to the sink and do a quick golden gloss on her?"

"But, Richard"—Mrs. P checked her watch, a diamond-encrusted chronograph on a pink lizard band—"I'm running late."

"Trust me." Richard flashed his most winning smile. "You will be tickled pink with the result."

He took the hunk of Mrs. L's hair from my fingers and gave me a little shove toward the sink. I knew from experience that the nicer Richard was to the client, the more furious he was

74

with the people around him—namely, me. I tried to breathe deeply as I guided Mrs. P to the sink. How would Faith Honeycomb handle this moment?

I wrapped a fresh towel around Mrs. P's neck and quickly washed off the offending gloss.

"Nothing's wrong, is there?" Mrs. P asked. From my angle above her, I could see the way gravity worked on her face lift. Her whole face moved in one piece, as if all the muscles were frozen.

"Nothing at all," I said in what I hoped was a soothing voice. In truth, her hair had turned a delicate shade of violet. "I'll just be a minute while I mix the gloss."

I hurried to the back room, praying all the while that Mrs. P wouldn't decide to sit up and look in the mirror.

I knew that a golden gloss wasn't going to do the trick. She was too far gone. So I made a quick calculation: Which would piss off Richard more? To do as he asked and leave him with a miserable client? A client who, if memory served me correctly, was the wife of a famous lawyer? I shook my head hard, trying to think straight. I needed to take care of this myself.

So the professional in me—I was, after all, Doreen's daughter—did the only possible thing. I snuck quickly into the back room and mixed up a series of glosses that might just do the trick. Then I worked with the precision of a chemist, painting Mrs. P's scalp with first one and then another potion that restored her highlights—the proper auburn streaks slowly appearing—to what Richard, had he been paying attention, would have originally intended. Then I sent Mrs. P off to have her complimentary blow-dry and gingerly made my way back to Richard's side. He had by now moved on from Mrs. L and their shared glee at silk flowers and personal trainers and was doing a single-process on an elderly woman who had been brought over by one of the senior stylists—squeezing one more client into his impossibly busy schedule.

I stood by his side for at least five minutes before he spoke to me. Nor was he speaking to his client, who seemed like a perfectly nice little old lady but had committed the unforgivable sin of wearing polyester pants, carrying a fake Gucci handbag (the Gs were backward, a dead giveaway), and wearing a Timex watch.

Finally, after apparently having decided that I had squirmed long enough, Richard turned to me.

"I suggest you use your lunch break," he said, his accent even heavier than usual, "to go shopping for some new clothes. You look"—he swept his hand up and down like a scepter—"like a cocktail waitress."

The little old lady's eyes—round as saucers—met mine in the mirror. It was all I could do not to burst into tears, or at the very least run out of Jean-Luc Salon never to return. But Doreen hadn't raised a quitter. I nodded slowly, as if contemplating the wisdom of Richard's point of view. I studied myself in the mirror, casting a critical eye at what I had thought to be a creative interpretation of the Jean-Luc dress code. I was wearing black tights (opaque, shiny), black hot pants, square-toed high-heeled boots with gold buckles, and a white tuxedo shirt, open at the neck. I had felt sexy and cute when I'd left my apartment that morning. Now I felt cheapened by Richard's scorn. Maybe he was right. Maybe I didn't know how to dress in order to fit into the universe of Jean-Luc.

"Okay, I'll head out now," I said, trying to keep my voice from trembling.

"Here, honey, let me give you something," said the little old lady, reaching into her handbag.

"You don't have to tip Georgia," said Richard. His voice

dripped over my name as if I were just a total joke of a human being. I tried to bathe him in a sea of white light. It wasn't working.

"No, really . . ." The little old lady kept digging for her damned wallet. I hoped for her sake that it wasn't a fake Gucci.

"No, I *insist* you don't," said Richard. "Our assistants are very well compensated. And we wouldn't want to spoil them."

He winked at her, an oily wink, and then looked at me in the mirror, as if daring me to speak. It was a complete lie. I mean, we *lived* on our tips. The salon paid us next to nothing. Jean-Luc even made us pay for our own business cards. And this wasn't the first time that Richard had done this. He was always telling clients that they really shouldn't tip me. I kept trying to figure out why. I mean, was he trying to get more for himself? What could my pennies possibly mean to him? *It's because deep down he knows that you're the real thing*, Patrick had told me over and over. *And he's just a big fat fucking fraud.*

As I left the salon and headed out onto Fifth Avenue, I felt like an insect. No, smaller than an insect. Richard had reduced me to something invisible. A speck. An amoeba, like we studied under the microscope in biology class at Weekeepeemie High. I passed a pay phone and stopped. I dug into my purse for the loose dimes I always kept there. There was one voice I needed to hear more than anything in the world. I slid dime after dime into the coin slot. It wasn't the first time I had done this, and I knew that it required twenty dimes to call Weekeepeemie from Manhattan.

"Doreen's, can I help you?"

"Mom? What are you doing answering the phone?"

"Oh, you know." She laughed. "Just waiting around for my next appointment."

"Oh." Standing on the corner of Fifty-seventh and Fifth, I

was hit by a wave of homesickness so intense that my teeth ached. I couldn't keep talking or I was going to cry. I mean, what was I doing in New York City, anyway? I wasn't making enough money to send home. What was the point?

"Georgia?" My mother's voice wafted through the phone lines. She was far away—too far away. "George? You okay?"

"It's nothing." I gulped. "I just miss you, that's all."

"Oh, honeybun."

I tried to pull myself together.

"But you know what? Pretty soon I'm going to send you five hundred bucks," I said. "I know it's not much, but with my tips, I should be able to—"

"Don't you worry about me," said my mother. "You just take care of yourself."

"I love you," I said.

A fire truck sped by, siren wailing.

"I love you, too, baby," said Doreen. It sounded quiet on her end, that kind of midday Weekeepeemie quiet where you can hear people talking on the street outside the salon. My knees felt weak, and I was afraid I was going to just lose it.

"I gotta go," I said.

Fifty-seventh Street east of Fifth Avenue was one long line of luxury shops, their windows glittering with gems and fur and supple leather, cottons so fine that they looked like silk. I recognized clients of Jean-Luc's as I walked. I smiled at them, but they had no idea who I was. A tall, beautiful blond girl who worked at *Vogue* climbed out of a chauffeur-driven Mercedes, one perfect leg unfolding at a time. She had just been in the salon the day before—Jean-Luc had cut her hair and Faith had done her color—and one of the other assistants showed me a photo spread of her in that month's *Town & Country*. She was an It girl; that's what girls like her were called. In one of the pictures I saw, she was lying on a hammock at her family's estate in Portugal. In another, she was riding a horse bareback on the beach. And here she was, ducking into Hermès as her driver waited at the curb.

I waved, then faltered. What kind of idiot was I, anyway? She looked at me with a quizzical, gentle, well-bred expression, as if to ask, *Do I know you from somewhere?* Like maybe I had been her masseuse in Biarritz. Or given her a facial at Georgette Klinger.

I kept my head down, huddled against the cold. Where was I going to find something I could afford in this neighborhood? Finally, I remembered one store. Ann Taylor was a place I never would have been caught dead in, full of conservative blazers and sweater sets, attire for the young aspiring businesswoman. But I couldn't exactly walk into Hermès or Gucci or any of the places favored by the clients, senior stylists, and colorists of Jean-Luc. In fact, I had walked into Hermès only once, on my first day in New York. I had wanted to send my mother a present, wrapped in the handsome orange-and-brown wrapping that I had seen immortalized in *Vogue*. In the end, after looking at the smallest items—the scarves, the pens, the wallets—what I was able, and just barely, to send Doreen was soap.

"May I help you?" a salesgirl asked.

I looked at my watch. I had fifteen minutes in which to transform myself. I took a couple of deep breaths.

"Yes, please. I need black pants—trousers—the plainest you've got. And a white shirt. Also plain. Oh, and black shoes."

"Do you work at Jean-Luc?" the salesgirl inquired, smiling.

I was instantly relieved, and also curious. Which of the stylists had stooped to Ann Taylor? Or was there just not that obvious a difference between a ninety-dollar pair of pants and a five-hundred-dollar pair? Maybe if an It girl wore ninety-dollar pants, they would look like a million bucks. Not that she ever would. I left Ann Taylor exactly fifteen minutes later with a lighter heart and two outfits that would fit perfectly at the salon.

Back at Jean-Luc, after I ducked into the bathroom, slipped into my new Ann Taylor ensemble, and stuffed my own clothes into my knapsack, it was time for Richard's lunch. All of the other senior stylists and colorists ordered their own lunches or brought in whatever they planned to eat during the day. But not Richard. No. Richard expected me, as part of my duties as his assistant, to order his mozzarella on panini and cappuccino from Nello's on Madison and to fork over the twenty bucks that it cost. For which, it will come as no surprise, he often forgot to reimburse me. When Richard's lunch arrived at the salon, I took it from the delivery boy and brought it up to the staff room.

The staff room was the beating heart of Jean-Luc, the one place where the assistants and junior stylists and senior stylists and colorists all caught their breath. It felt a little bit like back-stage at a play. The main action, the drama, the illusion of per-fection, was out there on the salon floor, and the staff room was where all the unsexy details got taken care of. When clients or-dered their lunches from the local coffee shop, the paper bags, plastic forks and knives, and plastic plates were disposed of, and Paco, the salon's resident busboy, brought out the carefully arranged Cobb salads and fruit medleys on cloth-lined wicker trays that could be balanced on the clients' laps while they re-ceived their treatments. You haven't lived until you've seen a client get a blow-dry and a manicure while trying to eat a sand-wich without smudging her nails.

Patrick was already in the staff room, grabbing a quick bite with *his* senior colorist, Lois. Lois was the coolest thing going at Jean-Luc: a great-looking, sandy-haired wisp of a woman who wore white cashmere sweaters and elegant, man-tailored trousers.

"Hey!" Patrick said as I walked through the door. "Where'd you go?"

"Don't ask."

"Come sit."

Lois patted an empty chair next to her. She was a lipstick lesbian—a term I had never heard until Patrick used it—and she lived up to her description. Her lips were perfectly lined in her signature crimson, stark and beautiful against her otherwise bare face. She was rumored to be dating a famous and famously closeted actress, but nobody knew for sure.

"I can't," I said. "I've got to get Richard's lunch ready."

Lois rolled her eyes. "That guy really needs to—"

"Wait a minute," said Patrick. "What are you wearing?"

"I—"

"That wasn't what you had on this morning."

"Richard said I—"

"Richard!" Patrick exploded.

"—looked like a cocktail waitress," I finished weakly.

"The cocktail waitress of my dreams," said Lois.

The door to the staff room swung open and Jean-Luc came in, along with Massimo, the über–senior stylist. Massimo and Jean-Luc had worked together at the same salon before Jean-Luc got the backing to open his own place, and Massimo was understood to be a) more talented than Jean-Luc; and b) secretly pissed off at the way Jean-Luc got all the glory. He was also one of the most decent of all the senior people. He always stopped and said hello to me in the morning, and he had a warmth to his brown eyes that made me instantly comfortable, when really I should have been totally intimidated. I mean, the guy was a genius.

"*Alors!*" exclaimed Jean-Luc. "It is fucking insane out there, so be quick about it—*mangia, mangia!*"

Massimo scowled, irritated that even this—his mother tongue—was being appropriated by Jean-Luc.

"Did you see Sigourney Weaver this morning?" Lois asked Jean-Luc. "I noticed her on the books."

"She sent her assistant," Jean-Luc said with a flutter of his fingers, as if waving good-bye to the whole experience. "She tricked me—that Sigourney—as if I would ever have made myself available at the last minute for a secretary."

Jean-Luc's purplish black lip curled in scorn.

"Was that the girl with the curly hair?" asked Patrick. "You did a beautiful cut on her."

"*Merci,*" Jean-Luc said with a small, formal bow. "But still—to be honest—do we care?"

I caught Lois's eye. What did she think of all this? I wondered if Jean-Luc really meant it or if his cynicism was all part of an elaborate act. Certainly, on the other side of the staff room wall, on the stage set of the salon—where the polished wood gleamed and the magazines were set out in a perfect fan, where the staff was trained to always smile, to be helpful to a fault— Jean-Luc was the embodiment of charm. He would never be impolite to a client. He knew that, ultimately, service was what mattered. There were half a dozen salons in New York City that could compete with Jean-Luc when it came to talent. But none offered Jean-Luc's level of service. Half-caff-decaf-cappuccino with skim milk? No problem. A manicure *and* pedicure during a blow-dry? But of course. Heated waxing tables, telephones at every station, a concierge to take care of every whim from restaurant reservations to theater tickets. Clients brought their little dogs, fluffy, groomed, with names like Poofy and François. Sometimes they brought their babies, along with the requisite baby nurse. Whatever made them happy—special— was what would make them return.

I retreated to the counter near the coffeemaker to put Richard's lunch on a plate for him. He always took his lunch at exactly one o'clock, whether or not he had clients waiting. The other senior stylists squeezed in a bite to eat if and when they had a fifteen-minute break.

Jean-Luc knocked back a double espresso and let out a deep and dramatic sigh. "And now I have Mrs. Z," he said. Mrs. Z was one of the salon's more, shall we say, *generous* customers. She was . . . well, her age was difficult to pin down: forty-seven? fifty-five? older? She had gone under the knife so many times that the skin behind her ears was as hard and knobby as an alligator's. She made her entrance into the salon the way a man might walk into a high-priced strip club: with fifty-dollar bills flying. No one got less than fifty dollars for attending to Mrs. Z. Esmeralda, who took her coat and gave her a robe, got fifty. Jing Su, who shampooed her, got fifty. If you said hello to Mrs. Z, you pretty much were guaranteed a fifty.

Massimo slumped down at the table next to Lois and Patrick as Jean-Luc made his exit. He unwrapped a plastic bag filled with green stuff that looked like something washed up on a beach.

I looked at him quizzically.

He grinned back at me and shrugged. "My nutritionist. He says it is good for detoxification."

In my three short months at Jean-Luc, it never ceased to amaze me how focused everyone who worked there seemed to be on their health: special brews, concoctions, and bottles of vitamins filled the staff shelves. Yet at the end of the day, you could find any of them at the hippest bars and restaurants in town, drinking martinis and smoking cigarettes and in the bathrooms of those establishments doing a whole lot more. Though I didn't know whether that was the case with Massimo. He was so gorgeous—maybe he was just a health nut.

Richard pushed through the door just as Patrick and Lois were clearing their plates. "Where is my lunch?" he asked me.

"I—it's ten minutes before one," I stammered. "I've got it right—"

His ponytail had come loose, and the hair around his temples had curled, so he looked like a cross between a beach boy and a Hasidic Jew. His eyes blinked rapidly.

"*Excusez-moi.* I don't think I asked you for the time," he said. "I asked you where the fuck is my lunch?"

Everyone in the staff room fell silent. Lois, Patrick, Paco—who was unpacking a client's lunch at the sink.

"I was just unpacking it," I said. I tried to keep my voice steady.

"Do you know what your problem is?" Richard asked.

I shook my head. My cheeks were hot, blood pounding through my head. My ears rang. Maybe I really didn't belong there. Maybe I should have stayed exactly where I had come from and continued to be the coolest girl in Weekeepeemie.

"You think you know something," said Richard. He was raising his voice, and if he wasn't careful, a bit of New Jersey was about to slip in. "You know *nothing!*"

"I'm sorry," I mumbled. "I—"

"Excuse me." Patrick's sweet voice filled the room. I closed my eyes. *Don't get involved,* I sent him a silent plea. I didn't want him to lose his job on my account. He was the only thing I was living for in all of New York City.

Richard wheeled around and stared at Patrick. "Yes, my pretty?"

"Lay off her," said Patrick.

"Why? Are you *laying* her? I didn't know you had it in you."

"Stop it, *Ricky.*"

Patrick said it quietly, but with enough emphasis. Richard took a step back, his forehead creased in puzzlement. It was so quiet in the staff room that you could hear the hum of the refrigerator as it clicked on.

"I must go now," he said stiffly, "to check on my client."

Lois pinched the bridge of her nose, frowning. As the door swung closed behind Richard, she walked over to me and gave me a hug.

"I'm sorry, love."

"It's okay."

"No, it's not. No one should ever speak to anyone like that."

"What a total jerk," said Patrick. "Are you okay?"

"I'm fine," I said, perhaps too vehemently. I wanted to put the whole episode behind me as quickly as possible.

"Let's go out tonight," said Patrick. "My treat."

"No, *my* treat," said Lois.

"That's right, guys. Fight over me."

"By the way, why'd you call him Ricky?"

"Because he's really—" Patrick stopped when I flashed him a warning look. Richard was a jerk of the first degree, but I understood his desire to reinvent himself, and I didn't want to be the one to ruin it for him. Who knew how many years it had taken him to learn that perfect French accent or to become a person who knew about silk flowers in window boxes and all things Hermès? Sometimes, when I looked at Richard, I caught a glimpse of the weird, outcast kid from Verona, New Jersey, he must once have been. We were all like that, all of us who ended up doing hair.

"I'm going back on the floor," I said.

"I'll join you," said Patrick. "Our one-fifteen is probably waiting."

"But wait," Lois called after us. "You haven't told me why—"

"Some other time," said Patrick. Even though he hated Richard almost as much as I did, I could see that he understood.

THREE O'CLOCK, WE had one of the girls from Click come in. This was a regular occurrence. Click, Ford, Elite, and Wilhelmina all sent us their models—particularly their brand-new models, just off the bus from Nebraska or the boat from Iceland. They wafted through the doors of Jean-Luc, fawnlike, delicate creatures, improbably tall, with features that rendered their faces somehow unique and beautiful. A pair of puffy lips, or hooded blue eyes, or a mass of auburn curls—as was the case with this particular model, who crossed her legs and folded her arms as Richard regarded her in the mirror.

"I think we need a bit of chestnut," he said, his hands resting on her narrow shoulders. "To create more contrast with the red."

The girl shook her head, curls flying. "My agency says not to change it. Just a few natural highlights. That's all."

"Trust me," said Richard. "This will make your career. You will go from being just another pretty girl to—*et voilà!*—a supermodel. I have done them all. Elle MacPherson. Cindy Crawford. You name it."

The girl shook her head again, and this time she scowled. "I said no. Really—my booker will kill me."

"Georgia . . ." Richard turned to me. "Would you please go mix the light auburn with the chestnut brown?"

"You're not listening!" said the girl.

I followed Richard's orders, propelled by my resolution to do whatever I had to do to get along with him. The only way anyone moved up at Jean-Luc was by assisting a senior person and eventually getting noticed. I suppose I could have gone to the staff manager and asked to be switched to another colorist, but the risk was too great that I'd simply be asked to leave.

In the color-mixing room, I pulled down two tall cans of light auburn and chestnut and measured one ounce of each into a bowl, along with two ounces of developer. The girl's hair would actually look quite pretty, I thought. Not that it wasn't pretty already. I was stirring it all together with a plastic paintbrush when I heard Jean-Luc's voice, coming closer.

"What do you think you were doing over there?" he asked as he and Richard pushed through the curtains separating the color-mixing room from the shampoo area.

"She was trying to tell me how—"

"She is the *client*," said Jean-Luc. He was speaking very softly, but his face was only inches away from Richard's.

"She's a model. She doesn't even pay," said Richard. "What do you expect me to do? Kiss her ass?"

At this, Jean-Luc moved even closer. I wasn't sure either of them was aware of my presence in the room. I had pressed myself against the wall, wishing I could disappear. Jean-Luc's eyes bulged, and a white string of spittle formed at the corner of his mouth.

"I'm Jean-Luc," he hissed. "And I kiss ass."

Then he swiveled around and strode back into the salon.

Richard wiped his forehead and sighed deeply. For a moment he looked almost human. As though he might even cry. But then he noticed me. He took the bowl of light auburn and chestnut from my hands and dumped the whole thing into the sink.

"What are you looking at?" he snapped. "Get back to work."

"I THINK YOU should talk to Jean-Luc," said Lois.

It was close to midnight, and we were all beyond tipsy, edging toward the land of drunken oblivion. Paddy's Pub was hopping, though, perched as it was just a few blocks north of Times Square, full of frat boys and a few straggling theatergoers who had just come out of *Cats*. We were sitting in the darkened window, Patrick, Lois, Kathryn, and me. Kathryn, the assistant who seemed to know it all, was a last minute addition to our evening—one I hadn't been too happy about. But whether it was the five Baileys on the rocks or something about Kathryn herself this evening, I had decided that she was all right.

"I can't," I said.

"She can't," said Patrick at the same moment.

"Why not?" asked Lois.

"Have you forgotten what it's like?" Patrick responded. "We are all—every single one of us—totally expendable. He doesn't need us. He doesn't give a shit." He turned to Kathryn, who was bent over her Irish coffee, her silky blond hair spilling over her shoulders, which were bare, gleaming under her black tank top. How did she get her skin to gleam like that? "Except you, of course," said Patrick.

Kathryn looked up, her green eyes wide and exquisite. She

88

was so shockingly beautiful that it made it difficult for people to get beyond that—to think anything else about her.

She blushed. "That's not true," she said. "He'd let me go in one minute."

Lois laughed. "Yeah, right."

It was a well-known fact, so obvious that no one even bothered to gossip about it, that Jean-Luc had a wicked crush on Kathryn, who had been assisting him since the salon opened. *Kath-e-run,* he would practically sing her name, dividing it into three syllables, *watch this angle,* and he would snip long, layered bangs on a client, performing for both the client's benefit and Kathryn's. All the assistants assumed she would be the first of us to be promoted, to be given her own chair on the floor of the salon, and to be allowed to book her own appointments.

"What are you going to do, then?" Lois asked as she lit one of her many Marlboros. "You can't keep taking his shit."

"I have to," I said. I closed my eyes. The room was spinning just a bit, and I wondered how I was going to manage in the morning. Shaking hands were simply not an option. Could I forbid a hangover, scare it away?

"Are you all right?" asked Patrick.

"Yeah." I tried to take a deep breath. "I don't feel so hot." I pushed my chair back. "I'm going to find the ladies' room."

"I'll go with you," Kathryn said quickly.

We wove our way through the bar, past a group of guys wearing football jerseys and I LOVE NY sweatshirts. Even in my drunken state, I could see the way they were ogling Kathryn. In Weekeepeemie I had been one of the prettiest girls around, but in New York I didn't even begin to measure up.

"Here . . ." Kathryn steered me to a door that said "Dames." She flicked the light switch and a fluorescent bulb blinked on overhead. She pulled a paper towel from a dispenser on the wall and wet it with some water. Then she pressed it against my forehead.

"That sweet stuff will get you sick every time," she said.

"Don't remind me."

"Sorry."

I leaned against a stall door and stumbled backward as it gave way. "Oh God," I said. "I don't know how I'm going to get up in the morning."

"Call in sick," said Kathryn. She kept wiping my forehead and cheeks with the cold towel.

"You know I can't."

"Listen," she said. "Let me talk to Jean-Luc. I don't think he has any idea how bad Richard is."

"That's really nice of you, but—"

"Really, I'd be happy to. I promise I won't get you into trouble. I know how to talk to him."

I was reminded of the one rumor that I felt slightly guilty for believing—and gossiping about—which had to do with the nature of Kathryn's relationship with Jean-Luc.

Kathryn blinked and took a step back, as if she could read my mind. "I've been assisting the guy for three months," she said quietly. "I know how he thinks."

"Let me think about it," I said. Then, impulsively, I reached over and gave her a hug. She was okay. It wasn't her fault that she was gorgeous and talented and clearly destined for a fabulous life. I couldn't hold that against her. After all, wasn't that what all of us wanted?

"Patrick's such a nice guy," she said, changing the subject.

"He is, isn't he?" I answered dreamily.

"It's too bad, really."

Kathryn was examining her lipstick in the mirror.

"What's too bad?"

"You know. That he's gay," she said.

"What are you talking about?"

She gave me a long, searching look. Then she just shook her head slowly from side to side.

"Oh, honey," she said. "Don't even think about it."

WE PUSHED OUR way back to our window booth, where Patrick and Lois sat bathed in the pink neon lights of Times Square. Through the fog in my head, I was freaking out. All the pieces of the puzzle came tumbling . . . no, *crashing* . . . into place. Patrick was gay. Of course. Patrick was gay—of course, of course. I was a moron for not figuring it out sooner, I know, but back in Weekeepeemie it just wasn't something you thought about people. And he had told me he loved me, hadn't he? I should have understood that he meant something different, that he could never love me *that way*. Those late nights in our pajamas, cuddled up together watching television, were all that was ever going to happen between us. And it was just like him not to tell me. How could he tell me? It was something he had probably only recently figured out for himself. Besides, the last thing in the world he wanted to do was break my heart.

I took a deep breath, steadying myself. I was drunk, yes. Drunker than drunk. And I loved a boy who was never going to be able to love me back. I looked at Patrick and raised my glass. My eyes were spilling over, but I didn't care.

"I love you," I said.

"I love you, too," he said back.

Kathryn was watching us, her eyes bright as a hawk's.

We all clinked our glasses.

"A toast," said Lois, slurring slightly. "To you three beautiful kids. You're going to be stars, each and every one of you."

"Oh, stop," said Patrick.

"No, you are," said Lois. "A hundred bucks says you three will be working on the floor before the end of the first year."

In Which Richard Moves Up in the World, or Beach Hair

The Hamptons, the Hamptons. Oh, what could be said about the Hamptons? Well, for one, nobody who really went there (as in owned, not rented, and not only owned but had been there for at least two generations and could talk about summering there as a child) called it the Hamptons. That much I had figured out. Apparently, referring to the spit of land on the eastern end of Long Island as "the Hamptons" was a dead give-away—a sign of the nouveau riche, the arriviste, as clients liked to say. To call someone an arriviste was the worst form of insult. It meant she was no more significant than a flea, a person who could be flicked off a tanned, gleaming shoulder on the beach at the Maidstone Club.

Those truly in the know (or very, very good at faking it) referred to the Hamptons only as "the east end" or, simply, "the beach." So here we were, on our way to the beach, traveling on that last refuge for those with no private jet or helicopter or fab convertible at their disposal: the Hampton Jitney. The jitney was like a cross between a limousine, a singles bar on wheels, and the glorified Greyhound bus that it really was. A girl in short shorts and a tank top—it was the last Friday in August—came walking down the aisle with the complimentary orange juice, bottled water, and copy of *Hamptons* magazine that were part of the twenty-six-dollar bus fare.

Patrick, Kathryn, and I were on our way to Southampton. Though I had never been there, I had figured out from clients that each Hampton had its own personality. East Hampton was where the movie people went. Sagaponack, next to East Hampton, was full of magazine editors and television people—there was even a beach there nicknamed "media beach" and spoken of sneeringly by those who had summered there as children, before the media had descended. The one saving grace of media beach was the fact that you could catch a glimpse of a Kennedy there. Even in the blasé world of Jean-Luc, a JFK Jr. sighting—particularly a shirtless JFK Jr. sighting—was something to swoon about. Then there was Bridgehampton, where hundreds of modern atrocities (this was the term the clients used) had been built on potato fields, as if spaceships had landed there, ruining the view. Sag Harbor was for the writers and artists, because by Hamptons standards it was affordable. Finally, there was Southampton. Home of the pink-and-green ensemble. Of the faded Lacoste shirt and beat-to-shit Docksiders, and the private club you could join only if your name was Muffy, Binky, or Buffy, and so was your mother's and grandmother's, and . . . well, you get the picture.

In the salon, day after day, I listened to clients talk about the Hamptons. (Look, I'm going to call it the Hamptons, okay? Why pretend?)

"Suki Singer's party on Lily Pond Lane is this weekend," a

client had said just the day before. I nodded encouragingly and made a mental note to find out who Suki Singer was, since clearly I was supposed to know.

"It's a white party," the client went on.

I didn't know what this meant, either. I feared it might mean that ethnic people weren't invited.

"Maybe I'll wear the Dolce miniskirt with just a simple tank top," she mused. "If I wear my white Gucci pants, they'll get grass stains."

The jitney ticket was going to be our only expense over Labor Day weekend, because we had been invited by Roxanne Middlebury, third wife of Edgar Middlebury, known to me only by black-and-white photographs of his shiny bald head on the society pages of *The New York Times*. Roxanne was, one way or another, the client of each of us. Kathryn gave her the sexy, layered bob she favored, I gave her honey gold highlights, and Patrick regularly styled her magnificent mane into sleek, glossy perfection.

We had arrived, Patrick, Kathryn, and I, stacked up like dominoes, falling one after the other, with seemingly little effort and—as Lois had predicted—great speed, onto the floor of the Jean-Luc Salon, where each of us was quickly developing a following. Patrick had been featured in *New York* magazine's "Best Bets" as the best blow-dry in the city. *W* had dubbed Kathryn "a young stylist to watch." And though I had yet to be written about in a national magazine, something even more amazing—at least to me—had happened. Faith Honeycomb had taken me under her wing. She liked my work, and she had begun to refer clients to me, because she had more than she could handle. I had even overheard Sweetie, the receptionist, on the phone with a client, referring to me as "Faith's protégée."

"Do you think Roxanne will pick us up?" asked Patrick. He was looking particularly, scruffily gorgeous, with three days' growth of stubble and a New York Yankees baseball cap (given to him by the wife of the general manager, a client) pulled low over his eyes. I noticed his gorgeousness with a certain degree of detachment, a hard-won distance that I had developed to shield the sadness I always felt around Patrick. *Why?* I always felt inside, a silent wail. *Why do you have to like boys?*

"No way," I said. "She'll send the maid."

"Or the driver," said Kathryn. "The maid probably doesn't drive."

"Good point."

"You know, she said her house was a cottage," I said. "They're so rich—there's no way they live in a cottage, right?"

Kathryn laughed. "Cottage doesn't mean the same thing out east," she said. "You'll see."

Kathryn was clearly more comfortable than Patrick or me in the world of the clients. She knew how to seem like one of them. She had attended many charity benefits on the arm of Jean-Luc and had the slightly world-weary air of a girl who has seen one too many canapés.

"Hey, look at Esme!" Patrick said, stopping on a page of *Hamptons* magazine that he had been idly flipping through. "What did they do to her hair?"

Esme, a Ford model who was, of course, a client, was featured in a fashion layout that seemed to be an homage to Bo Derek in *10*. She was spread out on a rocky cove in Montauk, her hair braided into dozens and dozens of cornrows.

"That look just doesn't work on a white woman," Kathryn said dismissively. "The body is great, though."

"Yeah, and the lips," said Patrick.

I had noticed that all of us at the salon, myself included,

talked about the clients, particularly the models, this way. The face. The body. The nose. The lips. As if each of these features was separate and distinct from the whole person.

"Dr. Taylor," said Kathryn. She really did seem to know everything.

"Collagen?" asked Patrick.

"Collagen," said Kathryn.

"You're kidding! She's, like, twenty," I said.

"You can never start too young, according to Dr. Manfred Taylor," said Kathryn. She should know. Manfred Taylor— Manny, for short—was a client of Kathryn's (formerly of Jean-Luc's) who snuck into the salon first thing in the morning to have the few remaining gray hairs on his head snipped a centimeter and dyed dark brown.

"Southampton," announced the jitney driver as we pulled into a disappointingly nondescript parking lot where every single thing seemed to be called "Hampton": a gym, Sports Hampton; a dry cleaner, Clean Hampton; and a small gourmet store, Food Hampton.

We got off the bus with many of the other passengers. Judging from the traffic on the Long Island Expressway, nobody was left in the city. Tanned, fit men in their thirties with faces that looked older, wearing expensive sports shirts in colors no New Hampshire man would ever be caught dead in (pale pink, bright lavender), donned their mirrored sunglasses and checked their vintage Rolexes, wondering why their wives weren't waiting for them in their Mercedes station wagons. Girls around our age seemed to congregate in groups, every once in a while letting out the kind of high-pitched squeal that made you embarrassed to be of the same gender.

"Group share," said Kathryn.

"What's that?"

"Oh, you know. A bunch of them find a house—it's never one of the good houses—for thirty, forty thousand—"

"Dollars?" interrupted Patrick.

"Yeah. And then they come here every weekend trying to land a rich husband."

"I'd like to get my hands on that one," I said, pointing to a frizzy, bleached blonde.

At that moment a black Range Rover pulled into the parking lot. A tinted window on the driver's slide slid down, revealing Roxanne Middlebury herself.

"Yoo-hoo!" she called, waving a hand upon which flashed a diamond so large that it looked fake in the afternoon sun. I had noticed that most women who were clients of Jean-Luc's could be divided into two categories: those upon whom real jewels and haute couture were made to look somehow—well, there's only one word for it—cheap; and others who could mix designer pants with a great-looking top, and if asked where they got it would whisper "Costco" or "Sears" with a crafty little smile. On these women, costume jewelry bought on the streets of SoHo or in some far-flung ethnic bazaar looked like the real deal.

Sorry to say, Roxanne Middlebury was not one of these.

"Yoo-hoo!" she called again, waving us over. "Have y'all been waiting long?"

We clambered into the car, which smelled of new leather and—despite Roxanne's twin toddlers—had nary a crumb on the floor.

"Sorry," she said, backing up expertly, then making a screeching right turn onto Route 27. "Carlos, that's our driver, had to pick Nicky and Nora up from a play date in Wainscott, and Rosa doesn't drive, and I had to finish my Pilates or else my trainer would have killed me!"

"We were hardly waiting," murmured Kathryn.

"But I'm going to make it up to y'all," said Roxanne. From the backseat, I could see the teeny tiny bit of dimpling where her otherwise glorious thighs met the leather seat. She would have been horrified, former aerobics instructor that she was, and immediately booked an appointment for liposuction.

"Roxanne, we're so happy to be here," Patrick began. "You don't have to—"

"I got three extra tickets to tomorrow's benefit!"

Patrick nudged me with his leg. We had been sort of planning on a quiet day at the beach. I hadn't even brought anything fancy to wear.

"What's the benefit?" asked Kathryn, stifling a yawn. "Sorry, not enough oxygen on the jitney."

"Le Chic Chien," said Roxanne as we pulled off the main route and onto a sun-dappled street of pretty, modest houses.

"What is it?"

"Le Chic Chien," Roxanne repeated, as if of course we all would have heard of it.

"The chic dog?" asked Patrick.

"Yes, isn't that fabaroo? It's a doggy fashion show!"

Outside the tinted window, the houses started to get a bit bigger, the lawns more spread out, smoothly manicured and green.

"I'm dressing Fang in a Burberry raincoat," said Roxanne. I had seen pictures of Fang—a tiny white Maltese with a pink nose—at the salon. Roxanne had shown me Fang's photo one day when she was in town getting her portrait done—with her dog.

"Wow," I said. What else was there to say? Back in New Hampshire, dogs generally served a purpose: hunting, protection, Seeing Eye dogs, what have you. Okay, fluffy white dogs no bigger than possums were being dressed in clothes I couldn't begin to afford for myself. "Are any of the pooches wearing Calvin Klein?" I asked in a kind of ha-ha way.

"Well, Calvin's dog, I would think," Roxanne said thoughtfully. "But wouldn't it be hysterical if Calvin dressed his dog in, say, Marc Jacobs?"

She spun the wheel and turned onto what I thought was another street until the gates closing behind me tipped me off that it was, in fact, her driveway.

"Here we are," she sang out.

Patrick nudged my leg harder. Don't get me wrong. We liked Roxanne Middlebury. In a salon full of women with attitude, women who struck poses and made demands on us as if we were servants, Roxanne was real. She was just who she was. Which was, specifically, the ex–aerobics instructor from Body Design by Gilda who had lucked into the incredibly lucrative situation of becoming (and quite suddenly, I might add) the third wife—and second trophy wife—of Edgar Middlebury. Specifically, Edgar Middlebury of *those* Middleburys, whose money was so old that all it needed to do was multiply.

But in truth, we hadn't had any idea. Not really. Because when you see mansions photographed in magazines, you don't get a true sense of scale. We drove under a tall hedge sculpted into a bridge and past swans floating in a pond. A gardener rode a lawn mower the size of a small tractor over a vast expanse of lawn.

Cottage indeed.

Roxanne pulled, finally, up to the carved wooden doors of a home that reminded me of a French château.

"Who lives over there?" I asked, pointing to another equally grand house that seemed, in the scale of things, to be quite close by—meaning I could see it.

"Oh, that's the guesthouse," said Roxanne. "That's where y'all will be staying."

I pulled my overnight bag—still the trusty black LeSportsac that I had worn on my first visit to the city—out of the back of the Range Rover. At the time it had felt quite chic, but now it looked pathetic, out of place when set against the grand stone steps of Château Middlebury.

"Carlos will bring your things over to the guesthouse," said Roxanne. "Come on in. I'll show y'all around."

We were hit by a cool blast of air-conditioning as Roxanne opened the doors, shooing us inside. The heels of her bronze mules clicked against the black-and-white inlaid marble floor.

"Nice place," said Kathryn. I watched her eyes drift over an enormous print of Marilyn Monroe that dominated the foyer. It looked familiar to me, as if maybe I had seen a picture of it in an art book.

"Andy Warhol," said Roxanne.

"Amazing," said Patrick.

"This is the library," said Roxanne, clicking her way into an oval-shaped room with a cantilevered glass ceiling. "We designed it after the Temple of Dendur? You know, at the Met?"

We all nodded, but only Kathryn seemed to even vaguely know what she was talking about. A temple? I didn't think the Middleburys were Jewish.

The walls of the library were lined, floor to ceiling, with leather-bound books. This—more than the Marilyn Monroe painting—impressed me. It seemed like a lifetime of books. No, several lifetimes. I imagined generations of Middleburys, seated on old leather club chairs in front of crackling fires in their libraries, handing down these volumes to children and grandchildren. I ran a hand along the books and began to pull one out, but it didn't budge.

"Nooo!" Roxanne screeched.

I stopped, my fingers frozen in midair, shocked. What had I done? Had I committed some horrible social gaffe? I searched my brain for anything I might have read in *A Debutante's Guide to Life* about not touching books.

"They're not real!" said Roxanne, visibly shaken.

"What do you mean?"

"They're just the—what do you call them—the spines," said Roxanne. "Our decorator found the whole library somewhere in England, but we didn't want to lug all those books back here—imagine the expense!—so instead we had the spines removed."

We looked at her, dumbfounded.

"It's all right," said Roxanne, one hand to her ample chest. "No harm done. Please—come see the rest of the house."

The house tour took a full hour. There were the public rooms, of course: It turned out that the library, living room, and grand foyer were the public of the public rooms, meant for the huge amount of entertaining that the Middleburys, because of their social position, were called upon to do. There was a separate catering kitchen precisely for these rooms, and as Roxanne stood in the middle of it, looking not unlike Vanna White on *Wheel of Fortune,* it was clear to me that she almost never set foot in this kitchen. She probably didn't even deal with the caterers. When the invitation came to spend the weekend at the Middleburys', it was through Roxanne's social secretary.

"I love the living room drapes," said Kathryn.

"What?" Roxanne momentarily looked confused. "Oh, you mean the window treatments. Jad is a genius, isn't he?"

"Jad?" asked Patrick.

"Oh, you *must* know Jad," Roxanne said. It was clear that she was one of those people who assumed that all gay people know one another. "Jad Michaels?" she continued helpfully. "His name used to be Michael Wasserman before he changed it?"

"Doesn't ring a bell," said Patrick.

"Well, he'll be at the benefit tomorrow—you must meet him then," said Roxanne.

We followed Roxanne into the family area of Château Middlebury. Another living room and library, though this library did appear to be outfitted with real books. I wasn't entirely positive—but I wasn't about to find out. The shelves of the library, as well as scattered inlaid wooden end tables that looked centuries old, displayed Middlebury family memorabilia. Here, a photograph of Edgar Middlebury with his arm around a tuxedoed Ronald Reagan. There, a more recent picture of Edgar and Roxanne dancing with Barbra Streisand and Ted Kennedy. I wasn't sure what to make of the politics. Were the Middleburys Republicans? Democrats? Or just friends of the famous? And to top it all off, a framed photo of Eddie Murphy flanked by the Middlebury toddlers had a central spot above the ornately carved fireplace.

We wandered into the cavernous living room.

"That was Edgar's first antique." Roxanne pointed to a mahogany side piece. "He bought it when he was twenty-one years old. Seventy-five thousand dollars, and he was putting his boxer shorts in there. Can you imagine?"

We all shook our heads. This, at least, was true. We couldn't imagine it. I trailed after Roxanne up the stairs, vacuumed so that our steps left impressions in the plush, cream-colored carpet, as if we were walking through freshly fallen snow. Roxanne was talking, and though I kept nodding and pretending to listen, my mind had wandered four hundred miles north. I wished I had a hidden camera—or at least a tape recorder—so

I could share this with Doreen. I mean, she was never going to believe it. I had called her the day before to tell her I had been invited to a client's house for the weekend.

"Roxanne who?" Doreen had asked. My mother never read the society pages. Her idea of reading the paper was scanning the police blotter in the *Weekeepeemie Register.*

"Middlebury," I said. "Roxanne Middlebury. They're one of the oldest families in New York."

"Hmmm . . . why are they having you for the weekend?" Doreen asked.

"What do you mean? She just likes us."

"Uh-huh," Doreen said vaguely. "Well, you'll tell me all about it on Monday."

As Roxanne led us up a grand staircase, I noticed a towering grandfather clock on the landing. According to its golden filigreed hands, it was five-fifteen. Doreen was probably finishing up her last clients of the day: old Mrs. Appleby, or maybe Jane Clark, who came regularly on Fridays for a wash 'n set that would last her through the weekend. I felt a pang of loneliness, a cold, sharp ache between my shoulder blades. The air in the Middlebury house felt too clean. It had been vacuumed and dusted and waxed and polished until there was nothing left of the flesh and blood who lived there.

After the bedrooms (canopies, crisp white linens monogrammed with the Middlebury family crest), the children's rooms (murals of farm animals on the walls, complete with real antique barn doors that opened up to another mural of the rafters and cows inside the barn), the master bath (two bidets), and a guest wing that—given the guesthouse—had never, to Roxanne's knowledge, been used, we found ourselves back outside, gingerly making our way across a lawn so smooth that it looked like Astroturf.

Roxanne's princess heels left tiny pockmarks in the grass, as if golf tees had been sunk there. As we followed her swaying bottom toward the guesthouse, I wondered if her tan was real. Would she risk prematurely aging her skin in the name of vanity? Or was there a tan-in-a-bottle that could look so golden and natural?

"My masseuse is coming at six," she tossed over her shoulder. "If y'all would like massages after mine, be my guest."

She slid open the heavy glass doors on the ground floor of the guesthouse—or, rather, guest minimansion—and we walked into a state-of-the-art gym as big and as well equipped as any professional facility.

"Edgar built me this," she said.

She flipped a switch next to the door, and an easy-listening station filled the room.

"This is the best part," she said, guiding us over to a fogged-up glass door. Patrick opened it, and even Kathryn's jaw dropped. Inside was a swimming pool—it may have been Olympic size—with a glass ceiling that opened, in the shape of a clamshell, to the sky.

"Y'all feel free to take a swim and sauna," said Roxanne. The humidity of the pool room had caused her stick-straight blow-dry to frizz a little bit. "You did bring your suits, didn't you? Otherwise, I've got plenty."

It was impossible not to like Roxanne or to begrudge her any of her good fortune. She was just a big, happy kid who had wound up in the candy store of her dreams. And she wanted to share it. With us. She had a generous spirit, that Roxanne. I felt graced and lucky; the previous wave of loneliness drifted away.

"By the way," Roxanne said, "I almost forgot. Tomorrow? Before the benefit? Do you think y'all could do something with this great big old mess of hair?" She flashed a grin that would make any Park Avenue dentist proud. "Say, around eleven in the morning?"

"Of course," Patrick said. Had he expected this?

"Eleven it is," said Kathryn. Of course, they both knew this was coming.

"And Georgia?" Roxanne turned to me. "Do you think you'll be able to put in just one or two chunky highlights with that secret formula of yours?"

"Sure," I stammered. "Absolutely."

She winked at me. "I *knew* you had your formula in that big nylon bag."

I smiled and hoped I didn't look as scared as I felt. I had no idea what I was going to do.

THE UPSTAIRS OF the Middlebury guesthouse was outfitted like a four-star hotel. Not that I had ever been inside a four-star hotel, but I had seen some of the rooms displayed on *Lifestyles of the Rich and Famous*. Three bedrooms with en suite baths were decorated identically, but each was in a different color. The doors of each bedroom were adorned with a small ceramic plaque, upon which had been engraved, respectively, THE PINK ROOM, THE VIOLET ROOM, and THE CRIMSON ROOM.

Patrick had insisted on the violet room, Kathryn wandered into the pink, and I was left with the crimson. I closed the door behind me and sat on the crimson-on-crimson duvet and stared at the crimson brocade covering the windows. I lay back on the bed and looked up at the crimson fringe on the canopy. I felt as if I were in a bordello. Or perhaps inside someone's small intestine. The color was relentless, impossible. I closed my eyes and still saw crimson.

Kathryn knocked on my door, then cracked it open.

"Hey, can I switch with you?" she asked. But then she actually took a look around. "Oh. Never mind."

"Right."

She plunked herself down on the bed next to me. "Wow. It looks like blood," she said. "My room just looks like puke. This is definitely worse."

"Did you know she was going to do that?" I asked.

"Do what?"

"Ask us to—"

"Why do you think I brought my scissors?"

"I didn't know."

"What did you think?" Kathryn asked, biting her thumbnail. "That she was just inviting us—her hairdressers—for one of the primo weekends of the summer?"

"I guess. I don't know. I don't know what I was thinking." I closed my eyes again. "Why didn't you tell me?"

"I figured you'd know," said Kathryn.

I stretched out on the bed and sighed. It seemed that every time I got someplace I thought I wanted to be, it turned out that there were hidden signals, mixed messages—a whole code I still hadn't begun to crack. Maybe it was like skiing. Or tennis. Or any of the sports the clients started their kids on when they were three or four years old. Maybe I had simply entered the game too late to learn.

"Well, you'd better come up with something before eleven tomorrow," said Kathryn. "Or you and your bags will be parked on Further Lane."

"You mean she'd kick me out?"

"Oh, she's probably too polite for that," said Kathryn. "But she'd be mighty pissed off."

"Stop," I moaned. "Okay, okay. I'm going to take a walk."

"You'll miss your massage."

"Yeah, right. Like I can lie on a table right now and relax."

"Where are you going?"

"Town."

"It's at least a mile from here!"

"I'm from New Hampshire," I said. "Walking is one of the few things I can handle."

THE CVS IN Southampton was stocked, as it turned out, with every possible hair color known to woman. Shelf upon shelf of boxes displaying blond models, brunette models, redheaded models. Nice'n Easy, Frost & Design, and Preciously Right were lined up next to one another, colors nearly identical, differentiated only by name: golden wheat, honey mane, sunshine bliss, copper hue, night raven. I knew for a fact that the models who posed for these boxes did not use these colors. I had myself done the highlights of the blonde on one of the boxes and had not used anything remotely like the brand advertised.

I kept walking. Under the fluorescent lights of the CVS, the people of Southampton looked like people anywhere. Well, almost anywhere. The two skinny girls carrying matching Fendi baguettes, with hair so light that it almost looked white, carried two Yorkshire terriers with matching pink ribbons in their fur. I wondered if they were planning to attend Le Chic Chien the next day. But for the most part, I found the CVS comforting. I could have blinked and been back in New Hampshire, surrounded by Prell shampoo, Head & Shoulders, value packs of Charmin, and racks and racks of magazines that leaned more heavily to the *National Enquirer* than to *Vogue*.

I wandered the aisles, feeling lost and alone, not to mention hopelessly stupid and naive. What had I expected? That a woman like Roxanne was going to take a beauty school graduate from Weekeepeemie under her wing? That she really *liked* me? No. She needed me. And I was only as important to her as her last perfect highlight. So I drifted aimlessly through the CVS until I stumbled upon the exact thing I had been looking for: a small, green-and-white box of Jolen Creme Bleach. It was meant for smaller jobs—eyebrows, upper lips—but it would do the trick. I was better off with the Jolen, which I could control in its application, than any of the brands of color that might, given the amount of highlighting already on Roxanne Middlebury's head, go terribly wrong. A few chunky highlights were what she wanted, and that's what she'd get.

Along with the Jolen, I bought a small, plain plastic bottle into which I planned to put the harsh-smelling bleach. I stuffed the package deep into my knapsack and said a quick prayer to the god of hairdressers that Roxanne would never find out.

IT WAS BLAZINGLY hot the next day, and the grounds of High Bridge Farm wavered and baked in the noonday sun. The humidity was oppressive—a condition that was the bane of our clients' existence and the one beauty factor over which neither the wealthy nor their hairdressers could exert any influence. No matter how perfectly highlighted (the Jolen having worked its magic), no matter how sleekly straightened and glossed, Roxanne Middlebury's hair was going to more closely resemble that of Fifi the sheepdog than that of a cover girl. Hence the hat: Pink, wide-brimmed, made of the most delicately woven straw, it perched atop her head like a flying saucer. And Roxanne was not alone. As we walked from her car to the tent, under which dogs and Hamptons denizens sweltered, I could see dozens upon dozens of pastel hats, with only the littlest bit of hair—a fringe of bang, a small, wilting flip—exposed to the elements.

"Why?" Roxanne moaned. "Why, oh why did it have to be so hot?" In her southern accent, the "why" sounded more like a baby's wail: *waa*.

She paused as another behatted woman stopped to say hello. Their two hats bumped brims as they attempted the triple-cheek kiss in fashion that season.

"Darling! You look ravishing," Roxanne said to the lady in question, who most certainly did not. She was a stocky, flat-faced woman whose miniature pug strained at his Hermès leash. Whoever had said that dogs and their owners resembled each other must have known this woman.

"Ariana, please allow me to introduce my colorist, Georgia," said Roxanne. "And my stylist, Kathryn. They're from Jean-Luc."

The woman smiled coldly, her eyes drifting instantly over our heads. Then she teetered off, the heels of her Manolos sinking into the soft green grass. Roxanne grabbed my arm and squeezed.

"Ariana Arianopolis," she whispered.

I looked at her blankly.

"Shipping," she explained, as if to a toddler. "*Greek* shipping."

"Of course," said Kathryn.

In sharp contrast with the ladies at the benefit, Kathryn had somehow managed to look cool. She had on a simple sheath the color of banana cream pie, which she had bought straight out of Calypso's window. It set off her pale blond hair to perfection. Like many hairdressers, Kathryn had the kind of hair that pretty much didn't need anything done to it. Her color was natural (though she told clients who asked that she had highlights), and even on this worst of possible days, it remained silky and sleek. She wore flip-flops on her tanned feet and somehow managed to make them look like the height of fashion.

"Picnic basket chic," Patrick murmured as we entered the tent. The music playing was—could it be?—the sound track from *101 Dalmatians*. Patrick gestured with his chin to a bevy of forty-something ladies standing in a cluster, their skirts precisely the same length, tanned aging knees just visible. They were each holding purses that resembled picnic baskets: wicker, brightly lined in tropical prints.

We made our way over to the buffet, where dog bowls of chicken salad and bone-shaped biscuits awaited us.

"I'll catch up with y'all later," said Roxanne as she abruptly slipped off into the crowd. I watched as she headed over to the runway, where the dogs were being gathered. Was she really going to put Fang into a Burberry trench coat in ninety-degree weather?

"Boy, she couldn't wait to get rid of us," said Patrick, munching on a dog biscuit. "I guess we served our purpose."

"Well, it's cool to hang out with your stylists, but only to a point," said Kathryn. "She wouldn't notice now if we just left and caught the next jitney home."

We watched as Roxanne air-kissed a rail-thin socialite with gleaming white teeth.

"Oh, my God," I suddenly blurted out.

"What?" The two of them turned to me.

"Isn't that . . ."

"Oh, my God," echoed Patrick.

No more than twenty feet away from us, there stood

Richard. He was wearing ivory linen trousers and a perfectly cut black T-shirt. His hair was in his trademark platinum ponytail, and his diamond stud was visible, even from where we stood by the canapés.

"What the hell is he doing here?" Kathryn asked.

"I can't imagine," said Patrick.

"Maybe his dog is in the show?" I offered.

"Yeah, right."

At that moment, the reason for Richard's presence at Le Chic Chien stepped forward from behind the effervescence of Richard and presented herself.

"No . . . ," breathed Kathryn.

"It can't be."

Jane Cooke. As in Jane Huffington Cooke, the fourth wealthiest woman in America, according to *Forbes* and the gossip pages of *Women's Wear Daily*. I knew this because in order to be a top colorist in New York, it was crucial to know who was rich, famous, or otherwise important (if there was, indeed, anyone important who was not rich or famous), and I now studied the financial and society pages the way I used to study *People* magazine. In any event, Jane Cooke was attached to Richard's arm, or it might be more accurate to say that he was attached to her, like a jewel: a shiny, impossible-to-miss sparkling bit of gaudiness that stopped—if only for a split second—the buzzing crowd, which began once again to buzz more loudly, like a swarm of excited bees.

"But he's gay," I protested. My naïveté about gay men had finally fled, along with any of my hopes and dreams about Patrick. I figured that every man in the beauty industry was gay.

Kathryn looked at me with equal measures of sympathy and amazement. "Yes?" she said. "And?"

Richard caught sight of us from the edge of the tent and

cocked one eyebrow as he turned in the opposite direction, guiding Jane Huffington Cooke ever so gently in the direction of the bar. She was—there is no way to put this kindly—downright homely. No amount of grooming could help her. Her chic, highlighted bob, her Chanel sundress and enormous, tortoiseshell sunglasses, served only to exacerbate the problem, because they looked as though they belonged to another woman entirely and had somehow misguidedly migrated onto Jane Cooke's broad, fleshy back.

"We must go say hello," said Kathryn.

"Are you out of your mind?"

"No, really, we must," Patrick said with a wicked little smile.

We wove our way through the behatted ladies, their faces shining, beads of perspiration escaping through layers of carefully applied foundation and pressed powder. Several of these ladies (and a few of the sweating gentlemen) were clients of the salon, but if they recognized us, they didn't let on. Their gaze slid over each of us, coolly assessing, never breaking the flow of banter. *Did you see it in his private screening room?* I elbowed past one woman who paid thrice weekly visits to Jean-Luc. And then another: *We're sending Alice to Geneva to finish high school. The schools here have really lowered their standards, I think. Very arriviste.* Finally, we were right behind Richard, so close that I could smell his citrusy aftershave.

"Ladies and gentlemen," a woman in a striped dress with a matching striped hat suddenly announced from the U-shaped runway set up as if we were in Bryant Park, "I present to you the spectacular dogs of Le Chic Chien, along with their equally fabulous owners!"

The microphone screeched as she stepped to the side and made way for the parade of pooches. A briard stuffed into a fire-engine-red Azzedine Alaia led the pack. A bichon followed in a jaunty yellow slicker from the new Marc Jacobs collection. A brown standard poodle pranced down the runway wearing a silk La Perla robe tied around his (or her) middle. The owners clearly took the whole fashion show seriously. They handled their animals like pros, as if this were one step away from the Westminster Dog Show. Roxanne made her appearance with Fang in his Burberry, his tiny pink tongue hanging in what I hoped wasn't dehydration.

Kathryn tapped Richard on his gym-perfect bicep. He pretended not to notice, so she tapped again. He turned to face us, and along with him turned Jane Cooke.

"Oh, hello," he said smoothly. *"Bonjour."*

"What a surprise," said Kathryn, "to see you here!" She was fearless; she was just having fun with this.

"Frankly," said Richard, "it is *quite* a surprise to see *you* at this occasion."

"We're here with Roxanne Middlebury," I said. I hadn't known I had it in me. Roxanne had defected from Richard to me, and I knew that it killed him.

His eyes flashed. "Darling," he said to Jane Cooke, "I'd like to introduce you to some of the . . . staff . . . from the salon."

"We're not exactly—"

"Patrick, Kathryn, Georgia," said Richard, "may I present to you my fiancée, Jane."

She pressed herself even more closely against him. Up close, I could see the telltale smoothness of her glasslike brow. She'd had an eye lift. It made her look perpetually surprised.

"Really!" said Kathryn. It was the first and last time I ever saw her at a loss for words. "Well! When did this—surely we would have read about—"

"Just last night," said a blushing Jane Cooke.

"Congratulations," said Patrick.

"Yes, yes. Congratulations."

"Ah," said Richard, his eyes floating above our heads. "Darling, there's C.Z. and Cornelia."

"Guest? Cornelia Guest?" I said.

"Please excuse us," Jane murmured as they disappeared into the swirling vortex of the crowd.

"What do you think?" asked Patrick as the three of us stood there, our mouths agape. "Do you suppose she calls him Ricky when they're alone?"

I laughed and slapped Patrick's arm.

"What are you talking about?" asked Kathryn.

For once, there was something she didn't know.

Doreen Gets the Works

A year had passed. And then another, and perhaps another. In the world of Jean-Luc, the days fell together, the weeks collapsing in a haze of blow-dryers, chemicals, French pop music, and the rhythm of the ladies, the endless parade of ladies who came through the salon's doors. The trends changed with each season (red is the new blond! bangs are in! waves are out!), and a new generation of clients appeared as mothers brought in their thirteen-year-old daughters.

The salon visit seemed to be a rite of passage that corresponded with the bat mitzvah or the communion ceremony. These girls sat in our chairs, all lanky limbs and smooth, acne-free cheeks (thanks to frequent bookings at the dermatologist), foils and chemicals touching their virgin hair for the very first time as their mothers beamed proudly from beneath the heat lamps where they, too, were having their color done. I mean, why miss a multitasking opportunity? Here the client had the chance to a) spend quality time with her daughter; b) get her own hair done; and c) have us match her color as closely as possible. *Georgia, darling? See how Zoe's hair has that contrast between the dark blond and the whiter, blonder pieces? Can you do that to mine?*

But for the most part, as the years flipped by like pages on a calendar, the salon didn't alter so much as a single hair (if you will) on its head. Every once in a while, at a staff meeting, some hapless creature would bring up a new idea. What about curtains between stations, for privacy? How about redoing the color scheme?

"Idiot!" Jean-Luc would thunder. The word sounded so much better in a French accent—both less crude and more insulting than its English counterpart. "If it is not broke, why fix it?"

And it would be an understatement to say that the salon was not broke. It was thriving, bursting at the seams. Jean-Luc had accomplished the seemingly impossible: He had created a salon that was both exclusive and hugely popular. Its popularity had not lessened its snob appeal. The ladies loved running into one another in their burgundy robes, their wet heads wrapped in towels. What Jean-Luc had figured out was something that my mother, back in New Hampshire, had known forever: The beauty salon was a club, the equivalent of men's poker night. Business deals went on, private school contacts were initiated, sons were fixed up with daughters, interior decorators were recommended. Where else would Muffie Von Hoven and Tamara Stein-Hertz find themselves seated next to each other on the banquette while their nails dried? Muffie, from the East Side. Tamara, from the West. Muffie, need I say, a WASP from Old Greenwich. Tamara, a Jew from Short Hills. These two ladies, in what is now a near historic event, met, bonded, exchanged all their numbers (home, husband's secretary, mobile, country home), and within a matter of months had formed Von Hoven–Hertz, a soon-to-become-multimillion-dollar manufacturer of decoupage items for the home.

They often came into the salon together, brainstorming as they sat side by side under the heat lamps.

"Trash cans," said Muffie, "that look like aquariums."

"Brilliant," said Tamara, who had begun to have just the teensiest bit of a British accent to go along with her great business success. "Tissue-paper boxes," she proposed, "with . . . wait, I've got it—teardrops streaming down the sides."

"Maybe too much of a bummer," said Muffie, who sounded just like her fourteen-year-old daughter. Muffie had taken to wearing faded jeans, Robert Clergerie work boots, and perfectly cut T-shirts that showed off her trainer-sculpted arms. You could always tell when a client was veering toward some sort of huge life change. Muffie, who had long favored tailored Chanel suits, was definitely going through something big. So it came as less of a shock, later that year, when I found out that Muffie and Tamara had both left their husbands and moved—together—into a duplex on Central Park West.

Many ventures such as Von Hoven–Hertz Decoupage began at Jean-Luc, in the idle hours of hair processing, nail drying—in short, the hours of waiting. And while salon life bravely ventured forward, what had, in fact, changed quite dramatically in those early years of the Jean-Luc Salon were the lives of several of its employees.

1. Richard had indeed married Jane Huffington Cooke and, much to the astonishment of everyone who knew him, had fathered a child with Jane Huffington Cooke—a beautiful little girl named . . . well, named Huffington Cooke. Huffie, for short. Richard still worked at the salon, though of course (as he reminded us all, at every opportunity) he didn't ever have to

work a day in his life, ever again. He was—if this was even possible—more gay. Gayer. The diamond stud in his left ear was a flawless two carats, and he walked like an elegant cat, slithering around the salon from client to client as if just waiting to be petted. And, though it kills me to admit this, I had developed something of a soft spot for Richard. He wasn't so bad. He had mellowed a lot since marrying Jane and signing a prenuptial agreement that reportedly gave him ten million dollars for every year they stayed married.

2. Kathryn. As Jean-Luc's favorite, she had risen to the top of the pyramid of stylists, second only to Jean-Luc himself. In most such cases of meteoric rise, talent—huge buckets full of talent—would come into play. And though I fear I will be accused of cattiness, or professional jealousy, or just plain old green-eyed envy—I have to say that in Kathryn's case, the reason for her stardom, the one and only reason, was that she had figured out the perfect way to whip Jean-Luc into a blind frenzy of desire. She was seemingly the one woman on the planet who refused to sleep with him. Rejection was so foreign to Jean-Luc, so peculiar and impossible, that it turned him into a puppy dog. Did it matter that Kathryn could literally not cut hair in a straight line? Did it matter that she looked at herself in the mirror more often than she looked at her client? Hell, no. Kathryn had been anointed by Jean-Luc and thusly was anointed by all of New York. She was, as I have mentioned, exquisitely beautiful. And in the manner of many exquisitely beautiful women, she had what appeared to be an innate style—a style and beauty that might just rub off on whoever happened to be sitting in her chair. And if clients went home, washed their hair, and discovered that it poufed out in back in an unflattering way, or hung lower on the left side than the right, they assumed that it was somehow their own fault.

It is true: I had grown to hate Kathryn.

3. Patrick—my darling Patrick. I still loved him. I couldn't help myself. I knew we'd never be together—I was missing the essential ingredient—and believe me, I had made my peace with that fact. Doreen had told me all my life that men disappoint you, and so far she had been right. Every day, Patrick and I worked alongside each other, just as we had in beauty school. We were a perfect team. He dreamed up the styles for clients, and I did the color, and anywhere from fourteen to twenty-two times a day we changed the way someone looked—and therefore felt—for the better. How many people can say that at the end of their workday?

Patrick kept his love life out of the salon. I don't know whether he did this to be sensible about not mixing work and play, or if he did it because he knew I'd feel a pang. But either way, we had finally reached a point where we could talk about it.

"What are you doing tonight?" I'd ask.

"Hot date."

"Yeah? Who?"

"A guy from Oribe," he'd say, invoking the name of another salon down the street.

"Can't you date some nice doctor or lawyer?" I joked.

Patrick looked at me, aghast, even though he knew I was kidding. None of us ever went out with doctors, lawyers, bankers, accountants, what have you. Those people were the clients. Don't get me wrong—we loved our clients. We just didn't want to socialize with them. Besides, I had long since learned, after the Roxanne Middlebury weekend, that they didn't really want to socialize with us, either. No. We went out with each other. In every salon across the city, there was cross-pollination. This stylist went out with that colorist. That colorist had a clandestine affair with the cute assistant. And so on and so forth, from the Upper East Side down to the cobblestone streets of SoHo. Except for me.

4. Me. Georgia Marie Watkins. A lot had happened to me, if you didn't count my love life. That part was . . . well, I'll come right out and say it: That part was a pathetic mess. Here was the equation. I went over and over it in my head, but it always wound up the same. People who worked in salons only dated other people who worked in salons. All the men who worked in salons were gay, with the seemingly solitary exception of Jean-Luc. Therefore, if I wanted a romantic life, I had one of two choices: a) I could fall in love with a gay man, which I had already tried, and not just Patrick, either—I had developed a teensy, quiet crush on the gorgeous Massimo but knew better than to pursue this no-win romance. I contented myself with his sweet smiles and occasional words of encouragement, just as I did with Patrick. Or b) I could venture outside the world of beauty, which I had also tried—to decidedly unhappy results. I mean, I know my clients meant well when they fixed me up with their cousin/nephew/friend from college. But these dates were a waste of time. What did I have to say to a guy who traded stock options or, for that matter, removed gallbladders? And what did he have to say to me? *Oh sure,* you're probably thinking, *you just didn't really try.* Trust me when I tell you that you don't know what you're talking about. People in relationships need to have stuff in common. Otherwise what do they talk about at the end of the day? So my love life was on hold. On long hold. That phone had been taken off the hook.

And speaking of the clients, I had begun, finally, to truly understand the world of the salon and the ladies who went there. We were not cut from the same cloth, and we never would be. These ladies were not from towns like Weekeepeemie. And as for the few of them who had grown up poor and married extremely well—they didn't ever want to be re-minded of where they'd come from. So when the clients invited me to parties, or openings, or to spend the weekend at their beach or country houses, I usually declined—unless, of course, the offer was just too damn good. Like, say, courtside seats at a Knicks game. But I knew there was always a price to pay. They always wanted something in return. More attention. Special fa-vors. I may not have gone to college, but I'm a quick study, and I learned my lesson back in Southampton.

But I've got to say, the biggest thing that had happened to me during those years is that I had become a big-deal colorist. I owed a lot to Faith Honeycomb—she really put me on the map. When *Elle* or *Vogue* would call her for a quote about how clients were matching their hair to their furs, or how red was too red, she always referred them to me. *Talk to Georgia,* she'd say. *She's young and trendy, just like your readers.* I remember the day I realized I had truly arrived. A first-time client came to see me—a Greenwich wearing the newest designer jeans and a Robert Cavalli blouse straight out of that month's *W*—and she pulled a clipping out of her Prada bag. It was a postage-stamp-size picture of me from one of the women's magazines, naming me the best colorist of that year. The Greenwich told me she had waited three months for an appointment. And I thought to myself, Greenwiches *never* wait three months for anything.

So I had finally started making some real money. Patrick and I had each moved from the shitty little apartment Ursula had helped us find into our own chic, funky apartments. Mine was a third-floor walk-up above a French clothing store on upper Madison, and Patrick had moved down to a two-bedroom in Chelsea. I mean, we weren't rolling in it, at least not by the clients' standards. But for the first time in my life, I was in financial heaven. I had never had extra cash around; never once had I not counted pennies. And now here I was, able to send at least a thousand dollars home every single month to Doreen and Melodie. Mel had made the dean's list at Boston University every semester, and even though she was on a full scholarship, she still needed money for books. I was so proud of her. My geeky little sister was going to do something important with her life—I just knew it. She had book smarts, and I had street smarts. And if my street smarts could help my mother and sister, well, that was all I wanted to do. As for Doreen, she had taken out a business loan to keep her shop afloat, and finally, now, she was able to pay it back. Doreen's salon was doing well. She even updated the decor, taking down the old (and, I have to admit, hopelessly lame) photographs of models with bad makeup and spiky hairdos and putting up some museum art prints. She threw out the sagging sofa she kept in front and bought a pair of sleek new fake-leather love seats. And she got all new magazine subscriptions. The clients were happy, and happy clients come more often—even if they don't need their hair cut or colored, they just like to hang out and be pampered.

IT WAS MY third autumn at Jean-Luc when Doreen finally worked up her courage to come visit me in New York. I had been back to Weekeepeemie a whole bunch of times, for weddings of my high school friends, and their various kids' christenings, and to see Mel and Doreen. But Doreen had never made it down to the city. I knew this was no reflection on how much she missed me. She was a country girl, that's all. And I think she was afraid of coming down to New York, though she never would have admitted it.

I arranged for her to meet me at work at eleven o'clock on

a Tuesday morning. Usually this would be a relatively quiet time of day in the salon. But what I hadn't thought through was that this was the Tuesday before Thanksgiving, which meant that the ladies of Jean-Luc were in full panic pampering mode. The in-laws were coming, or there was a quick trip to London, or the custom-ordered leaves for the dining room table were lost in Germany. It didn't matter. Whatever the crisis, there was only one way to respond. When faced with extreme circumstances beyond their control, the ladies pressed Jean-Luc on their speed-dials. Pedicure, manicure, waxing—the works. Hair was the finishing touch, the coup de grâce (as Jean-Luc liked to say), but all those other services, the ones that would be hidden beneath close-toed shoes and pencil-slim trousers—those were, in fact, the very thing that made the ladies of Jean-Luc feel in control of their lives. The in-laws would behave. The trip to London would go off without a hitch. The dining table leaves would be located and arrive, just in time, by FedEx. All because the ladies had smooth, hairless, self-tanned legs (not to mention bikini lines) and their toenails were polished cotton-candy pink.

It was into this storm, this Joy de Patou–scented madhouse, that Doreen walked—several hours early—having made a better bus connection than she'd previously thought she could. I did not see her when she walked into the salon, because I was at the sinks with my fifth client of the morning, but I knew she had arrived because, over the strains of the morning violin music that Jean-Luc preferred, I heard the unmistakable sound of Sweetie's voice.

"Well, I'll be! I'll be damned! Excuse me while I just fall over and die!"

I closed my eyes. Even as I washed the remaining chemicals from my client's wet head, I tried to take a deep breath. Doreen was here. At Jean-Luc. My past and my present colliding in a big bang, like the crash of cymbals. I cast a quick glance over to the banquette, where six of my clients were waiting. I had no idea what to do.

I left my client with her head in the sink and bleach on her eyebrows, said a little prayer, and walked quickly to the reception area, where dozens more clients sat, some of them flipping through that week's magazines and others watching with unveiled curiosity as the salon's famous head receptionist, Sweetie, engulfed Doreen in a full-on drag queen bear hug.

"I never thought I'd see the day!" Sweetie exclaimed. "Georgia Watkins has a mom!"

Over Sweetie's red satin–encased bicep, my mother shot me a pleading look. I feared Sweetie might be cutting off her blood supply.

"Oh, honey—you're just so . . ." Sweetie was at a loss for words. He held Doreen at arm's length, looking her up and down so deliberately that it would have been rude if this were anywhere other than the Jean-Luc Salon. "You're like an untouched work of art," Sweetie concluded.

I looked at my mother, leaned over, and gave her a big kiss. It was so strange to see her here. And it was true, what Sweetie said. She was untouched. And this was the one thing we never, ever saw at the salon. From the time mothers started bringing in their daughters for highlights and eyebrow waxes at age thirteen, there was simply no such thing as natural, completely natural, beauty.

Something was buzzing at the back of my head, as if there were something I was forgetting to do that I couldn't quite grasp. I looked at my beautiful mother with hair spilling down her back, hair that had never seen a chemical, and her glowing face free of makeup, expensive cream, not even so much as eyebrow pencil . . . and there it was again, that buzzing.

Oh, my God! Eyebrows! My hand shot up to my mouth in horror. I had left my client at the sink with her brows covered in bleach!

"Excuse me for a moment," I said, then raced back to the sinks. There she was. What was her name again? She had picked up a copy of French *Elle* and was leafing through it nonchalantly.

"Let me check those eyebrows," I said calmly, quickly removing the bleach with alcohol-soaked cotton. And then I breathed a huge sigh of relief. The patron saint of colorists must have been smiling on me. It was okay. Her brows were just the right shade of blond. Another minute and they would have started to go orange on me.

I helped the lucky woman up and out of her chair.

"Shen will blow you dry," I said, bringing her over to one of the new assistants.

THE SIX CLIENTS were still waiting on the banquette, plus two already in chairs at my station. Even though they'd almost never express their irritation, there was a limit. And I was getting close to exceeding it. I could see the tension mounting in their perfectly crossed legs, high heels jiggling like schoolchildren's impatient sneakers. A few discreet glances at wristwatches. I was on thin ice.

"Mom?" I went back to the reception area, where Doreen was examining the glossy black-and-white photographs of models whose hairstyles had been designed by Jean-Luc. Cindy Crawford's dark waves spilling over her bare shoulders. Claudia Schiffer peeking out from beneath long, piecy bangs. Naomi Campbell with her hair slicked back. Doreen seemed mesmerized, hypnotized. Or perhaps she was just in shock.

"Mom?"

She spun around, startled. And the thin shell of hardness around my heart, the one I needed all the time to survive in the world of Jean-Luc—that shell cracked and spread open. My mother looked exactly the same as always, although I realized that she had put on her best city clothes, the ones she wore on the rare occasions when she ventured to Portsmouth or Boston. The tan slacks from Marshall's, the sweater set ordered from the Spiegel catalog, bangles on her wrist, and—ever practical— clean white sneakers. I was so happy to see her. So extremely happy that it was all I could do not to break into a little dance right there on the mosaic tile floor of the reception area.

"Look at you," my mother said with a wide, beautiful smile. It was the kind of smile you just didn't see in New York, at least not the New York I was familiar with. Her face was creased into a dozen lines and wrinkles—the *good* kind of wrinkles (which didn't exist, according to the ladies of Jean-Luc) that came from a lifetime of . . . well . . . living.

"You look like such a grown-up lady," said Doreen. She looked me up and down, not in the fashionista sweep of the eyes that tallies up the designers and prices in a single glance, but in the way only a mom can. She knew me by heart and was taking inventory, to make sure all the pieces were there.

"Mom, I've got to—"

"My, what a pretty watch," Doreen said, lifting up my hand and examining my wrist. I flushed, embarrassed. The watch had been my present to myself after my first big promotion at the salon. It was a Cartier tank watch: simple, elegant, and very expensive. I suddenly felt that I shouldn't have bought it for myself. I hoped my mother had no idea what it was or how much it cost.

"Thanks. Listen, I'm kind of backed up. I didn't know how busy we'd be here today . . . I was thinking maybe I could give you the keys to my—"

"Nonsense!" I suddenly heard Jean-Luc's voice behind me. He came around to my side, then grasped Doreen's hand. "Allow me to introduce myself, madame." He drew himself up to his full height, made even taller by his wavy, brilliantined hair. He still came up only to Doreen's nose.

"I know who you are," my mother murmured. "You're Georgia's boss."

"*Oui*," said Jean-Luc with a small bow. He was still holding her hand, and now he bent to kiss it. "*Enchanté*. You have a very talented daughter, madame."

"Thank you," said Doreen. "I think so, too." Her voice was softer, smaller than usual, and it occurred to me, with a slightly nauseated lurch, that my mother was intimidated. I had never, ever seen her be cowed by anybody, and I didn't like it one bit.

"For you," Jean-Luc said, "the works! You will spend the afternoon right here in the salon." He snapped his fingers as if expecting an army of staff to appear. "*Le manicure, le pedicure. Le waxing. Baliage.* And, of course, a haircut—with yours truly."

"Oh, I couldn't possibly—"

"But I insist!" Jean-Luc waved his hand. "Come. I will take you to get a robe."

I cast a nervous glance over to the banquette. It was a disaster. My clients now looked openly irritated, and worse, they were talking to one another. If I didn't do something, there was about to be an all-out revolt. Jean-Luc was already steering Doreen away by the elbow. My tough-as-nails mother was being docile as a child.

As quietly as I could, I asked, "Mom—are you okay with this?" After all, she was, as Sweetie put it, untouched. Which was the way she had always liked it.

She swiveled around and grinned at me. Her eyes were shining. "Are you kidding me? I'm in heaven," she said.

I HAD NO SENSE of how many hours had passed before I laid eyes on Doreen again. I dealt with client after irritated client, my fingers burning from the nonstop exertion. No one tells you about this in beauty school—the pain involved. I knew from watching Doreen come home when I was a kid and soaking her hands, but it was different to actually feel it. On days when I had back-to-back clients without a break, my hands felt stiff, almost arthritic, and I wondered how an older woman like Faith Honeycomb handled that kind of volume, the relentless pace we dealt with at the salon.

Baliage, single-process, foils, low lights, double-process, one after the other. And, as luck would have it, I had not one but *two* nightmare clients on my schedule. The first was a woman we referred to in the salon simply as "the editor from hell." The EFH was not quite at the tippy-top of the masthead of one of the chicest women's magazines, but she expected to be treated like royalty. And just like royalty, she didn't carry any money with her, because she had become accustomed to never paying for anything. Magazine editors generally don't have to pay for their meals, their car services, their travel, or—in the case of the more powerful ones—their clothing. But we had a policy at Jean-Luc that magazine editors did, in fact, pay for their hair. We gave them a thirty percent discount, and Jean-Luc felt that was more than enough. But the EFH would simply come in for highlights and a trim, then slip out without paying. It had happened a dozen times, and Jean-Luc was pissed.

This time, he had asked me to be absolutely certain that the EFH paid her bill. Easier said than done. She sat in my chair in her perfectly cut black pants (Costume National or Prada, I wasn't sure which) and little black cardigan (the EFH always refused to change into a robe and instead simply put the robe over her clothes; this made me nervous, because a speck of bleach on that sweater would be a minor tragedy) and talked to me nonstop about "the shows." She had just come back from Milan. So dull, so dreadful, to always have to be dressed, to be courted by the department store buyers! Her lovely upper lip curled in disdain.

I was barely paying attention to a word she said, though I spent a lot of time nodding as I wove the *baliage* through her blond hair, separating the layers with Saran Wrap. I was wondering how my mother was doing, and also wondering what Jean-Luc would do to me if the EFH walked out of the salon once more without paying. I had instructed Sweetie, at the front desk, to make sure to stop her.

I was three clients beyond the EFH when I heard the commotion.

"I will not! I absolutely will not! This is ridiculous!"

The EFH marched back to my station, holding her Hermès Kelly bag in front of her chest like a shield. Sweetie trailed her.

"I don't pay for my hair," she said to me.

"I'm sorry, but Jean-Luc insists," I said. "We have an editorial discount, which you're more than welcome to—"

"I don't pay for my hair," the EFH repeated. "I don't pay at Christophe in Paris. I don't pay at Privé in Los Angeles. I don't pay at John Frieda in London."

"Well, you have to pay here," I said as nicely as I could muster. God, I didn't like this woman.

"We take Visa, MasterCard, and American Express," Sweetie said helpfully.

"I don't have my wallet," said the EFH. I eyed her huge Hermès bag. Like hell she didn't have a wallet in there.

"There's a cash machine right down the street," Sweetie said. Boy, he was one transvestite with balls.

The EFH glared at both of us. The client in my chair—a nice Wall Street trader—was watching the whole thing, her head whipping back and forth between me and the EFH as if we were playing a tennis match.

"I'll have my secretary call you when I get back to the office," said the EFH. "But you'll be sorry. You're never going to see me again!"

I had to bite my lip to keep from telling her how very sad I was to hear that news. But before I could even respond, she had turned on one high, Stephane Kélian heel and stormed out.

NEXT, WOULDN'T YOU know it, I had Claudia G on my schedule. It was just too much, having the EFH, Claudia G, and *my mother* all in the salon at the same time. What had I done to deserve this? Claudia G was known, inside the salon, simply as "the diva"—the deev for short. As in, "Oh, my God, please, tell me it isn't true, please-please-please don't let the deev be on my schedule today." But there she was. It was a mood buster. Hell, it might even be a week buster. Claudia G was a one-woman wrecking ball. When she wasn't busy having a nervous breakdown, she was busy giving one.

For those of you unfamiliar with Claudia G from the party

pages of the Sunday *New York Times* Styles section (which, by the way, are the only party pages that matter—forget about *New York* magazine, and by all means forget about *Gotham*), Claudia G was a star in the firmament of Upper East Side society. Claudia, with her signature waist-length hair, the precise color of a silver fox. (She had actually brought her silver fox coat to the salon and asked me to match it.) She was usually standing, in these photos, next to her wealthy and famous husband, Tommy G, who had founded, and then after ten years walked away from, one of Wall Street's largest hedge funds and started a second, equally lucrative career as a sculptor of much-sought-after granite boulders, which now dotted the lawns of the country estates of the very rich.

And there she was, breezing into the salon as if she owned the place. Claudia was one of our few clients with a house charge. Jean-Luc was all but forced to open one for her, since she—like the EFH—never carried a wallet, cash, or even a single credit card. Why would she? She glided around Manhattan in her chauffeur-driven Mercedes, her driver waiting curbside wherever she went—and she never went anywhere she wasn't already known. I often had fantasies about kidnapping Claudia G and depositing her below Fourteenth Street all by herself. What would she do? How would she ever get home?

"Georgia!" She waved her fingertips as she walked past my other waiting clients.

I had been praying to the hair gods that she might cancel or just not show up. But it seemed that I had already used up my daily favor with the hair gods on my other client's eyebrows. Claudia lowered herself gracefully into an empty chair next to my station. She lifted her hair with both thin arms, then let it fall around her in a silvery cascade.

I went over to her, bent down as if to a queen, and bestowed a kiss on her cheek. She smelled expensive. She was wearing an unusually pure floral scent that you didn't just buy over the counter. I vaguely recalled her mentioning something about a private *parfumier* who sent her flasks from Paris.

"I'll be with you as soon as I can, Claudia," I said with what I hoped was a firm, don't-fuck-with-me smile.

"Define 'soon,'" she said, smiling back. Her don't-fuck-with-me smile sent mine scurrying like a small animal across the salon floor and out the door.

"Fifteen minutes," I said. What was I doing? There was no way I could possibly finish two full heads of highlights in fifteen minutes. But I couldn't have said a minute beyond fifteen to the diva. As I returned to my client and started to weave my comb quickly through her hair, creating layers of foils, I cursed Claudia. I cursed the whole privileged lot of them. And then, suddenly, I remembered my mother. It had been hours since she'd come in and gotten swept into the vortex of Jean-Luc.

Richard was in the next station, doing *baliage* on one of Jane Huffington Cooke's friends.

"Richard?"

He turned, narrow hip cocked. *"Oui?"*

"Have you seen my—" And then I stopped. The fewer people who knew Doreen was in the salon, the better. Out of the corner of my eye, I saw Patrick blow-drying a client with a short auburn bob.

"Patrick," I hissed over the sound of the dryers. "Hey!"

He caught my eye and gave me a questioning look. Then he excused himself from his client and came over to my station. He looked around at Claudia G, at my frantically weaving comb, at my other waiting client, and got the situation in a single glance. He shook his head ever so slightly. I didn't know if he was going to laugh, cry, or help me out. *Helllp!* I begged him silently.

"Claudia, darling!" he cried out, as if only just noticing the diva sitting there—as if each and every person in the salon had not noticed her grand entrance. "You look gorgeous!"

Patrick was good at flattering the clients, but, like me, he never said anything untrue. Claudia did look gorgeous, in that haute-faux-Bohemian way that certain women can get away with. The silver mane of hair, the distressed and yet buttery leather boots, the vintage Levi's, the arms loaded with turquoise bangles. On another woman it would look like a costume, but Claudia was someone who *made* fashion. She wore these over-the-top outfits and probably laughed (privately, of course) when other, lesser women followed suit.

The thing was, there really was nothing Patrick could do to help me. He couldn't take over my clients' highlights, and Claudia, judging from the way she was jabbing numbers into her cell phone, was not in the mood to be flattered.

"How's Doreen doing?" I asked Patrick.

"Jean-Luc has her," he said darkly. The biggest secret in the salon was that many of us younger stylists were not in love with Jean-Luc's creative vision. Don't get me wrong, he was a great, great cutter. His styles were precise, perfect. That was the problem: They were often too perfect. You could spot a Jean-Luc haircut a mile away. They looked a bit like . . . well, like helmets.

"At least Massimo's going to blow her dry," said Patrick.

"That's good."

"She's already seen Alicia for waxing, manicure, and pedicure," Patrick continued. "And Faith for color."

"Faith did her color? How could I not have known that?"

"Jean-Luc had her use the private room," said Patrick. We

had one small private room on the floor of the salon, reserved exclusively for movie stars so famous that they actually didn't want to be seen there—as opposed to the typical starlets, who really did.

"Why?"

"I have no idea."

All the while, I was weaving highlights at warp speed, grateful that my client had thin hair. How many minutes had passed? Each moment Claudia G was kept waiting felt like an hour.

"Georgia, I just need one highlight, right here," Claudia said, pointing to a piece of hair near her face. "Can't you just quickly do a single highlight?"

"Just a few more minutes, Claudia—I promise," I said, avoiding the question. Because in theory, yes, I could (and would) do a single highlight on her while my other clients with earlier appointments were kept waiting. But Claudia was a unique case. She required handholding—and I do mean handholding. Claudia had suffered a hair trauma as a child and had never gotten over it. Her mother had dragged her to a barbershop when she was ten years old and had left her there, where a mean, mean man had cut off all her hair. Hence, the trauma. So two things were true for Claudia G from that moment on: First, no scissors ever cut more than a centimeter from her hair, ever again. And second, when she got highlights—even a single highlight—she insisted that I stay by her side and hold her hand.

On busy days, it was a nightmare. Today of all days, it had exceeded the realm of nightmare and made me wonder what I had done in my life to deserve to be so punished.

"I'll check on Doreen," said Patrick, happy to move away from my tense little station. "As soon as I finish my client."

By some miracle, Claudia G was still in one piece by the time I had finished the two heads of highlights. I hadn't been able to bring myself to check my watch, but I knew that more than fifteen minutes had passed.

One of the assistants had already mixed Claudia's color, and it was waiting for me on a tray next to her chair. With my comb, I separated the precise chunk of hair, which indeed would look better with a single highlight, and slathered on the color, protecting Claudia's scalp with a cotton ball. As the color set, I sat beside her, holding her delicate hand.

Claudia's whole mood changed as soon as I put the formula on her hair, like a drug addict who'd finally gotten her fix. Her hand relaxed in mine, and I could feel her pulse slowing. The corners of her mouth began to turn up. How easy it was, really, to make her happy! Tommy G probably should keep a jar of my formula at home, just in case.

"It's Sydney's birthday tomorrow," she said in her trademark confidential whisper.

Which one was Sydney? Claudia and Tommy had three girls, very close in age. Ten, eleven, and twelve, if memory served. Sydney, Sophie, and Scarlet were beginning to be fixtures on the party pages themselves, showing up with their parents at Bridgehampton Polo or the annual Christmas party given by one of their friends who rented out Wollman Rink.

"Georgia?"

I looked up from Claudia's hand. I had fallen into a dreamlike stupor, at once wondering how she kept her skin so soft and what it must be like to be her daughter.

I gasped. I instantly wished I hadn't, but I couldn't help myself. Before me stood a woman who bore a slight resemblance to Doreen, if Doreen had been altered in every possible way except for surgery. Could an earth mother from Weekeepeemie be transformed into Madison Avenue Barbie? The answer—though I wouldn't have believed it possible—was an unfortunate yes. Yes! Oh, Jesus. I didn't know what to say. I opened my mouth, then closed it.

"So . . ." She pirouetted. "What do you think?"

"Excuse me," said Claudia. "But I was just in the middle of—"

"Just a minute, Claudia," I managed to say.

My mother's long blond hair was now above her shoulders. She had severe, Louise Brooks bangs across her forehead, hanging in a thick fringe just below her eyebrows. And her color . . . her color was a deep, shiny chestnut auburn that I would have admired as a masterpiece had it been done to anyone other than my mother. On her lined, bare New Hampshire face, it looked like a wig. A bad wig.

"Doesn't she look *magnifique*?" Jean-Luc appeared from behind her. That man was always sneaking around. "We pulled out all the stops."

"*Excuse* me," said Claudia G.

"Just a minute!" I said, perhaps too sharply. Honestly, I didn't care if I never saw Claudia G again.

"Who are you?" Claudia demanded of my mother.

"Doreen Watkins," my mother answered. She extended her hand. My God, she was trying to do the polite thing and shake hands with Claudia G.

Claudia took a quick, sharp breath and offered Doreen her limp, bejeweled fingers. I could see her thoughts as if a cartoon bubble were floating over her head. *Why the hell are you getting all this attention?* she was wondering.

"Well?" asked Doreen. She'd had her eyebrows done, too, I realized with a start. They were shaped and arched into perfect, groomed submission.

"You look . . . ," I began weakly. They were all staring at me expectantly. And then, suddenly—just in time—I realized that my mother felt, for the first time in as long as I could remember, like a beautiful woman.

"Amazing," I said. "You look amazing." Then I stood up, still attached to Claudia G, and led her over to the sink to rinse out her single highlight.

DOREEN HUNG OUT in the salon for the rest of the afternoon, partly because she was afraid to wander the city by herself and partly because she was enjoying the whole scene—particularly watching me. I didn't mind, not at all. I had grown up as a colorist under Doreen, feeling her eyes on me all the time, watching, weighing, making sure I got it right. Being under that constant scrutiny probably had something to do with my success at Jean-Luc. You had to be comfortable being watched if you were to survive there. Everyone watched everyone all the time, and not necessarily in a nice way. It was all about comparison and envy, and it was an art, really, to do it subtly, without being noticed in the dozens and dozens of mirrors that reflected, relentlessly, everything going on.

But Doreen's gaze was soft, generous. Even with her harsh new hairdo, she looked like a misplaced angel, sitting there on the banquette, clutching her woefully unfashionable nylon handbag in her lap. Doreen, I saw, had not been offered a plastic bag—which was a good thing, because she would have laughed out loud.

I was able to keep an eye on her now that she was finished having done to her all that could possibly be done to a woman in the name of beauty. She watched, amused, as clients passed through the salon. It was an okay day for people watching: Susan Sarandon had been in to see Faith, along with a few other recognizable but not hugely famous actresses, like the one who was married to Richard Gere. A supermodel who was a member of the British royal family sat on the banquette in her vintage Levi's and skinny tank top, a shock of boyish brown hair falling over her forehead. And then, of course, there was the usual bunch of New York media power elite. Lynn Mendelson, the formidable Hollywood publicist, teetered by on her four-inch heels. She had once told me that publicists simply had to be taller than their clients. The curly brown head of her teacup poodle poked from the top of her briefcase.

To top it all off, there were three unruly little boys loose in the salon—their mother had brought them in for haircuts. They shrieked and yelled, their shirttails hanging below the blue blazers of their school uniforms. Their hair was so white blond that the pink of their scalps showed through. The mother, meanwhile, was getting her nails done, oblivious to the dirty looks she was getting from all the women who were in the salon precisely to escape the sound of screaming children. But what could we do? At ninety dollars a haircut, Jean-Luc was not about to turn their business away.

"Can't you do something about those brats?" one client hissed. I knew for a fact that she had three children of her own in boarding school.

"Which one is the mother?" another client asked, and she looked so irritated that I was afraid to tell her. The salon was full of sharp objects: scissors, tail combs.

I had four more clients left, and then I'd be done for the day. I had big plans for Doreen. Dinner, then theater tickets to the newest, impossible-to-get-into Broadway play, given to me by a producer client. I had taken myself off the appointment book for the following day, in anticipation of Doreen's visit. We were going on a private tour of the Statue of Liberty (the mayor's girlfriend was a client), lunch at La Côte Basque (the owner's wife was a client), and then, finally, a few hours of shopping on Madison Avenue (all the boutique owners were . . . well, you know). I was dying to show my mother a good time. And I hate to admit this, but I also wanted her to see how well I was doing. I wanted her to be proud of me.

"WELL, WELL, WELL . . ." Doreen linked her arm through mine once we finally escaped the salon at the end of the day. "Well, well, well, well, well."

She tossed her head in a familiar gesture, but now, with her long blond hair gone, there was basically nothing left to toss. We turned up Madison Avenue, where the shops were just beginning to close for the night. It was already dark outside—a new, wintry dark. I still wasn't used to having turned the clocks back a few weeks earlier.

"Is it like that every day?" she asked.

"Pretty much."

"Unbelievable."

Yeah." I paused. "Well, maybe it was a little crazier than usual. With the holiday coming up and all."

"And who was that woman?"

"Which one?"

"With the long gray hair and the—"

"Oh, that would be Claudia G," I said.

"Is she somebody important?"

We waited for the light to change on the corner of Sixty-third and Madison. Smoke from the hot dog vendor down the street blew up and around us.

"They're all important," I said.

Doreen tossed her head again. I still couldn't get used to looking at her. It just wasn't right. She had always been exactly herself. Now she appeared to be impersonating someone else entirely: someone who shopped at Bergdorf's, had lunch at La Goulue, and got her hair done at Jean-Luc. Someone with two housekeepers, a country house, and stacks of cashmere blankets in her guest closet.

Doreen caught me staring at her. "You don't really like it, do you," she said.

"It's amazing work," I answered lamely.

I searched for something more to say that would be both flattering and true.

"I love the blow-dry," I said.

Doreen smiled. "Now he—what was his name? The very handsome Italian man who blew my hair dry?"

"Massimo."

"Right. Massimo. I really liked him."

"He's pretty great. Everyone thinks he's the most talented guy there."

"Sure, he's talented," said Doreen. "You're all talented." There was something about the way she said the word—as if talent and hairdressing didn't really belong in the same sentence. Talent and piano playing, or talent and algebra, or talent and sculpting—I knew those were things that made more sense to her. All my life, she had impressed upon me that what she did was a craft, not an art. But we at Jean-Luc considered it an art. How else were clients going to be willing to spend thousands of dollars a year on their hair?

"He seems . . . humble," said Doreen. Then she paused. "Is he a . . ."

"What?"

"You know."

"Oh." I had to laugh. I had forgotten how far away Wee-keepeemie was from Madison Avenue. "You mean, is he gay?"

She nodded.

"I'm sure he is," I said. "They all are."

We walked a few blocks in silence. There was something in the air between us, something unsaid, though I had no idea what it was. I dipped my toe into the water.

"So . . . what do you think?"

"About what?"

"About the salon . . . and me, working there . . . you know, what do you *think*?" I asked in that particular, whiny tone that all daughters everywhere reserve for their mothers, no matter how mature they might otherwise be.

Doreen slowed down and wrapped her scarf more tightly around her neck. "I think it's a fantastic opportunity for you," she said. And there it was again: that unsaid thing. I could feel it between us as surely as if a third body were there.

"*What?*" I asked.

"It's just . . . I don't know how the hell you do it," said Doreen. I was a bit taken aback. She never cursed.

"Do what?"

"Those women . . ." She trailed off.

"The clients?"

"My God, Georgia. I've never seen so many people stuffed so full of themselves—"

"They're not all bad," I interrupted. What was I doing? Why was I defending the clients to my mother, of all people?

"I just want you to be happy, sweetheart."

"I am happy."

I felt suddenly, inexplicably, on the verge of tears. I stared hard at the window of a jewelry store, diamonds glittering around the necks of brown suede mannequin heads, and willed myself not to cry.

"Do you know how much money I'm making in there?" I blurted out. "I made five hundred dollars today, just in *tips.*"

Doreen put her arm around me. "That's great, baby. You're doing unbelievably well. I'm so proud of you—you know that."

At those magic words, the tears that I had fought back spilled down my cheeks. *Shit.* I swatted them away.

"Oh, what's the matter? What's wrong?" Doreen hugged me closer. We passed a coffee shop. Rich, creamy desserts revolved slowly in the neon light of the window.

"Let's go in here," I said. Because it was clear to me that the last thing my mother wanted—and, in fact, the last thing I wanted—was to have dinner in a fancy restaurant and squirm in the audience of a Broadway show. So we plopped ourselves down in a red vinyl booth not unlike the hundreds of red vinyl booths in New Hampshire diners and ordered cheeseburgers, fries, and vanilla Cokes. The smell of oil frying, the sound of the metal spatula scraping against the grill, the sizzle of hamburgers as they cooked, reminded me of Weekeepeemie.

"You can always come home, you know," said Doreen. "You could be my partner."

The lump in my throat just wouldn't go away. I knew I would never stop missing certain things about Weekeepeemie, but I also knew that I was never going back.

"This is home now," I said softly.

Doreen nodded, then took my hand from across the table

and stroked my fingers, the way she did when I was a little girl and she was helping me to fall asleep.

"Talk to me, baby. Tell me what's going on," she said.

"Oh, same old, same old," I said, which was truer than I wished it were. My days were a blur of clients, and my nights were a blur of exhaustion and television. I really wanted to change the subject.

"So what's new in Weekeepeemie?" I asked.

Doreen blinked. I could practically see the gears shifting in her mind as she decided whether or not to let me get away with avoiding her question.

"Well," she began slowly, "Ann Cutbill just had her fourth."

"Her fourth?"

"They're all having three, four, five kids," said Doreen.

"How can they afford it?"

She shrugged. "You know Weekeepeemie folks. We don't tend to think too far ahead."

"Women in New York don't even have their first kid until they're, like, thirty-five," I said.

"I guess they're trying to fit it all in," said Doreen. It didn't sound like a compliment.

Our cheeseburgers arrived, and we sat there chewing in silence. I knew Doreen wanted to ask me all the deep, important, mother-daughter-type questions, questions about happiness and contentment and finding love. Even though she had raised me to be independent and make my own way in the world, underneath the diner's bright lights I understood something about my mother. She was proud of what I had done careerwise, but she wanted me to have something she hadn't: a man to share it with.

Outside, horns blared on Madison Avenue, but inside the

diner, my mother and I were in our own little bubble. We could have been anywhere.

"Where the hell am I going to find him, Ma?" I blurted out.

She knew exactly what I was talking about. Of course she did.

"Don't worry," she said after a long sip of vanilla Coke. "You will."

The Hair Show

"Ladies and gentlemen, I present to you . . . the world-famous J. Sisters!"

The announcer's voice echoed and bounced off the cavernous ceiling of the Jacob Javits Center, where thousands had gathered for the New York Hair Show. Jean-Luc, Kathryn, Patrick, Massimo, and I stood in front of a white canvas tent. Protruding from the tent's flaps was a massage table, and upon the massage table was the lower half of a woman's naked body, except for a tiny, and I do mean tiny, paper G-string. A heavy-set dark-haired lady wearing a professional white smock held up one of the naked legs and painted it with steaming hot, pale green wax. We all stopped, transfixed, as the lady then pressed a textured cloth into the wax and—faster than you could say "motherfucker"—ripped the wax off the leg, exposing a shiny and hairless expanse of skin.

"These famous Brazilian sisters are known across the world

for their Brazilian bikini wax!" the announcer's voice boomed. "They take it *all* off!"

The dark-haired lady now swung the leg over her shoulder and spread the wax along the inner thigh of the anonymous leg. With the gaping paper G-string, really, nothing was left to the imagination.

"Ouch!" Massimo grimaced. "That must hurt."

"Let's move on," Kathryn said coolly. "The real action looks like it's down there." She pointed to the ever swelling crowd that was still a couple of city blocks away.

Everywhere I turned, there was hair. By which I mean *big* hair. Teased and sprayed hair. Hair that had never left the 1980s. There were hot pink lips and eyes lined in kohl, ears pierced with a dozen tiny rhinestones, and—forgive me for sounding like a snob—platform shoes and pants that may or may not have been leather but looked, in any event, suspiciously like vinyl. A lot of the people milling about reminded me of my old friends from beauty school. These were the folks who worked at Hair Today, Gone Tomorrow and A Cut Above.

And why were we there? Why, you might reasonably ask, had we chosen to spend a perfectly glorious Saturday in the stale, cold air of the Javits Center? Because we were on a mission. Jean-Luc had decided that it was time for a product line. Vidal Sassoon had a product line. Frederic Fekkai had a product line. It was time for Jean-Luc shampoo, conditioner, hair masque, gel, spray, mousse. And we—his entourage—were here to pick up ideas. To spy and to sniff, to see who was up to what.

But there was an even bigger reason we were there, why being part of Jean-Luc's inner circle was so important. Jean-Luc had begun to drop hints about the possibility of expansion.

Jean-Luc Los Angeles.

Jean-Luc Chicago.

Jean-Luc Washington.

And although he hadn't made any promises yet, the feeling among us was that we might be able to have a piece of those franchises. I couldn't believe it. I mean, I had gone from literally sweeping hair off the floor to being one of Jean-Luc's chosen ones in . . . well, it wasn't exactly in the blink of an eye, but still. Most people work their whole lives and never have something like that happen to them. I thought about it all the time. Why me? I knew it had something to do with having a talent for it—Doreen had always said that being a great colorist was all in "the touch"—but there were lots of talented people out here. I was lucky. I had good hands and a good eye for color, but I was also in the right place at the right time. Lucky, lucky me.

We wandered, the five of us, like a lost group of tourists, around the beauty show. There were endless aisles of vendors. In the Conair booth, several salesgirls were demonstrating the various speeds on their blow-dryers. Next, there was a booth devoted exclusively to sinks. Flat irons, curling irons, salon chairs, heat lamps. I was beginning to long for the J. Sisters.

"This is just a waste of time," Jean-Luc fumed. "We can't learn anything here. We just need to start from square one—invent, instead of copy from . . ." He waved an arm as if dismissing every single person in the Javits Center like a bunch of swarming gnats.

"Well, maybe it's just a lesson in what not to do," said Patrick. He was always looking on the bright side.

"I do not need a lesson in what not to do!" Jean-Luc exploded.

Patrick looked at me. We knew each other so well that I could see exactly what was going through his head. Jean-Luc drove Patrick crazy. Massimo could shrug him off, Kathryn could cast a spell on him, and I just felt lucky to have been chosen by him. But he really got to Patrick.

"You know what?" Patrick said softly. "I don't need this shit." Abruptly, he turned away from the group and started off down a different aisle. "Catch up with you later," he called over his shoulder.

Jean-Luc looked after him, frowning. "What is he—"

"Just let him go," said Kathryn, touching his arm.

ON THE OPPOSITE side of the auditorium, we were finally able to see what all the fuss was about. A private room had been cordoned off with velvet ropes, and ticket agents stood in front of a huge, glittering sign.

"Oh *no,*" breathed Kathryn.

HIROSHI—SPECIAL GUEST STAR, read the sign.

"Oh boy," Massimo murmured.

We all looked at Jean-Luc, who had stopped in his tracks. His lips were white, and his breathing was audible.

"What is this?" he asked quietly. Too quietly. When Jean-Luc got quiet, you knew there was going to be hell to pay.

"Now, Jean-Luc. It's no big deal," said Kathryn, once again touching his arm.

"Of course it's a big deal," Jean-Luc sputtered. "Hiroshi? Hiroshi?" he repeated, his voice rising into a loud question mark. Several people who were waiting on line scowled at us. The thing was, Jean-Luc had worked for Hiroshi for the first twelve years of his career, until he ditched Hiroshi and went out on his own. And even though Jean-Luc had become a huge success, we at the salon knew that he still had some sort of weird jealousy thing going with his former boss. Because even though Jean-Luc had become a household name (well, that is if the household was accustomed to spending three hundred dollars on a haircut), Hiroshi was more of a superstar. He cut all the coolest people. Mick Jagger stopped in when he was in town. Sheryl Crow flew him to her VH-1 shoots. And there was a persistent rumor about Air Force One being kept on the runway because Hiroshi was giving the president a haircut.

Jean-Luc turned suddenly, viciously, to Massimo.

"That should be me up there," he said. "Not that little Japanese man. Why didn't our publicists know about this?"

"Because it's the stupid fucking hair show," said Massimo. "Nobody cares."

"I care!" shouted Jean-Luc.

"Of course," Kathryn said soothingly.

"Don't treat me like a fucking child!" Jean-Luc shouted.

"Let's go in and watch," said Massimo.

"Are you out of your mind?" asked Kathryn.

"No, actually I'm curious," said Massimo. "I haven't seen Hiroshi in a while."

I stole a glance at Massimo. What was he doing? This was going to inflame Jean-Luc even more.

"Let's get out of here." Kathryn tugged at Jean-Luc's arm.

"No, no, no," said Jean-Luc, his voice dripping with sarcasm. "Of course we must watch the great Hiroshi. Perhaps we can learn a thing or two."

We slipped through the door without anyone stopping us to see our tickets—thank God, because the only thing worse than Hiroshi being there would have been being forced to pay to see him. Inside, on a stage platform, stood Hiroshi, whom I had seen only in pictures. I recognized him by his own signature haircut: tawny jet black layers that fell around his face with edgy, rock-star perfection. He wore faded blue jeans slung low around his narrow hips and a black T-shirt. Hiroshi circled around a model, who was seated on a folding chair in front of him. He examined her from every angle.

"Such theatrics," Jean-Luc muttered.

Then Hiroshi began to cut. I remembered reading that he preferred to cut hair dry. The model's hair had been blow-dried absolutely straight. He chopped bold angles, instantly highlighting her bone structure. In a business where the word *genius* is tossed around a thousand times a day, the man was actually a genius. Massimo stood next to me, watching carefully.

Next to the stage stood dozens of women. They were waiting, like seals, for the fish bait of Hiroshi. They wanted to be chosen as his next model. Where else could you get a three-hundred-dollar haircut for free?

I stole a glance at Jean-Luc. His hands were clenched, and a muscle throbbed along his temple. He was breathing rapidly. I worried, for a moment, that he might have a stroke. I could just see the headlines of the next day's New York Post: HAIR WARS! FAMOUS FRENCHMAN FAINTS!

"I think we've seen enough," said Kathryn. She threaded her fingers through Jean-Luc's and gave him a tug. There it was, finally: They were an item, no question about it.

"I hold you personally responsible for this," Jean-Luc said to Massimo. Kathryn stood by his side, still as a statue.

"What do you mean?" Massimo responded. It was the first time I had ever seen him ruffled. "It is not my job to—"

"I will tell you what is or is not your job!" Jean-Luc thundered.

Massimo took a step back. Hiroshi paused, scissors in the air, and squinted into the darkness to see what the fuss was about. Without even thinking about it, I moved closer to Massimo.

"You're fired!" yelled Jean-Luc.

"Sir, you're going to have to leave," a guard announced.

Jean-Luc drew himself up to his full five feet seven inches. "Don't you know who I am?"

"Did he really just say that?" Massimo whispered.

I stifled a laugh, but not before Jean-Luc saw me.

Jean-Luc flung the guard's arm away from him. The guard's hand moved to his belt, and I wondered if he had a gun.

"Don't worry. I am leaving," Jean-Luc said with whatever grandeur he could summon up. "I am leaving this shithole and never coming back."

The crowd, which had completely turned its attention from Hiroshi to Jean-Luc, cheered at this announcement. Jean-Luc's normally olive-skinned complexion turned dark red.

"Come, *chérie*," he said to Kathryn. Then, almost as an afterthought, he tossed this over his shoulder: "And you, too, Georgia Watkins—you and Massimo are fired. Fired!"

"HE DOESN'T MEAN it," said Massimo, pouring me my third glass of wine. We had walked and walked until we stumbled upon a small French bistro on a downtown side street.

"It has to be French?" Massimo groaned. "I've had enough of Frenchmen for one day."

"It's here. We're tired. And I need a drink," I said.

So here we were. The last of the carafe of wine swirled around the bottom of my glass.

"Of course he means it," I said. I was already picturing myself back in Weekeepeemie, putting foils in Mrs. Foti's hair.

They didn't even call it "highlights" up there. They called it "frosting"—and that's what it was. It had all the sophistication and subtlety of frosting on a cake. Well, I had tried. I had made a good run of it. Years of experience at one of the most famous salons in the world, not to mention a little bit of money saved up in the bank. Things could be worse.

"What are you thinking?" asked Massimo. His dark eyes watched me intently above the rim of his wineglass.

"I'm thinking that I'm going to end up right where I came from," I said. "Weekeepeemie, New Hampshire. Population 3871. That is, if Mr. Miller hasn't died yet. If he's dead, it's 3870."

I was a little drunk, feeling just a tad restless. Nothing like getting fired to feel that you've got nothing to lose.

"And you?" I asked Massimo, elbows on the scarred wood table. "What are you going to do? Do you have a boyfriend?"

I just blurted it out. It made no sense, of course. What did that have to do with anything?

A smile played at Massimo's lips. "You are assuming a great many things," he said.

"What?"

"Well, first of all, you're assuming that we are really fired, which I assure you we are not. He needs us too much."

"But he—"

Massimo leaned across the small table and put a finger to my lips, a gesture so intimate that it shocked me into silence.

"Secondly, you and I could both get a job in any salon in this city. We can call our own shots. You realize that, don't you?"

A dark curl fell across Massimo's noble forehead, and he brushed it away. He signaled the waiter for another carafe.

"And third, why do you think I would have a boyfriend?"

"I just figured . . . I mean, you're so cute and all, and all the guys must . . ." I stopped. I could feel the heat rising in my cheeks. There's nothing quite like a blonde blushing. Massimo just continued to look at me with that little smile and those warm, intense brown eyes.

"I do not have a boyfriend," he said finally. And then he leaned all the way across the café table and kissed me softly on the mouth.

IN THE SPRINGTIME in New York City, there are always a few perfect evenings—the dusk pink over the gray blue of the Hudson River, the sidewalks washed clean, the air so soft that it feels at one with the body, as if moving through it requires no effort at all. The night that Massimo and I fell in love—and yes, I do mean fell in love, though Massimo would claim that for him it happened earlier, much earlier, and he was just biding his time—was just such an evening. After the second carafe of wine we walked farther downtown, into the West Village, where Massimo lived. It seemed that everyone in New York was outside. Parents sat along benches at the Bleecker Street playground, squeezing the last little bit of sunlight out of the day as their children raced up jungle gyms and down slides. Massimo held my hand gently as we passed, with exactly the right amount of pressure—not pulling or tugging the way boys in Weekeepeemie had done, but cupping my fingers with his, simply, protectively, as if to say, *You are mine.*

"I always stop to watch them, the children," he said. "These children, they could be in New York or in Italy or in China—it doesn't matter. They have a universal language. Full of joy."

We walked past a bakery where a line of people had formed outside, snaking halfway down the block.

"What are they waiting for?" I asked. I didn't know this part of town at all. I was always too busy working at the salon to take the time to explore.

"Cupcakes."

"You're kidding. Cupcakes?"

"That bakery—they are the Jean-Luc of cupcakes," said Massimo. "People wait and wait, they don't even know why."

At the mention of Jean-Luc, I got nervous again. Where was Patrick? Was he fired, too?

"Maybe we should call—"

Massimo steered me by the elbow up the wide stone steps of a brownstone.

"I have a better idea," he said. He checked his watch. "How long has it been? Three hours? I'll bet you Jean-Luc has already called us."

"No way."

"What do you want to bet?"

"I don't believe in betting."

"I'll tell you what," Massimo said as he unlocked the front door. "If I am right, you will come away with me next weekend."

I stifled a smile. It was true that I wasn't much of a gambler, but I could hardly lose that bet. *You've been right in front of me all along,* was what I was thinking.

Massimo flicked on the light in his apartment, revealing a shabbily grand room in the manner of New York parlors. The ceiling was high, with ornate moldings painted over so many times that they looked thick, like whipped cream. An old iron chandelier hung from the center of the ceiling, casting the room in a dim, orangey glow. A threadbare velvet sofa, covered with soft-looking throws, faced an enormous marble fireplace. A gilded mirror leaned against the far wall.

"You have such a beautiful place," I said.

He smiled. "I have lived so far from home for so many years, I had to make a real home for myself—do you understand?"

I nodded. I did understand, even though I had done the exact opposite. I had always lived as though I could pack up at any minute and head back to New Hampshire if things didn't work out.

But Massimo's apartment was all so homey, I hardly knew what to make of it. If I had seen the apartment before that afternoon, I would have been even more certain that Massimo was gay. What straight man who lived by himself lived like this? No one I knew, that's for sure. Straight men I knew had no interest in taking care of themselves or their surroundings. They let dirty dishes pile up in the sink, left wet towels on the bathroom floor, and lined up empty beer bottles on their windows.

"Ah, the machine, it is blinking," said Massimo as he helped me off with my jacket. "Shall we see who it is?"

I sank into the velvet sofa. On the mantel, there were photographs of handsome, dark-eyed people on a beach, in a restaurant, their heads thrown back, laughing. Massimo's family.

"My mother and father, and my two sisters," said Massimo. I recognized the tone in his voice. He missed his family.

Beep. Massimo pressed the button on the answering machine.

"Hello? . . . Massimo? . . . *Bonjour?* Is anybody home?" Jean-Luc's voice echoed off the high ceiling of Massimo's parlor.

"Hello?" A long pause. "*Merde*. Listen—call me, please?" Then the rattling of the receiver and a click.

Massimo shook his head ruefully. "That is just like him," he said.

"What?"

"He cannot bring himself to simply say he is sorry."

"How do you even know he's sorry?" I asked.

"Oh, he is. Not because he behaved like a total, excuse me, asshole. But because he has spent the rest of the day calculating how much money he will lose if you and I are both gone."

I pulled off my boots. My feet ached from all that walking. How was it possible that I felt so instantly comfortable?

"So, *bella mia* . . ." Massimo pulled me close. I nestled my head into his shoulder, and with his other hand he caressed my cheek. "I guess I win our bet."

"I guess you do." I laughed. Technically, of course, he hadn't exactly won. But who was I to argue? So I didn't. I didn't argue as Massimo lit a fire in the fireplace on that cool spring night or when he knelt in front of me and slowly, deliberately, unbuttoned my blouse, unhooked my bra, unzipped my pants, and moved his elegant mouth along the length of my body.

"How long have you known?" I murmured. There was such a sense of purpose in his touch, as if he had known for years that this would happen.

"For a very long time," he said. Then he kissed my thigh. "Very long, I have waited."

There was no thought in my head about whether this was the right thing, or too soon, or what would happen tomorrow. I reached out for him, the muscles of his arms taut beneath his crisp white shirt, and slowly the world faded away. There was no Jean-Luc, no fear, no uncertainty, no distrust. Just the crackle of firewood, the murmured Italian words, *bella, cara mia,* the blur of fingers and tongues and limbs, just the two of us floating in the space we had suddenly, amazingly, made our own.

THE NEXT DAY, when we arrived at the salon, Jean-Luc acted like a contrite puppy dog. I wouldn't have expected it of him. And anyway, as you can imagine, my mind was elsewhere as I floated through the first of my twenty clients, my comb moving as if it had a life of its own. I was deliriously happy, living inside of a bubble.

My second client arrived carrying her Mongolian lamb coat—you know, the kind that has sort of fuzzy, stringy bits of fur going this way and that.

"Georgia, dear—do you think you might be able to put a couple of highlights in my coat?" asked the client. "The fur has gotten a bit dull."

It was one of the weirder requests I had ever heard, to be sure, and on another day it might have put me in a bad mood—but on that day, nothing could bother me. I took the coat from her, hung it over the back of my chair, and had my assistant mix some bleach.

Massimo! I kept him in my line of vision—where he had always been—and felt both comforted and excited by his presence. Needless to say, we hadn't slept much the night before, and we certainly hadn't responded to any of Jean-Luc's half-dozen phone calls.

"Massimo! . . . *Allo?* . . . *Allo?* . . . Where are you? Call me, eh? As soon as you can—*tout de suite!*" *Click.*

"*Mon ami,* I am . . . I am sorry," Jean-Luc finally said into the answering machine. "Please, I am an idiot. I will see you in the morning, *oui?*"

Massimo chuckled, his bare chest rising and falling beneath my cheek. "The poor guy," he said. "He's probably thinking of what he'll say to all our clients tomorrow morning. Think of how many free manicures he will have to give to make them happy!"

"Well, I guess he'll be relieved when we walk in the door," I said, snuggling deeper into Massimo's chest.

He leaned up on one elbow. "What makes you think we're going in?" he asked.

"Of course we're going in," I said. Was he joking? This was my *job*.

He sighed. "Okay, okay."

So here we were. Massimo was cutting the hair of one of the anchorwomen of a morning television show, I wasn't sure which one. She had anchorwoman hair: shoulder length, slightly layered, with a face-framing fringe in front. I watched as he meticulously trimmed a quarter inch from her bangs. She was smiling at him, gesturing with her hands, and her whole face seemed animated, except for one thing: Her forehead didn't move. It was the most amazing thing—I had begun to notice it among certain clients in the entertainment industry—there was a new injection on the market that paralyzed the facial muscles, preventing wrinkles but also preventing any expression at all. It was called Botox, and it was replacing eye lifts and face lifts, or at least putting them off. The anchorwoman's forehead was as smooth as a skating rink.

"So what are we going to do today?" my client asked, jolting me out of mooning over Massimo. She was a longtime client, a Wall Street trader who wore four-inch heels and carried an Hermès briefcase. I had done the exact same thing to her hair for the past five years: subtle golden highlights to give some life to her mousy brown.

"What do you want to do?" I asked.

She shrugged. "I need a change."

I glanced down at my tray. My assistant had already mixed the usual. Then I took a closer look at my client. What was her name? Alice? Alison? I never forgot a face, or a head of hair, or the details my clients always shared with me about their personal lives. But names I wasn't so good on. Anyway, whatever her name was, she didn't look so good. She had lost too much weight, crossing the line from chicly thin to emaciated. And just as the anchorwoman's face was glassily serene, this woman looked so haggard that I wanted to go get her some Botox myself.

"What's the matter?" I asked.

"Nothing. Just a bad day."

"Do you want to go blonder?" I asked. Blonder was often the answer. There were so many blonds. Icy blonds. Honey blonds. Golden blonds.

But as I studied her skin tone, debating about which blond, she suddenly blurted out, "Red!"

"Red?"

"Yeah," she said. "Let's do it."

"Listen"—I stole a glance at her index card—"Amanda. I don't think red is such a good idea. Maybe we could go strawberry blond, give you a few pieces around your face—"

"No," she said. "I really want red. Real red." I saw a tear trickle out of the corner of her eye.

"Listen," I said gently. "Whatever's going on with you, now is not the moment to make a big change. If you still want to do something drastic a month from now, come back to me and we can talk about it then. But you're going to hate anything I do to your hair today—I just know it—and then you'll end up hating me, and I'll lose you as a client."

She started slowly to nod and wiped her cheek with the back of her hand.

"So go buy yourself something expensive that you don't need," I said, waving my hand in the direction of Fifty-seventh Street. "At least then if you don't like it, you can always return it."

She—Amanda—got up from her chair and gave me a kiss on the cheek. "Thank you," she said quietly. "You're right. I know you're right."

"I hope you feel better," I said.

As she left, I saw Massimo watching me. How long had he been watching? He gave me a small nod and blew me a kiss. And then, in the endless row of mirrors, I saw that Patrick had seen us. He looked at me, eyebrows raised, and broke into a huge, face-splitting grin.

For the rest of the day, everyone behaved very oddly at the Jean-Luc Salon. Patrick and I giggled every time we looked at each other, Massimo and I stole kisses in the laundry closet during our break, and Jean-Luc—poor guy—I almost felt sorry for him. He had no idea what was going on.

Single-Process

The key to Jean-Luc's success was his burning, naked ambition. It was why guys like Hiroshi and John Sahag and Oscar Blandi drove him insane. You could see it in his eyes—his need, above all else, above food and sex and sleep, to be on top. So it was no wonder, really, when Jean-Luc started talking seriously about expansion. It wasn't enough for him that the salon was a huge success, that it was mentioned nearly every month in *Vogue* and *Bazaar* and *W.* It wasn't enough that he and Kathryn—they were now officially a couple—were invited to everything from the Metropolitan Museum's annual gala to the chicest art openings and film premieres.

No. None of this was enough for Jean-Luc, because, as my mother had long ago drilled into me, envy and greed were powerful things and could motivate a person to do just about anything. *There's a reason they call it "the green-eyed monster,"* she used to say. And now, whenever I looked at Jean-Luc, that's what I saw: a lumpy green ogre with little bits of brioche stuck in his teeth.

It was a Thursday around Christmastime when Massimo, Patrick, and I found the invitations in our staff mailboxes. (Presumably Kathryn had had hers hand-delivered.) On heavy, vanilla-scented paper, it was written in Jean-Luc's unmistakable elegant script: *Please join me for a drink at the Carlyle,* it read. *Tonight at seven o'clock.* There was no number for responding. Hadn't the French invented the RSVP? And it was last minute, of course. During the holidays. All in keeping with Jean-Luc's assumption—which had never let him down—that any invitation from him would trump all others.

"What do you suppose this is about?" asked Patrick. He, Massimo, and I stood in the small staff room, grabbing a quick coffee before the clients began to arrive.

"I'm sure he wants to take us out for a drink to show us how grateful he is for all our excellent work," I said.

"Ha, ha, ha," Patrick said dryly.

"I think I know," said Massimo. "But I don't want to say. We will see, won't we"—he checked his watch—"in just ten hours."

The staff room was nearly empty except for the few modest tables where we ate our quick lunches. You'd never know it was holiday time. There were no decorations—not so much as a wreath or a stocking, much less a Christmas tree. The only signs of life were a few scattered knapsacks and shopping bags that the staff dumped at the beginning of each day. The refrigerator shelves were stocked with food in labeled Tupperware containers that the assistants and shampoo ladies, who couldn't afford Fifty-seventh Street take-out prices, brought with them from Brooklyn or Astoria.

But down in the salon, it was Christmas! The windows of

Jean-Luc were lined in twinkling white lights; a Christmas tree hung with antique ornaments from Provence stood in the corner near the heat lamps; and in deference to our sizable Jewish clientele, an electric menorah was lit at the front desk. Christmas carols were piped through the sound system. I often found myself humming along to the tune of "Jingle Bells," but my personal lyrics went: *Cash, cash, cash. Cash, cash, cash . . .*

Gifts were everywhere. Many of the clients did, in fact, give us cash—a hundred here, two hundred there, and the occasional, insane, check for a thousand—but quite a few clients preferred to give us actual gifts. Magnums of champagne, pounds of Belgian chocolate, cashmere scarves and sweaters, and my personal favorite, which I had come to expect every year and had just received the day before: In a Tiffany's bag, inside a small orange-and-brown Hermès box tied with a brown velvet ribbon, was a vacuum-packed ounce of pot. My client, a record industry mogul, always gave me the same exact thing, in different but equally chic wrapping. I didn't even smoke the stuff! I wished I could somehow convert it into actual money, but that, Massimo reminded me, would be drug dealing.

Holiday generosity was rampant—it was almost an epidemic. The night before had been our staff Christmas party, which was always held at the trendiest place in town. This year, the party had been held at a club called Edge that hadn't even opened yet. The manager was a friend of Sweetie's—Sweetie, of course, being the most glamorous transvestite in New York, was like the walking, talking *Zagat* guide of hip, cool places. In fact, by the time a bar or club was listed in *Zagat* or in *Time Out New York*, Sweetie had already moved on.

Everybody was drinking Cristal or Veuve Clicquot, and the floor of Edge was littered with gift-wrapping as staff members exchanged gifts. For a brief window of time, money became meaningless—there was just so fucking much of it. The senior stylists had all pooled together to buy the two Filipina shampoo ladies trips back home to visit their families (not both at the same time, of course). Leather jackets, Burberry mufflers, TAG Heuer watches, Ralph Lauren alligator belts (six hundred dollars at Bergdorf's, but *free* with a gift certificate), all exchanged hands. The music—deejayed by one of the junior stylists who had started out as a guitar player—was rocking, and everybody was dancing.

"Hey, pretty girl!"

"Shake it, baby!"

"Gimme some love!"

Just try to imagine a whole bunch of people—people who live for fashion and beauty—who have to wear black pants and white shirts every working day of their lives. Then imagine those people let loose for the night, with money to burn, at a club where they can wear their most outrageous clothes and get away with it. By the end of the night, the club was a blur of shiny, perfect gym bodies. Gorgeous people allowed, just for the night, to be their full-on gorgeous selves. Even Jean-Luc got down and boogied.

OF COURSE, THERE was hell to pay the next day. We were all suffering from one giant, collective hangover. The day continued to crawl by. I had twenty-two heads (Claudia G among them, and she was like having five extra clients), and every hour or so, a client would call with a holiday emergency. Nan Babtkis needed her roots done before Christmas—could I squeeze her in? Nina Jenkins had been to another colorist—and she was so, so sorry, but now her hair was a complete disaster, and could I fix it? Today? The three hardest weeks in the life of an Upper East Side salon are the week before Rosh Hashanah, the week before Thanksgiving, and the week before Christmas. I felt as though I couldn't say no to any of my clients, so I just worked faster and faster, my comb flying in a frenzy. Massimo had been trying to convince me to work a little less hard. *Bella mia, it's only hair,* he would say at the end of days like this as he rubbed cream into my dry, parched hands.

And sure, it was only hair. I knew that. But it was like a disease or something. I had to work myself into a state of total exhaustion or I didn't feel I deserved all my good fortune. So there I was—twenty-two clients. Actually, it was twenty-three, because it had completely slipped my mind that I had promised Ursula I'd do her hair that day. I had been giving Ursula a combination of golden and rich chestnut highlights for years now, but I could never, ever take any money from her—I mean, she was *Ursula*—so I never had her make appointments through the salon. She came waltzing in during her lunch hour, surprising me.

"Georgia-pie!"

I tried not to look dismayed. I couldn't believe I had forgotten. How the hell was I going to fit her in? But if she'd had the slightest idea that she was putting me out at all, she would have run right out of there. Right from the beginning I'd had to twist her arm even to get her to come to me in the first place. *I don't want to take advantage,* she'd said. And I had told her I'd be insulted if she didn't let me do her color and have Patrick do her cut. That did it. She went from having big, frizzy, overprocessed hair to a sleek, shiny, golden chestnut style. And it was amazing—after that, she'd gotten three promotions, bing, bing, bing, and was now the executive secretary to the chairman of the whole bank. Good hair. I'm telling you. Not that I'm trying to take credit or anything.

"Look at you," Ursula said. "Every time I see you, I'm so proud I could burst."

I wished she wouldn't say that. It was embarrassing. I mean, at some point your life just becomes your life. I sort of understood some of the clients, rich men's wives who had started out as flight attendants or aerobics instructors—at some point, they just didn't want to be reminded.

But then there was a Bedford, sitting right next to Ursula.

"I saw that article about you in *New York* magazine!" said the Bedford.

"What? What was that? How could I have missed it?" asked Ursula.

"It wasn't an article, really," I said quickly. "Just a mention."

"Listen to her," Ursula said. "Just a mention."

I finished Ursula's highlights, then gave her a huge hug before turning her over to Patrick. She still smelled exactly the same—"Jean Naté, Jean Naté . . ."—and breathing in her scent, for a split second I was eight years old again, watching her make me a TV dinner back in Weekeepeemie.

I PEEKED OVER at Massimo as I did *baliage* on Jessie Adams. Jessie was a starlet in the making who had been sent to me by her agent, whose hair I also did.

Massimo wagged an envelope at me and crooked his finger, motioning me to come over. What could be so important?

"Excuse me for just a second," I said to Jessie, who had her head buried, in any event, in the December *Allure*; she was studying a picture of a starlet who was just a notch further along in her career. I hurried over to Massimo.

He handed me the envelope. "Take a look at this." He smiled mysteriously.

Out of the envelope, I slid two plane tickets—first class, I noticed—and several photographs of the exterior of a very grand-looking building. I couldn't figure out where it was at first, so I looked at the plane tickets again. New York/JFK to Paris/Charles de Gaulle.

"For us," said Massimo. "From—you will never believe it— Claudia and Tommy G."

"You're kidding me. I'm seeing her later today."

"She had her driver drop it off."

It had become common knowledge in the salon, among both the staff and the clients, that Massimo and I were a couple. We had always shared many of the same clients, and Claudia was among them, as was Tommy, who snuck in at odd hours to have his hair colored.

"But she doesn't have a generous bone in her body," I said.

"Shh," said Massimo. "She seems to have forgotten that."

"So this is her apartment?"

"Yes. On avenue Montaigne. Which, unfortunately for them, they are not able to use this holiday season."

He said the address reverentially, but he could have named any Paris street and it would have meant the same thing to me. I had never been to Europe. I had barely been off the East Coast.

I was dumbstruck.

"When?" I examined the ticket. "Wait—this is for next week!"

"The day after Christmas," said Massimo.

"But—"

"Why do you always say 'but'?"

"But we can't just—"

"There you go again!"

I laughed and looked over at Jessie Adams, who had finished reading *Allure* and was now jiggling one long, skinny leg.

"I need to get back to work," I said.

"My last client is at five-thirty," said Massimo. "So I will see you at the Carlyle, okay?"

"Okay," I said, and there it was, that secret, sharp pang I felt whenever Massimo said or did something unexpected. Where was he going? What was he doing? I wondered when I was going to reach a point of not being afraid that he was going to disappear.

"I have to buy some things for our trip," said Massimo, as if he had read my mind. "Because we are going to Paris the day after Christmas, yes?"

These things raced through my mind: Weekeepeemie, Doreen, Melodie, their disappointment if I didn't make it home.

"Yes," I said. It was like falling off a cliff. A single word—yes—the hard part. And the rest of it was up to the forces of nature.

I finished Jessie Adams's *baliage* (for which, of course, she neither paid nor tipped me) and was on my third to last client of the afternoon when Claudia G swept in.

"Darling!" She kissed me on both cheeks, French style.

"Claudia, Massimo showed me your incredibly generous gift this morning, and I can't even—"

She waved one hand dismissively. "It's nothing, really. Trust me. The apartment is just sitting there empty, and Tommy gets all these free plane tickets—"

"It's not nothing," I interrupted. Oh, my God, was I going to cry? *Snap out of it, Georgia.* I was an emotional basket case.

Maybe it was PMS. I tried to get a grip. I mean, for Claudia, it truly wasn't that big a deal. People like her really do live in a universe where trips to Paris could be handed out like Halloween candy.

"Well, you can thank me by putting in one highlight"—she held up a chunk of hair near her face—"right here."

SEVEN O'CLOCK. The Carlyle. We were all there on time—that is, Massimo, Patrick, Kathryn, and me. Jean-Luc was late. Ten, fifteen, twenty minutes late. We sat on a kilim-lined banquette, gathered around a small, low table, eating chips and waiting.

"Do you know what's going on?" Patrick, fearless as always, asked Kathryn. "Excuse me, let me rephrase that. Of course you know what's going on."

"Of course," Kathryn said mildly.

She wrapped a silky strand of honey blond hair around her finger, then let it go. She crossed one bare miniskirted leg over the other and took a sip of her Bellini. I noticed the other patrons of the Carlyle bar noticing us. We stood out, I suppose, in that environment. Blue-blooded, blue-blazered gentlemen with snow white hair and coiffed ladies carrying alligator Kelly bags and wearing marble-size strands of South Sea pearls sat daintily on the edges of their seats, nibbling nuts one at a time.

"Well?" Patrick asked Kathryn. "What's up?"

"Why don't we just wait for Jean-Luc," she said.

Patrick rolled his eyes.

"What's your problem?" Kathryn's anger flashed.

"Nothing. No problem at all," he said.

Patrick was looking even dreamier than usual. Each year that he was in New York—it was now going on nine—he got a little more comfortable in his own skin. By which I mean he allowed himself to be gay, and now he even had some money. Give a gay man money, and trust me, he will spend it on clothes. Tonight, Patrick was wearing perfectly cut black leather pants, a vintage, soft cotton men's shirt, and a shearling coat—this year's Christmas treat to himself.

"Why do you suppose Jean-Luc picked this place?" Massimo wondered out loud. "It's a bit . . . out of the way. Especially after last night's party—we all need to go to bed early."

"It's out of the way for you, perhaps. But Jean-Luc and I are staying here while our apartment is being renovated," said Kathryn. She had made the transition from lowly assistant to muse to full-on girlfriend seamlessly, as if all this had always been part of her master plan. She had even developed—could it be?—the vaguest hint of a French accent.

At that moment, along with a blast of cold air (since Jean-Luc never used revolving doors, only doors that clearly said USE OTHER DOOR), Jean-Luc arrived, the lower half of his face covered with a cashmere muffler.

"Good evening, good evening," he sang out as he unbuttoned his overcoat. He turned to Kathryn. "I was at Waterworks," he said, mentioning the name of a bathroom fixture store where a single faucet could cost more than a thousand dollars, "picking out the tiles for the master bath."

Then he turned to the rest of us. "I am sorry I am late."

Patrick and I exchanged a look. No, he wasn't.

"So. I see you have started without me." Jean-Luc looked at our half-empty glasses on the table. "Hair of the dog, as you Americans say." He snapped his fingers for a waiter. This was a habit left over from his earlier life in France, where somehow it wasn't considered atrocious manners to summon a waiter in this way. At the Carlyle, however, it didn't go over so well.

The waiter, a man well north of seventy, approached our table with a disapproving glare. "Yes, may I help you?"

"Another round, please," said Jean-Luc. I was praying that he wouldn't snap his fingers again. "And for me, a vodka martini—Absolut—with two olives."

As I watched Jean-Luc, I tried for the life of me to understand what it was that Kathryn saw in him. Oh, he was handsome, I suppose, if you go for vain, overcoiffed Frenchmen. But to me, what was sexy about a man—what was sexy about Massimo—was a real, hard-core confidence. Massimo simply was who he was. And all Jean-Luc did, all day long, was pretend. He was very, very good at it, but from day one I had seen right through him. If there was one thing that being Doreen Watkins's daughter had taught me, it was how to read people. It was probably why I was good at my job. It wasn't so much how I colored people's hair, but how I saw them when they sat in my chair and figured out what they wanted.

Jean-Luc tented his hands beneath his chin, cocked his head slightly to the side, and surveyed us all. "I am sure you are all wondering why I asked you to come here this evening."

We all just sat there, waiting him out.

"I am sure," he continued, "that you wondered what could be so important as to drag you here, at the end of the day, at Christmastime."

The waiter arrived with a tray of our drinks. He set Jean-Luc's martini in front of him. The glass was brimming, but Jean-Luc picked it up with a steady hand and took a long sip.

"You were wondering"—he smiled insistently—"*oui?*"

None of us—not even Kathryn, it seemed—wanted to give Jean-Luc the satisfaction of a response.

He took another sip of his martini. "Well then," he said. "I will tell you."

A dramatic pause. Music was playing; somewhere a pianist was improvising on Christmas carols. A young couple walked past our table with their baby in a Snugli.

"It is time, finally time, to expand," Jean-Luc proclaimed. Under the table, I was sure he was stroking Kathryn's thigh. "I have been waiting for the right moment, and finally it is here. These ideas have been inside my head for a long, long time." He tapped his forehead with one finger to illustrate his point.

"Expand how?" Massimo asked mildly.

"First we will begin with one phenomenal salon," said Jean-Luc. "Bigger and better even than the Jean-Luc Salon we have now."

I was liking his use of the word *we*.

"And where will this new salon be?" Kathryn asked. Why was she even asking questions? She had all the answers. Jean-Luc whispered them to her late at night as they soaked in their Waterworks tub.

"One thing at a time, *chérie*. What was I saying?" He took another sip of his drink. "Ah, yes. First, the incredible new salon. A huge presence. Huge! And then"—he snapped his fingers three times, and out of the corner of my eye I saw our waiter stiffen—"rat-tat-tat, one after the next we will open smaller salons in cities everywhere. Perhaps eventually even in small towns. Jean-Luc will be everywhere!" He spread out his arms to emphasize his point, very nearly capsizing his drink. "Jean-Luc Greenwich! Jean-Luc Scarsdale! Jean-Luc Short Hills fucking New Jersey!" he crowed.

"How do you see us involved in this?" asked Massimo. His tone was casual, but of course he was asking the question at the front of all our minds.

"What do you mean?" Jean-Luc raised his nearly empty martini glass and toasted us. "You are all my *team, n'est-ce pas*?

You will be opening these salons, finding the proper locations, overseeing them from top to bottom." He paused, then, as he always did just before delivering an important piece of news. "And of course you will be owners, at least in part. I will franchise these salons to each of you."

"Wow," said Patrick.

"That's incredibly generous of you, darling," Kathryn murmured.

"So when do we begin?" asked Massimo, ever the pragmatist. "And where?"

Jean-Luc's eyes flashed. "Aren't you going to thank me?"

"My friend," said Massimo, "I am, of course, very grateful."

As for me, I was in shock. Even though I had suspected for some time that Jean-Luc had expansion on the brain, I had never imagined anything this huge. And it sounded like he wanted all of us to be really involved. If it was true, it was the biggest thing that had ever happened to me, professionally speaking. I grabbed Massimo's hand under the table and squeezed hard.

"What is the next step?" asked Kathryn. I noticed that she had drained her Bellini in two long gulps. How very unlike her. I wondered if she was nervous for some reason.

"Ah, yes. The next step," said Jean-Luc. "I know it is holiday time, but I would like to begin scouting locations for the next grand salon, next week."

"Next week!" Patrick exclaimed. "But that's Christmas!"

"*Oui,*" Jean-Luc said with a small, sheepish nod. "But I was hoping if you would not mind to go—"

"I can't be away over Christmas," Patrick grumbled.

"Then the weekend after, before the New Year." Jean-Luc shrugged, an elaborate, drawn-out thing. He seemed to do it with his whole body. Just as the Italians are famous for talking with their hands, just as Americans are known the world over for their back-slapping, high-fiving camaraderie, so the French are known for their shrugs.

"You, Patrick, will go to Los Angeles," said Jean-Luc. "Would that be all right?"

"I'll work it out," said Patrick. His whole tone had changed instantly. He liked L.A.

"Unfortunately, Kathryn and I cannot get away," said Jean-Luc. "We have the renovation of our apartment to tend to." He smiled at Kathryn, and she smiled back demurely. "And Massimo and Georgia, a little birdy tells me that you are planning a trip to Paris, yes?"

How did he know? Claudia or Tommy G must have told him. I guessed there wasn't much that went on at Jean-Luc that was kept secret.

Massimo raised an eyebrow. "Why, Jean-Luc? Are you thinking of Paris for the next location?"

Jean-Luc shrugged. "It is possible, yes. I don't know. But there is a very good real estate manager there I'd like you to meet—that is, since you're going to be there anyway. . . . And you, Massimo—you speak very good French, so why not?"

Massimo and I tried not to look at each other. Why not indeed?

CHRISTMAS IN WEEKEEPEEMIE. Think of small houses covered with a multitude of bright, blinking lights. Think of Rudolph and the other eight reindeer prancing across Mr. and Mrs. Appruzzesse's front lawn. The crèche in the center of town, on the green, held life-size replicas of Mary and the baby Jesus. And then there was the old Miller farm, where as long as I could remember, every tree (there were hundreds) was strung with silver stars that glimmered in the moonlight. Was it true only of Weekeepeemie, or the same in many other small, nondescript towns across America, that the less money people had in their bank accounts, the more they spent on Christmas? Meanwhile, the richest people in New York had, at the most, a small discreet wreath on their front door.

"Unbelievable," Massimo murmured.

We had come to Weekeepeemie, driven there on Christmas Eve day with our bags packed and ready to go to Paris. It was Massimo's surprise to me. He reorganized our flights so that instead of leaving from New York the day after Christmas, we'd leave Weekeepeemie at the crack of dawn, drive to Boston, and catch the afternoon flight to Paris.

So now we were taking a long, cold walk along the streets of Weekeepeemie, walking off the ten-thousand-calorie dinner Doreen had whipped up when she heard that I was coming home with a friend.

"A friend?" she had asked.

"Yes."

"What kind of friend?"

"His name is Massimo. He—"

"The cute Italian one? From the salon?" Then she laughed. "Don't ask me how, but I knew it. I just knew it."

"Knew what? There's nothing to know," I said snappishly. This was why I hadn't told her anything in the first place.

"Oh, sure, there's nothing to know," said Doreen.

"Keep this up, and I'm not bringing him home."

"Okay, okay," said my mother.

"UNBELIEVABLE," MASSIMO REPEATED, staring at the diorama of Rudolph and Santa's other reindeer.

"Stop saying that!" I said. "I can't help it—I grew up here!"

"Georgia . . . I meant it only in a good way." Massimo wrapped his arms around me, our breath making clouds in the cold air. "It is beautiful in its own way, yes?"

We stood on the corner of Elm Street, staring at the Appruzzesses' front yard. Massimo was right, of course. It was sort of beautiful—but like anything too close, too familiar, it was hard to see clearly. It was like looking at your own face for too long in the mirror.

"Does your mother always cook like that?" asked Massimo. "I thought my mother made a lot of food for holidays, but this"—he held out his arms—"this was huge!"

I laughed. "She did it because of you, I think. It's been a long time since she's had a man around to cook for."

"Your mother is wonderful," Massimo said as we walked. "She reminds me very much of you."

"Really? How?"

"Well, first—she is very beautiful." He slung his arm over my shoulder. "And then, she is also very brave."

"I don't think of myself as brave," I said. "Or beautiful," I added as an afterthought.

"For you to have moved to New York from a place like this . . . that requires bravery," said Massimo.

"Or craziness."

"That, too."

As we trudged back to Doreen's, I replayed the last two days in my mind. We had arrived from New York just after lunchtime, pulling into the small driveway of the house I no longer thought of as my own. Melodie was already there, home from her senior year of college. She was waiting to hear about her applications to medical schools, but I knew she'd get in everywhere. What school would say no to a genius like Melodie? And Doreen was still at her salon, of course, working up until the last possible minute. Christmas Eve was a big hair day everywhere, including Weekeepeemie. I opened the back door and there was my sister, whom I practically knocked down, I hugged her so hard. My nerdy, amazing, scarily smart little sister whom I loved and felt more protective of than anyone else in the entire world.

Massimo came through the door behind me. He waited patiently until Melodie and I finished hugging and squealing, then shook her hand with a small, elegant bow.

"You are Melodie," he said. "A lovely name. I would have recognized you anywhere. Georgia talks about you so much."

Melodie turned bright pink—magenta, really. I don't know if it was the attention of a handsome guy or the very fact that there was a guy at all inside our house. When was the last time that had happened? I searched my memory and couldn't come up with anything.

Something was different in the house, though. As Massimo and I put down our bags, I tried to figure it out. It took a minute, and then it hit me: The house smelled wonderful, full of the scent of delicious food cooking. I sniffed the air.

"What's going on? Where's Mom?" I asked Mel.

"At the shop," she said.

"That's what I thought. So what's the—"

"She started cooking at five this morning. She was like an insane person. I don't know what got into her."

"Your mother, she doesn't often cook?" asked Massimo.

"Never!" Mel and I chorused. Doreen's idea of a meal was a frozen dinner or take-out from Bob's Big Boy on special occasions. She had always been working too hard to cook.

"Where should we put our bags, do you think?" I asked Mel. She looked good, my sister. Nerdy girls can have their own, quirky beauty, and she was growing into that. I wished she'd let me give her a couple of highlights, though.

"What do you mean?" Melodie responded. "Your room. Where else?"

"But where will Massimo . . ." I trailed off. Clearly, I hadn't thought this through. Were Massimo and I going to sleep together? Under my mother's roof?

"We're all grown-ups," said Melodie. And it was true. I guess we were. I knew this much, though: There wasn't going to be any hanky-panky, as Doreen would say. Not in my mother's house.

Then the back door slammed, and there was Doreen. It had been a long time since I'd seen her. In fact, it had been since her visit to New York. Her hair had grown out nicely, and she looked like herself again.

"Baby!" My mother kissed me hello.

Massimo offered her the same courtly bow he had given to Melodie. "I am Massimo," he said.

"I remember you very well," Doreen said with a smile.

IT TOOK SOME adjusting for us all to get comfortable with one another. None of us were used to having a man around, much less a man who cleared and washed the dinner dishes and whipped up a flan with ingredients my mother already had in her kitchen (in her frenzy of cooking, she had forgotten dessert). But after that first dinner, and a long, fitful night of sleeping with Massimo, trying not to touch him on my small, girlhood bed, after Christmas morning and presents and then

Doreen's elaborate lunch, by the time Massimo and I took our long walk at dusk to see the multicolored lights of Weekeepeemie, the four of us had fallen into the rhythm and comfort of family.

"This is a special place," Massimo said to me as we rounded the bend by the old Miller farm. We stood still, watching hundreds upon hundreds of silver stars shine in the orchard.

"Yes, it is."

"We are all formed by where we come from," said Massimo. "And you—you are lucky."

And lucky was exactly what I felt that night, with Massimo's arms around me, looking out over the old Miller farm, with my mother and sister just a mile down the road, snuggled on the couch, watching TV. Nearly everybody I cared about, everybody in the whole world, was near me. And that, I realized, was how I liked it.

THE NEXT MORNING, Doreen got up at an ungodly hour to make us breakfast before we began the long drive to the Boston airport. What had gotten into my mother? She had turned into a domestic goddess.

"My goodness, Paris! How exciting," Doreen said as she placed two plates of scrambled eggs and bacon on the kitchen table. It was still dark outside. Through the thin white curtains, the faintest streaks of dawn were barely visible.

"Have you ever been?" Massimo asked.

"No," said my mother. "I've only been out of the country once, and that was to go to Mexico."

For her divorce, I thought with a start.

"Ah, Paris . . . Paris is the most wonderful city." Massimo's voice rose and fell, caressing the word *wonderful*. This was one of the things I loved most about him: his enthusiasm for life. He adored the world. He ate and drank of it in big, appreciative gulps.

"I've always wanted to see the Eiffel Tower," Doreen said dreamily.

"We will all go there together!" exclaimed Massimo. For a moment, I thought he meant *now*. "Sometime, we will all take a trip," he explained further, "all through Europe. We will go to Italy, and I will introduce you to my own mama."

Doreen looked at Massimo, then at me, then back at Massimo. I knew what she was thinking: *This is serious.*

"So what will you do there?" she asked.

"Well, we will spend much of our time scouting for a location for the new Jean-Luc," said Massimo.

My heart sank. I hadn't planned to tell my mother anything about that part of the trip. I kicked myself for not having told Massimo to keep his mouth shut.

"What do you mean, 'the new Jean-Luc'?" asked Doreen.

"Oh, it's nothing, really," I said. "At least not yet. I mean, nothing's firm, nothing's written in stone, it's just that Jean-Luc is thinking of expanding, and . . ." I tapered off.

"Expanding?" Doreen repeated mildly.

"He is offering us a franchise," said Massimo. I realized, as he said it, that he was very excited about this, much more excited than he had let on.

Doreen held a steaming cup of coffee between her two hands, warming herself against the frigid morning air. "Be careful," she said.

I had a momentary flash of anger at my mother for being such a party pooper. It was what she always said about everything. Be careful. Watch your back. Don't trust anybody.

"It's going to be great," I blurted out, even though I knew no such thing. "You'll see. It's going to be amazing."

I WAS A MUCH different type of traveler from many of my clients, the Upper East Side ladies who were used to spending thousands of dollars a month on their personal maintenance, going out to four-star dinners every night, and flying first class to Europe. Because I had never done any of it before, I soaked in every minute of it like a sponge. My clients had long since stopped thinking of their lives as anything special. They bought whatever they wanted, went wherever they wanted, mindlessly handing over their credit cards, knowing that the bills would be paid, easily and without question, by somebody else: husband, father, bookkeeper, personal manager.

So when Massimo and I were handed our glasses of champagne in the roomy first-class cabin of Air France's afternoon flight to Paris, when we snuggled together under a soft—could it be cashmere?—blanket and nibbled on delicious canapés of smoked Scottish salmon and crème fraîche, when I dozed into a sleep so deep and so comfortable that it seemed impossible, and when I awoke as we were beginning our descent into Charles de Gaulle—all I can tell you is that, inside, I was like a little kid shivering with joy.

Claudia G had sent a driver to meet our flight. A chauffeur in uniform held a placard with our names by the baggage claim, then escorted us to a dark blue Mercedes, which, he told us, was at our disposal for the duration of our stay.

"That won't be necessary," said Massimo. I was glad he'd said it. Because this was too much, really. The plane tickets, okay. The apartment, fine. But there was a limit to how much we could accept without feeling eternally indebted. I already had to hold Claudia's hand every time she had a single high-light. What would I have to do after this?

Massimo held me close in the back of the car as we were driven through the Paris suburbs. Small stone buildings were visible through the tinted windows of the Mercedes. It was late at night in Paris, no traffic on the roads, and my first impres-sion was how *old* everything looked. Against the ancient, or-nate buildings, in the yellowish glow of the streetlights, the few newer structures looked oddly out of place.

"I want to walk everywhere with you," he said. "Or if we must, we'll take the Métro. Paris is a city to be seen up close, on foot."

I nodded. I was tired and exhilarated, in that strange, dreamlike netherworld you're in after a long flight. Wake up in Weekeepeemie, go to sleep in Paris. Unsophisticated as this sounds, I could hardly believe it was possible.

"What do you want to do tomorrow?" I asked Massimo. We didn't have a lot of time; three days was the window in which Claudia and Tommy G's apartment was available—a fact about which Claudia had been profusely, embarrassingly, apologetic.

"It's just that Tommy's promised it to Beyoncé," she told me. "And you know how Beyoncé is," she went on, the way people who were constantly surrounded by famous people assumed that everyone knew everyone.

I had nodded. Beyoncé. Of course.

"I don't know," Massimo said. "Perhaps the Louvre? Or the Musée Picasso? A little shopping in the Marais?"

I could tell from the tone of his voice that he wasn't quite excited enough by the plan he was coming up with. There was something he wasn't saying.

"What about you?" he asked. "Any ideas?" The car had

now entered the part of Paris I recognized from pictures and movies. We sped along one side of a river strung by beautiful stone bridges lit from beneath.

"I thought maybe . . ." I stopped, self-conscious. What I really wanted to do was call the real estate manager and start scouting locations. To me, that was the most exciting thing we could possibly do, but I was afraid that Massimo would think I was being my usual no-nonsense, overly businesslike self. *Georgia, Georgia,* he would say, shaking his head. *Always the work. Never the play.*

"What?" he prodded me.

"Maybe we could start looking around for space? For the salon?" I asked tentatively.

Massimo slid closer to me in the backseat and engulfed me in a bear hug. Nobody hugged like Massimo. He made me feel completely safe; the whole world melted away.

"You are the woman of my dreams, do you know that?" he whispered in my ear.

"I was afraid you wouldn't think it was romantic," I said.

"Are you kidding? It's the most romantic thing I can think of," Massimo said as the car pulled up in front of the discreetly grand building I remembered from Claudia G's photographs.

TECHNICALLY, I SUPPOSE Massimo and I spent our entire time in Paris looking for the perfect location for the new Jean-Luc Salon. But in reality, what we did for those three days was walk around Paris in a little bubble of our own. We may have been accompanying the real estate manager from the seventh *arrondissement* to the sixth, from St.-Germain des Près across the river to the Marais, but we were both focusing much more on our imagined future together. It seemed so crazy, but some-how—how can I explain this?—it also seemed like fate. The country girl from Weekeepeemie and the Italian boy who had come to New York would move to Paris and open . . . how had Jean-Luc put it? *A phenomenal salon.*

Paris! I fell in love with the city. The cafés that Massimo brought me to, the restaurants that he knew from his many trips there, the scent of freshly baked bread and bitter choco-late that seemed to drift over every street corner. The boutiques with their beautiful, perfectly tasteful windows—and most of all, the Frenchwomen themselves. Where had they learned such style, such effortless chic? They were born with it, Mas-simo told me. But how? I mean, it just killed me the way a French girl could pull her hair into a chignon, throw on a pair of jeans, a T-shirt, and some high-heeled boots, tie a scarf around her neck, and—*voilà!* as Jean-Luc would say—she would look like a million bucks.

Suddenly, I could completely see having a salon in Paris. None of it felt impossible to me. I'd learn French. I'd figure out the Métro. Massimo and I would live in one of those great old apartments with a creaky elevator on the Left Bank. We'd tend to the hair of the chicest women in the world and raise a cou-ple of beautiful, French-speaking children.

Of course, I didn't talk about any of this with Massimo, be-cause to talk about it would have broken the spell. But as we walked the streets of Paris, my idea of our future was becoming clearer and clearer, like an outline slowly being filled in. We would be in an airy glass salon, Massimo and I, along with Patrick and a few of our favorite assistants from New York. The salon would be called Jean-Luc, but it would be ours, Mas-simo's and mine. Together, working side by side, building a life.

On our third morning, as he had each morning since we'd

arrived, Massimo went downstairs to a nearby *boulangerie* to bring me a croissant and a café au lait. And I went to my favorite spot in Claudia and Tommy G's apartment: the bathroom. There was a phone next to the toilet—a phone! next to the toilet!—and I finally gave in to the urge I'd had since first arriving. I picked it up, and using the handy international code printed on the inside of the receiver, I dialed Doreen. It was the middle of the night in New Hampshire. In my excitement, I hadn't taken into account the time difference.

"Doreen's, may I help you?" My mother's groggy, confused voice sounded as if it were just around the corner.

"Mom? Oh my gosh, I'm sorry. I forgot the time—"

"Georgia? Is everything okay?"

"Everything's fine," I said. "Guess where I am?"

"I know where you are. You're in Paris, right? What are you doing making such an expensive—"

"I'm on the toilet, Mom," I said. I had been dying to call her. Dying.

Outside the bathroom door, in the white leather and dark wood Paris pied-à-terre of Claudia and Tommy G, I could hear Massimo returning, carrying paper bags full of croissants.

"Sorry?" said Doreen. "I don't think I heard what you said."

"I'm on the toilet, Mom—and do you know what's outside my window? What I'm looking at right at this very moment?"

I paused.

"You're expecting me to actually guess?" asked my mother. She was talking to me the way she used to when I was a little kid.

"The friggin' Eiffel Tower," I crowed. "That's what I'm looking at while I'm—"

"I get it, Georgia," Doreen said, laughing. "But tell me, because I can't really tell—are you having a good time?"

ON THAT THIRD and final day, after a delicious breakfast in bed, Massimo and I wandered out onto avenue Montaigne. The sun was brilliant. I shaded my eyes and looked to the right and then the left down the grand avenue.

"Which way?" I asked. It seemed to me that we had already gone in every possible direction. Jean-Luc's fabulous real estate manager had shown us all over Paris, but she hadn't shown us a single thing that seemed right.

"I'm not sure. Let me think," said Massimo. He wrapped his muffler around his neck and pulled his baseball cap low over his eyes.

Then we turned, and I think we both saw it at the same exact moment. Was it possible that it had been there all along, in our own backyard, so to speak? A towering two-story space, with floor-to-ceiling windows done in green-tinted glass. It was both welcoming and hard-edged, sexy and industrial. Best of all, it had a small sign posted in the window: *A LOUER*. For rent.

"*Mama mia,*" said Massimo. "It is the place. How could she not have shown it to us?"

"Maybe it wasn't for rent until today," I said. "Who knows—maybe it's fate."

Gucci was on one side of the *A LOUER* sign, and Valentino was on the other. Chanel was down the street, along with every other famous French designer known to man. This would make Jean-Luc happy.

"I love it," Massimo said as we crossed the street. "It's perfect." He pulled a notepad from his breast pocket and scribbled down the number on the sign.

"I love you," I blurted out. The words flew out of my

mouth, and I clamped my mittened hand to my lips, but it was too late. There it was. I had said it.

In the middle of the avenue Montaigne, Massimo took me in his arms, in front of the two-story soaring glass salon of our future. He stared into my eyes for a long time as the sounds of Paris seemed to fade all around us. There was nothing but Massimo. Massimo and my life with him, unfurling between us like a map in the cold wind.

"I love you, too, my Georgia," he said.

Double-Process

Jean-Luc flipped over the space on the avenue Montaigne. How could he not? The location was, as we had suspected, the fulfillment of all his fantasies. For a poor kid from Marseilles to have arrived in the most fashionable neighborhood in Paris, to have his name in gilded letters on an elegant, tinted glass door, right there between Gucci and Valentino . . . well, what can I say without being crude? Okay. The guy was practically coming in his pants. Sorry about that. You can take the girl out of Weekeepeemie, but you can't take Weekeepeemie out of the girl.

A few weeks after Massimo and I returned from Paris, Jean-Luc flew there himself to negotiate a ten-year lease on the space. It was really happening. We were sworn to secrecy, for the time being. Only Patrick, Kathryn, Jean-Luc, Massimo, and I knew. Jean-Luc was planning to make a big announcement in the spring. He had a master plan: Our franchise was going to be the first of many. Patrick was going to come with us to Paris to help us open the salon, and then he was next. Jean-Luc Los Angeles was on the horizon.

So we set about planning. Every other night, after finishing at the salon, I trotted off to the Alliance Française for French lessons.

Bonjour, class.

Bonjour, madame.

Comment allez-vous?

Bien, merci.

On the nights that I wasn't learning the most basic French, Massimo, Patrick, and I were learning the most basic of business skills at a How to Run Your Own Business class at the Learning Annex. We learned the difference between working capital and net working capital. Within a few weeks, I was tossing off terms like "cash flow" and discussing the accrual method of accounting versus the cash method. This from someone who had never even bothered to balance her checkbook before!

After half a semester of business school, I became curious about a couple of things. Where was Jean-Luc getting his capital for the expansion? Did he have other investors, partners? When I asked Jean-Luc, he laughed. *You are worrying too much, beauty shop girl. Everything is under control. You are going to be very rich, my dear.* He made me feel like an ingrate.

So let's just say we were busy. We didn't have a minute to ourselves during that time, but it was a fantastic kind of busyness, because we had an amazing goal, and every single thing we learned, every night that we collapsed, exhausted, into bed, was a tiny step toward Jean-Luc Paris. The months passed in a blur of hair, the confusion of a new language, and the study of business skills that none of us had ever thought we'd need. And then—finally—it was spring.

"I HAVE SOME news—some very big, important news," announced Jean-Luc. It was a Friday near the end of March, a record-breaking cold day, as it happened. The salon had closed for the evening. It was nearly eight o'clock—but the entire staff, from us to the other stylists and colorists, Richard, Faith, the assistants, the shampoo ladies, even the managers and receptionists and front desk staff, had gathered in the center of the salon, crowded together, shoulder to shoulder, to hear the announcement that Jean-Luc had, well, announced he would be making that very morning.

Massimo was next to me. I could feel the warmth of his body, the excitement that was electric between us.

"My news will make some of you happy, and others, maybe not so happy," said Jean-Luc. He was looking quite handsome that evening, I had to admit, tanned from a long weekend in Anguilla with Kathryn, his golden skin set off nicely by his crisp white shirt. He was the very model of a hugely successful entrepreneur about to launch a new international salon. Which was what he was about to say. *Just spit it out!* I wanted to yell across the salon floor, but I restrained myself.

"Some of you may, in fact, feel quite angry with me. Others may be surprised," Jean-Luc continued. "And to that, I can only say I am sorry in advance, and to remember—this is business. And business is not always fun."

"Come on," Massimo said under his breath.

I looked around at some of the other salon staff. Patrick was standing right in front of me, and I could see small beads of sweat forming on the back of his neck. He was excited, nervous, just like Massimo and me. This was going to be huge, and there were going to be some people who would be pretty pissed. I looked over at Richard. His brow was trying to knit together, but he'd had so much Botox that his face simply couldn't scowl. Faith Honeycomb looked serene, as usual, as if Jean-Luc's announcement couldn't possibly affect her. And Kathryn stood off by herself, very still, very calm, arms crossed, watching Jean-Luc with a small smile.

"I have sold the Jean-Luc Salon to WXYZ," said Jean-Luc. There was dead silence on the salon floor; it was the most quiet it had ever been and ever would be. "You are all familiar with WXYZ?" Jean-Luc went on. He wasn't exactly looking at any of us, I noticed, not looking anyone in the eye. What the hell was he saying?

I felt Massimo's hand searching for mine, then holding it tightly, squeezing.

"It is a conglomerate," said Jean-Luc. "A very large conglomerate." He seemed to be enjoying saying such a big word.

"What?" I heard Patrick's disbelieving voice, just in front of me. "*What?*" he repeated.

"As I said, I know some of you will not be happy with this news," Jean-Luc said. "But it is what's best for the company. Nothing will change—and I must ask you to refrain from—"

"Fucking liar," Massimo muttered.

I was slow to catch on. It was hard to believe what I was hearing, to take it in. So Jean-Luc had completely deceived us—if there was going to be a Jean-Luc Paris, a Jean-Luc Los Angeles, a Jean-Luc franchise at all, it was going to be owned now by WXYZ. A tear rolled down my cheek, and Massimo gently wiped it away. Which only made me feel worse. Poor Massimo. Poor Patrick. That Jean-Luc was hurting them felt far worse than whatever he was doing to me. I hated him for it. I focused on the crystal chandelier above Jean-Luc's head and willed it to come crashing down on top of him.

"You will all, of course, continue to be employees of Jean-Luc, only now there will be new management—corporate management," said Jean-Luc.

I looked around the room. Who had known about this? Kathryn, of course. And no doubt for her this was nothing short of fabulous news. As I stared at her, I noticed—she must have just put it on, because, trust me, I wouldn't have missed it—a giant emerald-cut diamond sparkling on her left hand.

Of course. This move was going to make Jean-Luc a very rich man.

And then there was Richard. He did not look surprised, and I didn't think his placid expression was due entirely to being over-Botoxed. No. My instincts told me that Richard had known. He had known all along. Wait a minute. I just then remembered something. Wasn't Jane Huffington Cooke involved in WXYZ? Hadn't I read, in the endless trivia that I picked up in fashion magazines, that she had, until very recently, been a member of its very fashionable board?

"Well then. That is all I have to say," said Jean-Luc, dismissing us. "Now none of you will fall over in shock when it is in the papers tomorrow, eh?"

Next to me, Massimo was trembling ever so slightly. He looked stunned and shaken. My Massimo, who prided himself on covering every angle, on never being taken by surprise.

"What does this mean for us?" asked one of the braver assistants. "Who will be running the company?"

"We will have a superb woman from WXYZ," Jean-Luc said without missing a beat. "You will all meet her next week."

"Will the salon be moving?" another stylist asked. It was a

thought that hadn't even occurred to me. My brain was moving slowly, floating on a sea of shock.

"As a matter of fact, yes," said Jean-Luc.

"I cannot believe this," Massimo whispered, as much to himself as to me. "I cannot believe this," he kept repeating.

"We will move to a magnificent new salon, which we will build."

"Where?"

"In the WXYZ building," said Jean-Luc.

He paused, eyes scanning the crowd—this group of talented people who were at least partly responsible for his enormous success. He was fiddling with his pants pocket, probably craving a cigarette.

"Are our jobs safe?" asked one of the receptionists.

Jean-Luc's eyebrows shot up. "But of course," he exclaimed, spreading his arms wide as if to embrace every single person in the room. "You are my team! I need you now—every single one of you—more than ever! We will all be doing this together, yes?"

There was a faint ripple of approval in the room. A murmur of assent. But when I looked at Jean-Luc, all I saw was the fakeness of his smile. He must have practiced this moment in the mirror a thousand times: how to be reassuring but firm, a friendly barracuda. A green-eyed monster disguised as a suave Frenchman. He had sold three people in this room down the river. What else was he capable of doing?

Massimo tapped Patrick on the shoulder. When Patrick turned around, his face was white, caved-in. I hadn't seen him look so completely without hope since beauty school back in Weekeepeemie.

"Let's get out of here," Patrick said quietly.

Massimo nodded, then gave my hand a tug. I seemed to be

glued to the spot. The crowd was breaking up, the room buzzing.

"Come on, Georgia," he said quietly. Out of the corner of my eye, I saw Jean-Luc starting to make his way across the floor in our direction. That, I realized with a start, was the last thing any of us needed. Quickly, Massimo, Patrick, and I moved to the doors, shrugging on our coats as we walked, and escaped into the freezing night. We hailed a taxi and rode silently downtown, all the way to Massimo's house. It was simply understood that we were going to hang out together. Massimo and I certainly weren't about to let Patrick be by himself on such a lousy night.

When we got to the apartment, Massimo lit a fire and brought out a bottle of very good red wine, a Barolo that I knew he'd been saving for a special occasion.

After he'd poured the three of us healthy glassfuls, he raised his glass in a toast.

"I think we should celebrate tonight," he said, though if you had looked at all our faces, you would have seen three of the saddest, most pissed-off people in New York.

"I think we should celebrate," Massimo continued, "because every ending is a new beginning."

"Spare us the new age crap, please," said Patrick. "Not tonight. I just can't bear it."

"My friend, this is not crap," said Massimo, not in the least offended. "I think the only way we can see this is as an opportunity."

"Yeah," I chimed in. "Maybe the new ownership will be a good thing."

Patrick and Massimo both stared at me as if I had lost my mind.

"That's not what I meant," said Massimo. "Quite the opposite."

He buried his nose in the bowl of his wineglass and inhaled deeply, then took a sip. "The wine is beautiful," he said. "Please, enjoy. I brought this bottle back from Italy."

"So are you saying what I think you're saying?" asked Patrick.

"Will somebody please just speak English?" I said. I was still in shock, still so completely blindsided by Jean-Luc's announcement that I knew I wasn't thinking straight.

"Georgia, my beauty . . . my one true love," Massimo began. Why was it that Italian men could get away with this shit? If an American ever spoke to me that way, I would laugh. "We—you, me, and Patrick—it is time for us to go out on our own. How long have we all been working for Jean-Luc?"

"Nine years," Patrick and I echoed each other.

"Nine years." Massimo nodded. "And how many times have we said we'd do it differently if it were our own salon? Even if we had opened Jean-Luc Paris, it never would have been truly *ours*. Now we have a chance. Is Jean-Luc smarter than us? No. Is he a better stylist than us? God, no. It is time that we stop complaining and start doing. This is a great chance for us to finally make a real change, to be our own bosses—to do it our way."

He stopped and took a sip of wine. Patrick and I were riveted.

"Just think of it," Massimo said. "The three of us—true partners. Not slaves of Jean-Luc. Not killing ourselves to work for him and then watching him take all the money."

"How long have you been thinking about this?" Patrick asked.

"Forever," said Massimo.

196

"Go out on our own?" I repeated dumbly.

The wine had very quickly gone to my head. My tongue felt thick, inarticulate. I unbuttoned my sweater so that I was wearing just a tank top. It was warm by the fire. I looked back and forth between Massimo and Patrick, the only two men I had ever loved. Patrick had caught Massimo's excitement; glee had quickly replaced their anger and sense of betrayal. And—who knows—maybe they were right. Maybe going out on our own would be the best possible thing. To own our business! To have the roof over our heads be ours—our own place!

I don't know, I wanted to say. *I don't know, I don't think I can, it's too big a risk, I'm scared.* But watching their puppy-dog faces, I couldn't say any of that. The last thing in the world I wanted to do was disappoint them.

"Let's take it one step at a time," I said weakly.

"Bravo!" shouted Massimo, who had somehow taken what I'd said for a yes.

THE NEXT MORNING, we were back at our usual stations. What else were we going to do? It was a slow Saturday, typical for late March. Private schools were closed for spring break, so many clients were away. Mustique, Anguilla, St. Barths. I looked over my client list for the day. Mostly I was going to be doing single-processes, covering gray. Those ladies came in every other week like clockwork, the ones—usually brunettes—who had to suffer the indignity of gray hair sprouting all over their heads.

Covering gray was meticulous work. It wasn't just slapping on the dark color with a wide paintbrush. But even though I had to focus on what I was doing, there wasn't much artistry to

it, nothing to keep me absorbed the way I was when I did highlights and *baliage*.

And I needed to be absorbed. The salon already felt different, kind of weird. At lunchtime, I noticed Jean-Luc showing
around an impossibly chic fortyish icy blonde who was wearing that moment's Prada jacket, a pencil skirt, and suede boots
in a caramel color, the sure sign of a woman with a car and
driver. I mean, who else would wear such impractical boots on
the slushy winter streets of New York? As he walked around
with her, Jean-Luc was animated even more than usual, gesturing to various salon details: the sinks, the shelving, the spot-
lights above each station.

Patrick appeared behind me.

"Ms. WXYZ," he said, "looks like a piece of work."

"Oh, I don't know. Maybe she's very nice beneath that . . ."

"Beneath that sixteen-hundred-dollar jacket? Beneath that
premature eye lift?"

"Do you think?" I examined her from a distance.

"Oh, please."

Patrick was right. He was always right about pain-in-the-
ass people, and he was always right about cosmetic surgery. He
could spot both a mile away.

"What are we going to do?" he wondered out loud.

"What do you mean?"

"There's no fucking way we can stay here," said Patrick. "I
just hate Jean-Luc so much now that every time I look at him I
want to stick a tail comb in his eye." He leaned forward, looked
in the mirror, and brushed a few long dark hairs from his shirt
collar. "Not that I didn't hate him before, but this is a whole
new level."

"I don't know," I mused out loud. "Maybe it'll be okay. I

mean, the new salon—I know it won't be ours, but it still might be—"

"No fucking way," Patrick repeated, his tone bitter. I hated hearing him sound that way. "Don't you get it, Georgia? He's robbing us of our dream."

And it was true. There wasn't much I could say to that. But I guess I had spent so much of my life not really daring to dream big dreams that it didn't really surprise me to be robbed of mine. I felt fortunate even to be where I was in life. How many girls from Weekeepeemie end up on Fifty-seventh Street, doing what they love to do and making a boatload of money at it? So we wouldn't open a salon in Paris. At least we were here. Here wasn't so bad.

I looked down at the client who had just been brought over to my chair. She was a beautiful, curly-haired socialite-turned–breast cancer advocate. In fact, she was wearing a pin encrusted with pink diamonds shaped like the breast cancer awareness ribbon that women were wearing all over America. I had been with her through her own chemotherapy and hair loss, and when her hair first grew back in it was snow white. I kissed her hello, and as I did I felt a sharp pang, an intense love for her—and for all my clients. I was a lucky, lucky girl. All I wanted to do was hold on to that luck. Things were changing, and I was more than a little bit scared.

"Georgia?" Massimo leaned between two mirrors, beckoning me to come closer. "I noticed Mrs. K is on your list for today," he said.

Why was he looking at my client list? Usually he didn't care, and he was too busy himself, anyway.

"Yeah, so?"

"So"—Massimo kept his voice low—"you know who her husband is, don't you?"

I had a vague idea of the identity of Mrs. K's husband. He was some kind of big-deal business guy. What did he do again? Oh yeah. He helped entrepreneurs get their businesses off the ground. He had done a great job with a boutique a few blocks up on Madison that another client had opened. And a splashy yoga studio. And a brand-new trendy sushi place in Chelsea. All of the businesses he helped to start were booming.

Oh.

I looked at Massimo. Right.

"So Mrs. K, she is coming in at three o'clock, yes?" asked Massimo, again.

I glanced at my schedule. This was all moving fast, too fast, and I wanted to ask Massimo to slow down, but there was no slowing him down. He had lived for so long in Jean-Luc's shadow, had handled Jean-Luc's barbs and insults with what I had always thought was great delicacy. But now he had been betrayed, and enough was enough. No. There was no slowing him down. Him or Patrick.

"Yes," I said softly. "Three o'clock."

"Georgia, I want you to very discreetly ask her for her husband's business card," said Massimo. "I would do it myself, but it will look too suspicious. Believe me, Jean-Luc will be watching us like a hawk."

"I'll try," I said. My heart skipped a beat. I felt nervous, uncomfortable in my new role as the Mata Hari of hairdressers.

The hours ticked by until finally it was midafternoon and Mrs. K arrived for her appointment. I had halfheartedly hoped she'd cancel, but no such luck. I was on schedule when she got there, one of the benefits of a slow day.

She sat in my chair and my assistant brought her a cup of coffee. We exchanged all the usual gossip as I spread her hair, beginning at the front, and dabbed on bits of rich brown color to cover her gray. That day's gossip had to do with a particular investment banker involved in stock fraud—all the clients seemed to want to talk about him. Probably because he'd been a guest at so many of their dinner tables and his children went to school with their children.

"What in the world is he going to do in prison?" mused Mrs. K. "Read *War and Peace*? Find religion?"

Though I didn't say anything, I thought about another client of Jean-Luc's, a famous jewelry designer who had recently spent six months in prison for mailing empty boxes to his customers to avoid taxes. The guy—handsome, cultured, impeccably dressed and groomed—had come into the salon the day before he began his prison term. Six months later, we were his first stop on the day he got out.

"Didn't Jennifer Aniston look amazing at the Golden Globes?" I asked Mrs. K, changing the subject.

"What a body," said Mrs. K. I was working on the back of her head now. She had no idea how gray she really was. "Do you think she's had anything done?"

"No," I said. "But what about Meg Ryan? Those lips! I mean, what the hell did she put in there?"

My clients loved to talk about plastic surgery with me. They knew I had seen it all. And I didn't gossip—at least, I never gossiped about my own clients. Meg Ryan went to a rival colorist up Madison Avenue, so she was fair game.

What I needed to do, though, was bring up the subject of Mrs. K's husband. And I needed to do it when nobody was listening and nobody was looking—which was pretty much never. I was nervous. Ever since Jean-Luc's announcement the night before, I had been a bundle of nerves. As I worked on the underside of Mrs. K's hair, paying special attention because I knew she liked to wear her hair in a chignon, I kept playing out all sorts of scenarios in my mind. Scenarios that all pretty much landed me in one of two places: either on the street, homeless, or back home in Weekeepeemie. I didn't know which was worse.

If I didn't ask soon, it wasn't going to happen. I'd lose Mrs. K to the heat lamps and the shampoo station and whoever was going to be blow-drying her hair.

I cleared my throat. "Mrs. K?"

"Yes, sweetheart?"

"You don't happen to have—"

At that exact moment, Richard walked past my station, and I stammered to a halt.

"What, darling?" Mrs. K frowned slightly as she examined a microscopic chip on one very dark red nail.

"The time?" I finished pathetically. "Do you happen to have the time?" Fortunately I wasn't wearing my watch, or she really would have wondered.

"It's three-thirty, dear," she said with a quizzical tilt of her head.

I FELT LIKE a failure. I *was* a failure. I had never been any good at hiding anything or lying. Crazy as it may sound, I felt that Jean-Luc had been good to me. He had given me my start when I was an absolute nobody from Weekeepeemie, and now I felt like I was betraying him even by thinking of leaving the salon with Massimo and Patrick and making a go of it on our own. *On our own.* I didn't even like the sound of it. On our own might just be a scary, lonely place.

"I couldn't do it," I said to Massimo later that day as we stood on the corner of Fifty-seventh and Fifth, waiting for a cab. I was practically in tears. "I'm sorry—I just couldn't get his stupid card."

"It's okay . . ." Massimo stroked my hair. I searched his face for a sign. *Was* it okay? I wanted him to feel he could count on me. "Really," Massimo continued. "I got it myself."

"You what? No way." I slapped his arm. "What do you mean?"

He shrugged. His shrugs weren't as dramatic as Jean-Luc's, but he was getting there.

"I was outside on a cigarette break," he said.

"But you don't smoke!"

He smiled.

"You knew you'd run into her!"

"She even gave me their home number," he said.

"But how did you know I wouldn't—"

Massimo stuck out his arm, quick as lightning, and hailed a cab that had just let out passengers on Fifth Avenue. As he ushered me inside, he simply said: "Because I know you."

AND SO IT happened that the following evening, Massimo, Patrick, and I found ourselves in the living room of Mr. and Mrs. K, high above Park Avenue. I had been in clients' apartments before, all up and down Fifth Avenue, Park Avenue, even Madison. Basically anyplace west of Lexington Avenue was considered acceptable. The avenues were prime (though Madison had very few good buildings to speak of). Side streets were also fine as long as the buildings were white-glove co-ops, known, in the circles that mattered, to have difficult co-op boards. In the particular language of Manhattan real estate, a difficult board meant that you had to have at least three times the purchase price of the apartment in liquid assets. And, as I had learned in business class, a "liquid asset" did not mean other real estate, or trusts, or jewels, or artwork. No. Liquid assets meant cash. Therefore, to buy a three-million-dollar apartment (anything less being . . . well, just not good enough), you'd need to have nine million. Cash. Like, in your checking account.

My clients obsessed about this. Their obsession with real estate was second only to their obsession with private school, which began when their children were born. I had one client who actually took the preschool application for her newborn daughter up to the 92nd Street Y, with her infant in a Snugli. And I remembered that Mrs. K's two girls went to Spence, a school that was by any standard excellent but in the world of the clients was not quite top-drawer. It was all code. I had learned this over the years.

Where do your daughters go to school?
Brearley.
Where do you summer?
Ibiza.
Where do you live?
Nine-Forty Fifth.

This was all code, a language more difficult to learn than French, or Italian, or any of the languages that the clients' children were fluent in, in any case, by age ten. And according to this code, the Ks' apartment was . . . fine. As was their daughters' school. Just fine. But I knew that the snobbiest of the snobby clients would find the Ks' answers to the code questions ever so slightly lacking.

As we walked into their foyer, I was struck by how every single thing in their home was of the moment. The color of their eat-in kitchen, apple green, had just been featured in last month's *Metropolitan Home*. The white suede sofas were spotless, straight out of the D&D Building. The glassware was from the second-floor housewares section of Barneys. Even the music was this year's Grammy winner. There were no family photographs in evidence, no books, newspapers, magazines. Where did they put all that stuff?

Mr. K was not a client of the salon—something I had vaguely wondered about, since most of the wives eventually dragged their husbands in for a haircut at least once. But when he walked into the living room, hand outstretched, it all suddenly made sense. Mr. K was as bald as a cue ball.

"What can I do for you?" he asked as a casually dressed guy brought over a tray with a bottle of mineral water, a bottle of white wine, and a bowl of gourmet chips. The guy was their butler, of course. These people all had casually dressed unemployed actors working for them. The first time I had ever been to a client's house, I had mistaken the butler for their son and learned my lesson. Now I'd be more likely to mistake their son for a butler.

"We are thinking of opening a salon," said Massimo. His voice wobbled a bit.

Mrs. K breezed into the room carrying a bowl of nuts that the butler guy had forgotten.

"Fabulous!" exclaimed Mrs. K. "You three are the best people there, anyway. My God, I remember once going to that pretty blonde—what was her name?"

"Kathryn," the three of us chorused.

"Kathryn! That's it," she went on. "The single worst—"

"Let's hear more about your plan," interrupted Mr. K.

"Well, we don't know that much yet," Patrick said as he poured himself some Pellegrino. "Just that we're leaving Jean-

Luc and we want to open something . . . great. Something *different*."

"Different how?" Mr. K prodded. Mrs. K perched next to him on the sofa. Did she always take part in his business discussions, or was it because it was us? I figured it was because it was us.

"More . . . I don't know . . . intimate," said Patrick.

"Smaller—more personal," I chimed in.

"A place where everyone feels comfortable," said Massimo. "The clients, the people who work there—"

"It would be amazing if all the people who work in the salon could somehow make a percentage of the profits," said Patrick. I think he surprised himself by saying that, and he sat back, leaning into the soft pillows of the sofa.

Mr. K nodded. "Profit sharing," he said. "Very smart. Potentially very good business."

"How's that?"

"Gives people pride of ownership," said Mr. K.

The three of us exchanged a glance. *Pride of ownership*. Now, that was something we could all understand. My heart gave a little pitter-patter. Was this really possible? It seemed like a dream.

"But we're getting ahead of ourselves," said Mr. K. "Let's talk more specifically." He picked up a notepad from the coffee table. I liked that about him: In a world where people flashed their laptops like status symbols, in an apartment filled with all the latest gadgetry known to man, here was a guy with a simple notebook.

"Where do we begin?" asked Massimo.

Mr. K smiled. "Where we always begin," he said. "Money. It costs a lot to open a salon. That is, if you want to do it right."

"Oh, we want to do it right," said Patrick. "Otherwise there's no point doing it at all."

"That's the spirit," said Mr. K. "So. Money. Size. Location."

"We have money," said Massimo.

I looked at him. We did? I knew we all made a lot of money. But ever since I'd started, I'd been sending everything extra that I had home to Weekeepeemie. I had put Melodie through college and finally paid off Doreen's loan. It wasn't something I talked about, but I was proud of it. It meant, though, that I didn't have much in savings. It just hadn't seemed important.

"We have a million to invest," said Massimo.

I took a big sip of wine, which suddenly I needed. A million? Dollars? And clearly he and Patrick had already discussed it. When were they planning to say something to me? I didn't know how to feel. Shock, anger, pride, amazement—all rolling around inside me, banging like loose marbles against my insides. How much of that did they expect me to come up with?

Mr. K nodded slowly. "Well, that's a good start," he said. "You'll need more, of course."

More? I wanted to bolt from the Ks' well-appointed living room, zoom down the manned elevator, and run down Park Avenue as fast as I could, away from this insanity. I held on to the edge of my chair.

"You'll need not just enough to open a new space—demolition, renovation, equipment, staffing, advertising, and so on—but enough to float you all until the salon turns a profit," said Mr. K.

"And how long do you think that would be?" I asked, finally finding my voice.

Mr. K tapped his pen against the pad. "Ah, the great intangible," he said. "That's impossible to say."

"But you'll take them on, darling?" Mrs. K piped up. I could see that she was excited. Was she envisioning free hair for the rest of her life? I could see that she was the only reason Mr. K had even agreed to meet with three lowly hairdressers. Why else would he? What was enormous for us was small potatoes for him.

"Yes, yes, of course," said Mr. K.

"It sounds like fun," said Mrs. K. She startled her husband with a hug. For the first time in their marriage, his passion for business and hers for hair had found common ground.

So it was set in motion. As Jean-Luc began the process of creating his grand new multilevel salon on the top three floors of the WXYZ skyscraper, Massimo, Patrick, and I (with the help of Mr. K) started our quest for the right space. At first we looked on the Upper East Side, not far from Jean-Luc, but the combination of price per square foot and a desire not to be in direct competition with our soon-to-be-former boss made us turn elsewhere. And we were happy to turn elsewhere—believe me. The Upper East Side wasn't our idea of what was fun, hip, or homey—but it was where our clients, for the most part, lived.

The West Side was too granola crunchy. Midtown was a barren landscape of office buildings. Chelsea was too gay, Murray Hill too boring, the meatpacking district too industrial and smelly, even though there was one incredibly hip store, Jeffrey, that had opened there. There were already enough salons in SoHo, and TriBeCa was just too far out of the way. We looked and looked (on our days off, since of course we weren't going to leave Jean-Luc until we had someplace to go), until one day we got a call from Mr. K.

"I've got something for you," he said in that gravelly voice of his. "I'm not sure about it—the neighborhood's still a little funky, but one of my restaurant guys is going to be opening there . . . I think it's coming up in the world."

"Where's that?" Massimo asked. He hit the button on the speakerphone so I could listen. It was a Sunday morning and we were still in bed, half-asleep.

"NoLIta," said Mr. K.

"Where the hell is that?" asked Massimo.

"North of Little Italy. You know when a neighborhood gets an acronym, it's starting to catch on. Anyway . . . it's full of old tenement buildings. Some of them are starting to turn over."

"We'll check it out this afternoon," said Massimo.

IT WAS EARLY spring in New York—the one time of year when the city didn't seem to know what to do with itself. Dirty snowbanks had melted along sidewalks and curbs, creating puddles everywhere—and mud, endless mud. Buildings had air-conditioning instead of heat, or heat instead of air-conditioning. People sweated in down coats or froze in tank tops. Everyone was confused, out of sorts, waiting for warm weather.

Massimo and I stopped at a Starbucks on lower Broadway, then walked, venturing east into NoLIta. For a few long blocks, there was nothing. Then, as we rounded a corner from Prince Street onto Mott, we both began to see what Mr. K had been talking about. Shops had sprouted up, small ones. But we could see even just from the window displays that they were fashionable, young, and cool. One storefront had a mannequin in the window wearing a copper metal coat that, upon closer inspection, revealed itself to be made entirely of interconnected pennies. Another shop seemed to be selling nothing but hand-milled soap.

"Look at that beautiful church." Massimo pointed. "It is very old for America, yes?"

We walked closer and read the date carved into the stone above the doorway: 1809. The St. Patrick's Old Cathedral. An old redbrick wall surrounded the church, which rose above it, an edifice of dun-colored stone and stained-glass windows that took up the entire block.

"How could I have lived in this city for nearly ten years and never have known this was here?" I wondered out loud. I ran my hand along the brick wall, the stones smooth and cool to the touch.

"Georgia," said Massimo.

My eyes were still on the stained-glass windows. A slant of afternoon sun was hitting a pale yellow pane of glass.

"Georgia, look," said Massimo.

I turned around to see what he was looking at, what could possibly be more compelling than the St. Patrick's Old Cathedral. And there it was. Across Mott Street stood a five-story building, wider than a brownstone but not *too* wide. It had lovely brickwork on the front and an elegant glass-and-iron door.

"It looks empty," said Massimo.

"Of course it's empty. It's waiting to be our new salon," I said.

We crossed Mott Street and peered through the window grate on the first floor. The building looked like a mess inside—a beautiful mess. Massimo rattled the grate a little.

"There must have been some kind of business here," he said.

From behind us, there was suddenly a voice.

"It was a dress factory."

We wheeled around to see the littlest old lady I had ever

seen. She must have been under five feet tall, and she was made even smaller by her stooped-over posture. She was dressed head to toe in black, and she leaned on a cane. Her light brown eyes were bright, ablaze.

"It closed for good about six months ago," she said. Her accent was thick, Italian.

"Where are you from?" Massimo asked—in English, I'm sure out of deference to me.

"Padua."

"Padua!" Massimo exclaimed. And then they were off to the races, speaking Italian so fast that I figured most Italians couldn't even keep up. The three of us must have stood just off the corner of Prince and Mott for a half hour as Massimo and the little old lady, whose name, I discovered, was Giulia, spoke and laughed. Every once in a while, she and Massimo smiled at me apologetically.

"Giulia is from my hometown," said Massimo. A tear glistened in his eye. "She knew my grandmother—they grew up together."

I nodded, happy for Massimo, who I knew felt even farther away from home than I did. I mean, if I had come a long way from Weekeepeemie, how hard must it be for him, on the other side of the ocean from his family?

"She owns this building," Massimo went on.

My smile got wider. Sometimes things were simply meant to be. I was on a high, a brief moment free of worry, no fear of what the future might bring. We were really going to do this. And it was going to be fantastic.

He turned back to me, glowing.

"She will rent it to us," he said. "We will work it all out. She is a master seamstress. She says she will even help us to sew the curtains!"

And then I hugged her, too. We must have been an odd sight, the three of us—tall, dark Massimo, all-American me, and teeny-tiny peasant Giulia, hugging and dancing and crying amid the old merchants, cathedral-goers, and occasional hipsters who had found their way to Mott Street that dreary spring day.

Split Ends

The new Jean-Luc Salon in the WXYZ building—or, rather, the Salon Jean-Luc, as the new corporate parent had named it—had a three-hundred-and-sixty-degree view of the Manhattan skyline. Wherever you stood—sinks, manicure stations, even the bathrooms—you were looking at something awesome. Which was the point, of course. You were supposed to stand in awe. Awe was the theme, pretty much from the moment you walked through the doors of the new salon, where you were confronted with a huge marble fountain, brought from the south of France, which spouted water all day long. And if a client was uncool enough to toss a penny into the fountain (believe me, it happened every day), the receptionist would make note of it, and quickly, quietly, it would be fished out.

We were months away from being ready to make our move, and we hadn't breathed a word of it to anybody. That was something we'd agreed on from the beginning: Nobody must know. After we'd signed the lease with Giulia and begun demolition of the Mott Street building, we put a big sign in the window, announcing the arrival of the Mott Street Gallery. That's how paranoid we were.

Which was not an entirely unreasonable thing to be, paranoid. Jean-Luc was probably a little suspicious of us. He wasn't a stupid guy, and I'm sure he wondered why we were all so cheerful all the time, especially after he had screwed us so royally. But Jean-Luc had his own plate full of worries. Clients weren't exactly loving the new salon. It turned out that Jean-Luc, along with the WXYZ people, had made a massive and possibly lethal miscalculation: They had believed that the clients would be enamored of all things French. From the French fountain to the French vanity tables in the stations to the French cups and saucers in which their café au lait arrived, the clients of Jean-Luc were grumbling. They were New Yorkers. They liked being New Yorkers, and they wanted to be treated like New Yorkers.

The salon was beautiful, but not exactly functional. Jean-Luc, along with the WXYZ people, had in fact forsaken all things practical for the sake of a design that was more like a stage set than a real salon. Take the sinks, for example. They were *round*. Had nobody considered that water would splatter all over the clients? They did not like their perfect makeup smudged, and the poor shampoo ladies were constantly being yelled at and running to the staff room in tears. And then there was the floor. It was cobblestone. Had anybody thought of what it would be like to walk on the damn thing in high heels, much less stand on your feet all day? More than once, the concierge at the salon had to send a Jimmy Choo or Manolo Blahnik stiletto to the shoe repair place on Lexington while the client had her hair done.

But perhaps worst of all were the elevators. The Salon Jean-

Luc was spread over several floors, forcing the ladies to take the elevator wearing nothing more than robes, wet heads wrapped in towels. Need I say that the ladies did not appreciate this one little bit? The point of a salon visit was to be ensconced. Enveloped. Coddled in womblike surroundings while being taken care of and restored like a beautiful but slightly worn work of art. Not to be stepping into impersonal elevators, possibly even with civilians from other floors. The very thought set the clients' blindingly white, veneered teeth on edge.

In the midst of this, we just kept working and went down to check on the progress of the new place only at the end of our workday or on our days off. I knew this much: It was going to be the anti-Jean-Luc. We were leaving brick walls exposed, reopening fireplaces that hadn't been used in decades, doing the floors in wide planks of oak. Certain things were going to be urban and modern—the lighting, for instance, and the state-of-the-art treatment rooms for waxing, massage, and facials—but the overall look of the salon was cozy, downtown, functional glamour.

"How's it going to be okay that I can't contribute a lot of money to this?" I had asked Patrick and Massimo the morning after our first meeting with Mr. K. "I mean, I don't feel right about this. You guys are investing everything, and I . . ."

The two men—*my* two men—looked at me.

"We knew that going in," said Patrick.

"You mean, you guys discussed this?"

They nodded.

"Then how do you see this—this partnership?" I asked. I was trying to keep my tone businesslike, but inside I felt like a big pile of mush.

"Your talent," said Massimo.

"What about it?"

"It is worth a million dollars to us."

"Oh, give me a break."

"It's true, Georgia," said Patrick. "You're the best colorist in New York."

"Stop."

"As you make more money, you'll contribute more," said Massimo. "It's as simple as that."

But of course, nothing is ever really simple. The minute somebody tells you something is simple, you'd better watch out. I thought I had made my peace with leaving. I really did. I did my usual twenty, twenty-two heads a day, floating through my hours at Jean-Luc as if through some sort of alternate reality. I watched the other stylists and colorists from a remove, as if watching them on a movie screen. It seemed to me that my life was already elsewhere. Massimo and I were planning to move in together once the new salon was up and running. My whole life was in a state of suspended animation. Limbo.

One of the big questions that Mr. K had pushed us to really think about was whether or not the clients would follow us downtown. Each day, every time another client sat in my chair, I silently posed the question to myself: Given the choice of going essentially around the corner for all her hair needs or getting into her chauffeur-driven Mercedes, town car, taxi, or—God forbid!—bus or subway and schlepping all the way down to a neighborhood nobody had ever heard of—would she? It was impossible to know, yet I kept asking myself the question. Even though I had already committed to the new salon with Massimo and Patrick, I kept weighing the risks.

"I hate this place," announced one of my clients, the pale blond fashion director of a trendy women's magazine. "It looks like somebody tried too hard."

"Lots of people tried too hard," I said indiscreetly, chalking up one for the home team. She'd come downtown. Besides, she worked at a fashion magazine. Those women always kept two steps ahead of everybody else. I studied what she was wearing: a perfect black turtleneck sweater with three-quarter sleeves and—could it be?—cargo pants. Cargo pants?

"I wore pants like those in seventh grade," I said as I lifted a few strands of hair for *baliage*.

"They're coming back," she said with a crafty smile. "These are next season's Dolce."

The next client was an older woman, married to somebody important—I couldn't remember who. She had the tight, leathery skin of a woman who had lived hard and tried regularly to fix all that sun and booze and cigarettes with the cures *du jour*: microdermabrasion, collagen, nips here, tucks there. It didn't make her look younger—those things almost never did—but she sure looked well preserved.

"Wonderful!" she exclaimed, dipping a biscuit into a bowl of café au lait. "I just love it here—it's like a minivacation to Cap d'Antibes without the jet lag!"

I nodded, said nothing, continued to cover the gray. She wasn't going to be following us downtown. No way, nohow. She probably hadn't been south of Fifty-seventh Street in decades, except for the occasional Broadway show.

As I worked on her hair, I felt a tap on my shoulder. Jean-Luc's current assistant, a talented young Asian guy, handed me a note written on the newly corporate WXYZ message pad.

Meeting in the conference room. Six o'clock, it read. A meeting why? And with whom? A meeting at the Salon Jean-Luc was never a good thing. I looked at Jean-Luc's assistant questioningly, but he just shrugged (a tiny, assistant-size version of a Jean-Luc shrug) and walked away.

The clients were getting backed up, and according to

WXYZ corporate policy, we were no longer allowed to placate them with free services. M, a home design guru with her own cable talk show, had just been seated next to T, a publicist famous for her who-the-fuck-are-you glare. As I walked past them on my way to find either Patrick or Massimo, I overheard M say hello to T.

"Love your hair," said M. "Have you been using a flat iron? It looks so . . . modern."

T's Botoxed eyebrows struggled to shoot up, like two skinny worms wiggling on her glasslike forehead. Modern. Was that an insult or a compliment?

"You should try it," T recovered and parried. "You could use a new look."

Ding-ding-ding. The bitchiness factor had reached alarming levels that day at the Salon Jean-Luc. Was it something about the new salon itself? Some kind of karma or bad feng shui? The ladies' perfectly manicured nails seemed to grow into talons, and behind every tight little smile was a barb intended to wound, at least superficially.

"P, I haven't seen you in aeons!" said one client to another. It sounded harmless on the surface, but what it really meant was: *You know and I know that you just spent a month recovering from a full face lift in Beverly Hills.*

I hunched my shoulders as if shielding myself and scurried along until I found Patrick.

"What the hell is going on here today?" I asked him.

"Do you mean that note about the meeting?"

"Oh, good—you got one, too."

"Well, I don't know if that's good or not."

"The energy is so weird in here—don't you think?"

"Yeah. It feels like the clients all want to kill each other."

"Oh, thank God! I thought it was me!"

"Baby doll, there's not much you imagine that doesn't turn out to be true," said Patrick.

"I sure hope you're wrong about that," I said, once again picturing me, homeless, spending my last twenty-eight bucks on the bus fare back to Weekeepeemie.

Now, you wouldn't think that I'd be so freaked out. But I couldn't help myself, and I hated myself for it. I mean, the arrangement that Massimo, Patrick, and I had come up with, with the help of Mr. K and a lawyer Mr. K had found for us, was more than fair—it was insanely generous. I mean, I was going to be a full partner, and the three of us were taking out the business loan together. My boyfriend and my best friend—they simply understood that I didn't have the money, and they believed in me. What more could I possibly ask for in life?

"*Ciao, bella.*" Massimo stole a kiss between clients.

"Isn't that the name of an ice-cream store?" I asked.

"Very funny," said Massimo. "So are you ready for the meeting?"

"Do you know what it's about?"

"I have no idea. Nor do I care." He peeled off my plastic glove (I had just finished a single-process) and kissed my wrist. "But after, I want to take you down to Mott Street—"

"Ssshhh!" I hissed, giving a quick look around. What if someone heard?

"Don't worry so much, Georgia," said Massimo. A faint shadow of something—hurt? annoyance?—crossed his eyes, and instantly I felt bad. He was careful. I didn't trust him enough. That was my problem.

"Anyway, there is something I want to show you later," he

said. And then he went back to his station, where his assistant had just deposited a famously disheveled comedian whose wife had made him come in for a haircut.

The rest of the day limped along until finally it was six o'clock. The conference room in the WXYZ building—undoubtedly one of dozens of such conference rooms, though this one had been built and designed exclusively for the use of Salon Jean-Luc—was a plush and yet altogether businesslike affair. Jean-Luc's favorite colors, a deep burgundy and pale, pale cream, dominated the room. The windows were framed by heavy drapes, and upholstered swivel chairs surrounded an enormous, shiny dark wood table.

As we filed in, I scanned the room to try to figure out who was there and therefore what the meeting was about. There were about twenty of us in all (not counting Jean-Luc, who wasn't on time, of course, waiting to make his grand entrance), and what was immediately clear to me was that these were all senior staff. Senior colorists, senior stylists. Faith, Sophie, Enrique, Kathryn, and about a dozen others. That room held the core— the talent, if you will—of the salon. I took a seat next to Massimo and distracted myself by studying the black-and-white photographs of the French countryside that lined the walls of the conference room.

Finally Jean-Luc came in, his customary twenty minutes late. He was trailed by Ms. WXYZ and two of her minions. The women were dressed in crisp little navy-and-white outfits so similar that I wondered, for a second, if this was some sort of WXYZ uniform. Jean-Luc looked uncharacteristically pale and almost . . . uncomfortable. I had never seen the man look anything but supremely confident. It was a bit unnerving.

Jean-Luc took his place at the head of the oval-shaped conference table, and the WXYZ women sat to either side of him.

He leaned his elbows on the table, rested his chin on his hands, and looked around the table before speaking.

He cleared his throat. "A terrible thing has happened," he said.

My heart skipped a beat. What could be so terrible as to make Jean-Luc look so wan and at the same time so . . . furious?

"We have a traitor in our midst," Jean-Luc went on.

Now my heart was doing more than skipping beats. It was pumping wildly, a flapping bird caught in my rib cage. How had he found out? We had been so careful! I didn't dare look at Massimo or Patrick. I just kept my eyes pinned on Jean-Luc and tried to remain calm. My hands were shaking; I buried them in my lap.

"Richard has left the salon," Jean-Luc announced.

There were audible gasps around the conference table.

"And he has taken Amelia and Sam with him." Jean-Luc's lips, quivering with rage, appeared to be dark blue against his pale face, and his eyes burned.

I still didn't dare look at Massimo, but Patrick was sitting across the table from me, so I looked at him. I had to connect with somebody who felt the same way I did—a roller coaster mix of fear, then shock, and then a flood of relief. Richard! The one guy who actually seemed to be friends with Jean-Luc! Just the night before, the four of them—Richard, Jane Huffington Cooke, Jean-Luc, and Kathryn—had gone to dinner after the salon closed. Jean-Luc must have felt doubly screwed.

"He is opening a salon just up the street," said one of the WXYZ minions.

"I will tell my staff myself!" Jean-Luc thundered. The three WXYZ ladies visibly shrank away from him. Apparently, yelling and screaming were not a part of their neat, tidy corporate culture. I thought of a memo, sent around just that morning, about our burgundy-and-cream silk handkerchiefs, embossed with dozens of tiny JLs; we were meant to have those handkerchiefs visible on our persons at all times—"visible on your person at all times," was actually what the memo stated—either folded and peeking out of our shirt pockets or tied around our necks. One assistant had gotten creative and wrapped hers around her waist as a belt, and this was expressly forbidden.

"He will fail, of course," Jean-Luc was saying. "What does he think, Richard"—he spat out the name as though it were a bad taste in his mouth—"that he can just open a salon in my backyard? Do you all think it is so easy?"

He looked around the table, slowly making eye contact with every single one of us. Was it me? His gaze seemed to linger longest on Massimo.

"Do you know how many appointments have to be filled here *in a single day*—just to pay the rent? Do you know? I will tell you. One hundred and fifty. Just to pay the rent." Jean-Luc paused. "I will crush him," he said. He ground his thumb into the conference table, in case any of us might be missing his point. "I will crush him like the dirty cockroach that he is."

My nostrils stung, and I was filled with a cold wave of fear. I watched Jean-Luc's mouth move, but I could barely hear a word he was saying. My vision blurred. I was panicky. All I could see was our beautiful building on Mott Street with its huge, airy windows and high ceilings; it was still unfinished but starting really to take shape. I could picture it a few months down the road, with the antique mantels, the old terra-cotta pots of flowering plants leading to the small garden in back where clients could sip their coffee as their highlights were processed. The cozy workstations, the chandelier we had discovered in the Sixth Avenue flea market . . . And then I imagined a huge wrecking ball swinging into our new salon, the whole thing shattering, crumbling to the ground.

Who did we think we were, anyway? Jean-Luc was a world-famous hairstylist, and now he had the backing of a corporate giant. Massimo, Patrick, and I—we were just three people who had come from nothing. We should have been happy with what we had. It had been enough—more than enough. We had gotten greedy, and now Jean-Luc was going to destroy us. I was sure of it.

Jean-Luc's voice came back into focus. "If you are not for me"—his fist hit the table—"you are against me. Do you all understand?"

AFTERWARD, MASSIMO, PATRICK, and I walked a few blocks north on Madison. We passed Barneys, then an Italian restaurant, then a boutique known for its two-thousand-dollar sleeveless shift dresses. And then there it was, on the southeast corner of Sixty-fourth and Madison, on the second floor. All the windows were taped up, covered with construction paper, so no one could possibly see inside. In the center of the windows was a sign announcing the arrival of the Madison Avenue Gallery.

"I guess that wasn't such an original idea," said Patrick, breaking the silence that had descended on us all.

"What?" Massimo snapped. "Don't be ridiculous—it will be a completely different salon from ours. For one thing, it's uptown. Also, Richard has a totally different sensibility—"

"I meant the sign," Patrick said mildly.

"Oh."

"Don't get so defensive."

"Sorry," said Massimo. Then he turned to me. "Let's go

down to Mott Street. There's something I want to show you, remember?"

I couldn't. I just couldn't. My head was spinning, and for the first time since I had known Massimo, I wanted, *needed,* to be alone.

Massimo was already hailing a cab.

"Wait," I said, more sharply than I had intended.

They both turned to look at me, surprised.

"I can't," I said more softly. "I have to go home."

Massimo searched my face carefully. He had never heard me say that before. His home was my home, for all intents and purposes. I hadn't spent a night in my apartment, with or without him, in many months.

"What do you mean?"

"It's nothing, really," I said. "It's just—bills, paperwork. I kind of need a night to catch up."

Patrick was looking at me, too. He knew me maybe even better than Massimo did—better than anybody. And I could tell that he knew why I needed to be alone. He looked sad.

"I'll come down first thing tomorrow morning!" I said as cheerfully as I could. "Okay? We can have an early breakfast, check on the progress at the salon—whatever."

Massimo nodded. This was killing me. I needed to get away from both of them, get someplace that was just mine, where I could think. Quickly I kissed Patrick on the cheek, then Massimo on the lips.

"I love you," I whispered in his ear. Then, fast as I could, I headed toward my apartment.

DUST WAS EVERYWHERE. A thin film of gray covered the trunk I used as a coffee table, the top of the television set, the windowsills. The curtains were drawn, and my answering machine was blinking. Nobody ever called me either at the salon or at Massimo's. The red flashing light made me feel slightly more at home.

"This message is for Georgia Watkins. This is a courtesy call regarding your overdue AT and T bill—"

Beep.

"Hello, Ms. Watkins, this is Cablevision calling about an overdue—"

Beep.

I turned off the machine. I felt even worse. Clearly, I hadn't been on top of things. There was no excuse for overdue bills— none. I had been so busy, my head in the clouds between my love affair with Massimo and the work on the new salon, that I had let my responsibilities go down the toilet.

I opened the refrigerator. Nothing, of course. Nothing but a bad smell from a yogurt with an expiration date I didn't even want to look at. *Get a grip, Georgia.* I shrugged off my sweater, kicked off my boots, picked up the phone (which thankfully still worked), and ordered Chinese food.

It was eleven o'clock before I had a single thought in my head. I had gone into some kind of altered state, a cleaning frenzy. I vacuumed and dusted and scrubbed. I paid all my bills, then finally sat on my freshly plumped sofa and opened a now cold carton of moo-shoo pork. I picked up the phone and started to dial Massimo's number, but I hung up before the call went through. I didn't know what to say to him. I didn't think he could possibly understand how frightened I was. I needed to talk to somebody. I needed to sort all this out instead of just letting it swirl around inside my head. But the problem was that the two people I relied on the most were precisely the two people I couldn't talk to about this.

I picked up the phone again. It was late—very late by Weekeepeemie standards, where people tended to go to sleep when it got dark out—but what was a daughter to do? There was only one person I could trust. I needed my mother. I needed Doreen.

She answered the phone on the first ring.

"Doreen's"—her groggy voice came over the line—"can I help you?" I don't think she was even aware of it, but she always answered the phone that way.

"Hi, Mom."

"Georgia? What's wrong?"

"Nothing," I lied. There was silence on the other end. I could hear the sound of my mother breathing. Waiting. Because she knew that I wouldn't be calling at this hour unless something was really wrong.

"Everything," I then said.

"Talk to me, honey."

Suddenly, I could picture my mother as clearly as if I were there with her in Weekeepeemie. She propped herself up on one elbow, reached for the bedside lamp, and switched it on; her bedroom filled with a yellow glow. In my mind's eye, she was wearing a University of New Hampshire sweatshirt and flannel pajama bottoms so old that they were frayed at the knees.

"I don't think I can do it," I said. I started to cry. "I want to—or at least part of me wants to—but I just don't think I can."

"Slow down. Can't do what?"

Doreen's voice was calm, measured. It acted as a balm to my frazzled nerves. But I couldn't seem to stop crying. It felt to me, that night, as if my whole world were coming to an end. I tried to speak.

"The salon—I—I just—"

"Take a deep breath, honey."

I struggled to do as instructed. My chest felt tight, my whole body tense. First one deep breath, then another.

"That's better," said Doreen. "Now. Try to tell me what's happened."

My mother knew all about the new salon. She had asked, when Massimo and I had gotten back from Paris, so she had been kept up-to-date, through all the ups and downs, from Paris to Mott Street. And honestly, she had really surprised me. I had expected Doreen to be completely against the idea of our going out on our own, but it turned out that she hadn't been at all. *I just never trusted that Jean-Luc guy,* she said. *I thought he was going to sell you down the river.* What was it about my mother? So often she turned out to be right—and to her credit, she almost never said *I told you so.*

"I'm too scared," I finally said.

"What are you scared of?"

"You name it. I'm scared that the new salon won't work. I'm scared that the clients won't follow us downtown. I'm scared that it will take too long to turn a profit, and we'll go broke. I'm scared that Jean-Luc will come after us, I'm scared that—"

"Whoa there." My mother laughed. "Let's take one thing at a time."

"I'm not doing it," I blurted out. It was the first time I had actually said it. The words were a painful relief.

Doreen was quiet on the other end of the phone. I could hear her take a sip of water from the glass she always kept by her bedside.

"I understand your reasons for being frightened," she said

after a while. "But everything worth doing in this life involves a little bit of risk."

"I know," I said. But what I was really thinking was, *What about you? What about the risks you took in your life?* All it amounted to was a door slammed in the night, a mountain of debt, a lifetime of working too hard for too little.

"I don't regret anything I've ever done," Doreen said as if she were reading my mind. "I only regret the things I didn't do."

"I've already made up my mind," I whispered. I felt a cold stab of regret. Because I realized it was true. I hadn't called Doreen for advice or to talk it through. I had called because I needed to hear myself say it out loud.

"Does Massimo know?" my mother asked quietly.

I squeezed my eyes shut.

"No. Not yet."

THE NEXT MORNING was cool and bright—an unreasonably beautiful June day. It has always seemed to me that the hardest days in my life have been beautiful days, weatherwise. Why couldn't it have been dark and stormy? It would have made it somehow easier to face the task ahead. I rolled onto my stomach and willed myself back to sleep.

The phone rang at eight, waking me. I half expected it to be the phone company again, but it was Massimo. Kind, good-hearted, wonderful Massimo. I just prayed that he was kind, good-hearted, and wonderful enough to understand what I was about to do to him. I mean, Jean-Luc was like a second home to me. It was the place, outside of Weekeepeemie, where I had spent most of my life. And even though Jean-Luc could be a prick, he wasn't all bad. I found myself thinking of the nice things he had done over the years. The way he threw great Christmas parties for the staff and how he was always trying to get all of us publicity. He had a generous side. But more than anything, he had given a clueless girl from Weekeepeemie a chance.

"Good morning, *bella mia*," Massimo said. He sounded as though he had been up for hours.

"Good morning."

"Are you ready for a little cappuccino and croissant?"

"Just getting out of bed." I yawned. "Give me half an hour."

"I'll meet you at our place, eh?"

"Fine," I said, feeling sad. He was talking about a small café around the corner from the new salon, on Prince Street. I remembered how happy we'd been to stumble across it. We imagined that we'd have breakfast there every day before work.

"Are you okay?"

"Yeah, I'm okay."

"I can't wait to show you your surprise," he said. What kind of surprise could that possibly be? He was the one in for a surprise—a terrible surprise.

I threw on my clothes, didn't even bother to brush my hair, and raced downtown. The last thing I wanted to do was keep Massimo waiting. I knew that he'd be sitting in the window table at the café, flipping through the newspaper, checking his watch every five minutes.

He rose from his seat when he saw me rush through the door, miraculously on time. (Those European manners—try getting a boy from Weekeepeemie to do that!) He had a croissant and cappuccino waiting for me.

"I missed you," he said, taking my hand.

"I missed you, too." I felt sick, looking at him. I loved him so much. His face felt so familiar to me, it felt like home. I reached across the table and pushed his dark hair off his forehead. There were faint worry lines there. Had I never noticed them before, or were they new?

"Did you get everything done that you needed to?" he asked, watching me steadily.

"Yes," I said. I looked away from him, out the window, and took a sip of coffee. "My place was a mess. The bills! My phone was about to be turned off."

"That will all change soon—when we move in together," said Massimo.

"Yes," I said. And then urgently: "I can't wait." It was true. That much I knew: I was ready to take that risk—the risk of moving in together had long since stopped feeling like any risk at all.

"Just think—we'll be able to walk together to work in the mornings," said Massimo. "I am so much looking forward to that."

"Massimo . . ." My heart thumped.

He was signaling the waiter for a check.

"Massimo, I—"

"Are you done with your cappuccino?"

"Not yet."

He started to stand. I reached out and put a hand on his arm, stopping him. I needed to say it, to just blurt the words out. But saying them felt impossible. Once they were said, there was no going back.

"Massimo, listen to me. I'm sorry," I said. I started to cry. I could barely speak. "I can't do it."

"Can't do what? What do you mean?" He sat back down in his chair.

"The salon. I can't do it. I can't be partners with you and Patrick."

"Georgia—what are you saying?"

"I've changed my mind."

"How—why?"

"The only reason I can give you is that I'm too scared. I don't think I'm cut out for this."

Through all the months and all the disappointments, the shocks and the ups and downs, I had never seen Massimo look like this. His whole face seemed to fall and sag. He looked twenty years older.

"It's natural," he said. "Of course you're scared. You're getting cold feet. Don't worry, *bella*. Everything's going to be fine. The salon—it will be magnificent—"

"Massimo, I mean it. I can't do it," I said. My voice trembled. I had to stick to my guns. The whole Richard thing had spooked me.

"*Bella, bella,*" he said soothingly. He reached out and took my hand across the table. "It will be fine."

I shook my head. "No. It won't be fine. I've made up my mind."

Massimo let go of my hand, then leaned back in his chair, studying me.

"You mean this," he finally said.

"Yes."

"You'll walk out on us. Now. At this time."

"I have to."

"You trust Jean-Luc more than me? You believe all the things he said?"

"Massimo, it isn't about trust. It's about—"

"Of course it's about trust," he said. "What else could it possibly be about? You don't think I know what I'm doing."

"No, I—"

"Say it."

"*Please*. Stop. Don't do this," I pleaded.

"Say it," he repeated. He scraped back his chair. His elbow knocked a china saucer to the floor, breaking it in two.

I bent over to pick up the pieces of the saucer. A clean break. The waitress started to come over to our table to sweep it up, but she took one look at us and backed off.

"If you thought the salon would be a success, of course you would join us," he said, biting off each word angrily. "You wouldn't question it for a minute."

"Okay," I said. "Okay."

"Okay *what*?"

"I guess you're right."

"So you don't trust me."

"It's not you, Massimo. I guess I don't trust anybody."

"I'm finished talking to you." He started toward the door. The one other couple in the café had stopped talking to each other and were looking at us.

"Please, wait—"

His hand was on the doorknob. He was leaving. I crumpled a napkin into a ball in my hand and squeezed hard.

"Don't go."

"The only reason I wanted to do any of this—" He stopped, choked up. Then he tried again. "It was all about you. About you and me. Without that, there's nothing." And then he was gone.

I SAT IN the café for a few minutes after Massimo left, trying just to breathe. Everywhere I looked, the world was sharp, jagged.

I was dizzy, my mind swirling. What had I done? I was trying to protect myself, to keep myself safe. Now I felt like I had ruined my whole life. Finally, I dragged myself out to the street. The air was cool and crisp, the sun brilliant. I walked down Prince Street toward Mott, past the cool little shoe store that had just sprouted up on the corner. Pastel sandals with kitten heels, bright flip-flops in beachy colors, lay on the sand in the window. Just a few more steps and I was on Mott Street. I guess I was torturing myself, heading in the direction of the salon. I squinted in the strong sunlight, which was pouring across the steeples of St. Patrick's Old Cathedral. I could see the scaffolding on the salon as I moved closer. There was something new, something quite large hanging on the scaffolding, but it was so bright outside that I couldn't make out what it was. *There's something I want to show you.* I heard Massimo's voice in my head.

As I moved closer, I shielded my eyes and squinted at an enormous, hand-painted sign hanging on the scaffolding.

On it was written, in funky block letters, DOREEN'S.

Covering the Gray

I had never really understood the expression *between a rock and a hard place*. Those were just words to me, until the days and weeks following my breakup with Massimo. But after that . . . well, everywhere I looked was a hard place, and my back was pressed up against a rock, that's for sure. Massimo's blank eyes were everywhere, it seemed. They floated in front of me no matter what else I happened to be looking at, and in their blankness I saw the depths of his pain and disappointment. I felt he hated me now, and who could blame him? He was careful to avoid me, and when I tried to talk to him, he just turned his back and walked away. He was too much of a gentleman to yell at me or call me names. No. My punishment from Massimo, love of my life, was his disappearing act. The day after our fight at the café, a box with all my belongings, down to my toothbrush, arrived at my studio apartment. I searched the box for a note. There was none.

Patrick, at least, was still speaking to me, even though I

knew he was hugely pissed off as well. The difference between Patrick's and Massimo's reactions was that, on some level, Patrick understood. No one who, like us, had been raised in the cold, depressed small towns in the middle of New Hampshire took anything for granted. And some of us weren't big risk takers. It was genetic, I had convinced myself, something passed down to me by my ancestors, like the shape of my forehead or the sprinkle of freckles across the bridge of my nose.

But Massimo . . . Massimo had inherited no such gene, and he didn't understand. Of course he didn't. I had known he wouldn't. But what I hadn't known was just how personally he would take it. It had been stupid of me, incredibly naive, to think that maybe I'd be able to back out of the Mott Street salon and still be Massimo's girlfriend. What an idiot I was.

"He's acting like I cheated on him or something," I said, crying into my beer—literally crying into my beer—to Patrick one night after the salon had closed.

"Well, in a sense you did," said Patrick.

I looked at him, shocked. "How can you say that?"

"It's true. By not coming with him, it means you don't trust him. You don't believe in him. You don't have faith."

"But it isn't him—or you—that I don't have faith in," I said. "It has nothing to do with—"

"Oh, bullshit," Patrick snapped. I realized, with a start, that he was madder at me than I had thought. "If Jean-Luc was opening another salon, you wouldn't even have thought twice about it."

"But that's different."

"Why is it different?"

"Jean-Luc has already established himself," I said—the understatement of the day. I took a sip of my beer. "There's no . . . risk . . . involved in something like that," I finished weakly.

"That's exactly what I mean," said Patrick. "You're not willing to put yourself on the line, like, at *all*."

"But—"

"Don't you get it, Georgia?" he kept going, hammering home his point. "We were taking a risk—Massimo and me. We were prepared to have you be full partner without you putting money in. We just believed in you. In your talent."

I finished my beer and said nothing. I just sat there, staring at Patrick miserably. What was there to say? Of course he was right. I hated myself for the decision I had made, but I couldn't seem to change my mind, even though it was costing me almost everything I cared about.

"He still wants to call it 'Doreen's,' you know," said Patrick.

I shook my head slowly back and forth. A bunch of drunken businessmen let out a loud whoop at the bar as they watched their team score a run on the wide-screen television.

"Why? That makes me feel even worse," I said.

Patrick shrugged. "I don't know. Maybe deep down he thinks you'll change your mind. Maybe he just thinks it's a good name."

"What about you?" I asked Patrick. "Do you still want to call it 'Doreen's'?"

He looked at me with a small, sad smile. "You know how much I love your mother," he said, which somehow was not exactly the answer I wanted. "But I can't lie to you—this does affect the way I feel about you."

"Oh, don't tell me that," I cried. "I can't lose you."

"And me you, baby," said Patrick. "But I've got to tell you, this really feels like shit."

❦

MEANWHILE, MASSIMO AND Patrick were getting closer and closer to leaving. I no longer knew the exact date, because they obviously didn't confide in me. But by my calculations they could be no more than a couple of weeks away. They stayed away from each other when they were working at Jean-Luc, so as not to raise suspicions. And they both totally ignored me. My heart broke every day. It was hard even to do my work. My comb felt limp in my hand; I could hardly muster the energy to paint on highlights.

"What's the matter with you?" my clients asked, one after the other. The Bedfords, the Five Towns, the Short Hills, the Manhattan socialites—they all wanted to know.

"Nothing," I said, my voice hoarse. On top of everything, I had a cold I couldn't shake. My nose was running and my eyes were glassy. Just when I needed to look my most fabulous so that Massimo wouldn't be able to stay away from me, I looked instead like the pathetic wreck that I was.

But then the gossip started to spread through the staff of the salon that Massimo and I were kaput. It was bound to happen. The salon was a breeding ground for gossip, and besides, it was pretty obvious, I guess. Massimo was barely being civil to me. If he needed to let me know something about a client's color, he had his assistant relay it to me.

Massimo would like Mrs. Z's hair a little bit brighter, the assistant said. Or, *Massimo asked for a few lemony chunks along the front of the hairline.*

Massimo had never told me how to do my job before.

Massimo thinks this red should be less strawberry, more auburn.

Massimo thinks the back—see, along here?—is too dark.

After this happened half a dozen times, I exploded. "Oh,

really? Why don't you tell Massimo that if he has something to say to me, he can say it himself."

So the gossip spread from the staff to the clients, faster than you could say "double-process."

"Honey, I'm so sorry to hear about you and that handsome Italian," they said, one after the other. And they came bearing gifts: chocolate, champagne, a fur bolero bought at the J Mendel sample sale. "Come to the Mount Sinai benefit! I'll introduce you to my husband's partner."

Finally, I couldn't stand it another minute. I followed Massimo up to the staff room. He had to talk to me, he just had to. I walked into the staff room behind him. Fortunately, we were alone in there.

"Massimo—please. Won't you talk to me? This is too hard."

"Hard for who?" His eyes flashed. "No, I'm sorry, I cannot," he said, avoiding my gaze. He bent over and rooted around for his protein shake in the staff refrigerator.

"When?" I pressed on. "Please, Massimo. I love you. That hasn't changed."

He didn't respond. He opened his shake, poured it into a china cup. Then he started to head back out. He stopped for a moment and turned to me.

"We are on one side of something," he said, "something large, so large it feels like the ocean."

God. I missed everything about him. Especially the way he talked and made me see things.

"When we are on the other side of the ocean, then we will talk," he said.

Then he left the staff room, closing the door firmly behind him. What did he mean by that? Was there hope? I was pathetic. I clung to tiny wisps of signals—*he didn't hate me! he said five words to me!*—and just prayed that the ocean Massimo was talking about wasn't too wide or too deep—that whatever was left of us wasn't already dragging the depths.

A SWELTERING SUMMER Monday. The kind of humid day in New York City when heat rises in waves from the pavement and the smell of asphalt is in the air. Somewhere, not far from the WXYZ building, construction workers were digging, using a jackhammer. *Rat-tat-tat-tat-tat.* The noise was endless, unbearable. Even on the top floor of the WXYZ skyscraper, it gave me a headache. Why was I working on a day like this? Almost none of the regular clients came to the salon on Mondays, and this Monday in particular was the worst kind of day to sit in a salon for two hours, then go outside, hair instantly frizzing and wilting in the five steps it took to get from the lobby to the town car. I mean, what was the point?

But here I was. It was the policy of the new and woefully-not-improved Jean-Luc that senior people work three out of four Mondays of the month. And why? I supposed it was nothing more than a power play on the part of management, to keep us all in our place, remind us of who was boss.

On this particular Monday, Massimo and Patrick both weren't working. Which, on one level, was a relief—but it also made me feel empty inside. This was what it was going to be like every day once they were gone for good. It was as if someone had come along and ripped the heart and soul out of the salon—or at least that was what it felt like to me. Everybody else—Faith, Kathryn, even Jean-Luc himself—seemed pretty much the same as always.

I figured that Massimo and Patrick were probably downtown, putting the finishing touches on Mott Street (I couldn't bear, even in my mind, to call it Doreen's). I had given in to the urge, over the weekend, to check out the new salon. I know, I know. I shouldn't have done it. And even while I was heading downtown in the back of a taxi, even as I got out on the corner of Spring and Elizabeth streets, far enough away to duck for cover if I saw them, I kept trying to talk myself out of it.

But I was sick with longing—a kind of lovesickness—to see what they were doing, if only from a distance. After having been a part of the creation of the salon, I couldn't stand not being able to watch it grow.

Sweat streamed down my back, pooling behind my knees. You haven't experienced hot weather until you've spent some time stuck in traffic in the back of a New York City taxicab with broken air-conditioning. I walked the two blocks to the new salon, skulking in the shadows cast by the taller buildings, then ducked behind a Dumpster on the opposite side of the street from the salon.

My breath caught in my throat. The scaffolding had come down, and the repointing of the brick facade (one of the more expensive items on the line budget, as I recalled) was finished. The salon was . . . well, it was exquisite. It was everything we had dreamed of and more. The two-story entranceway with its enormous glass window—a piece of luck that we had been allowed to renovate in this way, given that it was a historic building—the boxwood hedges out front. Oh, just everything. It was perfect. I saw a shadow in one of the upper-floor windows, someone moving, and I quickly walked away with my head bent and my heart heavy. How could I not be a part of this? It felt as if someone had tied my hands and feet, crippling me.

"Georgia."

A voice brought me out of my reverie and back to the Salon Jean-Luc, the jackhammers, the steamy, boring Monday. It was one of the receptionists, her JL handkerchief tied around her neck in a jaunty little bow.

"I've got T on the phone," she said. "She wants to know if you can possibly squeeze her in today for a full head of highlights."

I searched the receptionist's face for the slightest hint of sarcasm and found none.

"I think I can probably manage to find room in my schedule," I said dryly. "Why don't you tell her three o'clock."

T was that publicist I mentioned earlier—but you probably know that already. Everybody knew T, or at the very least knew of her or had seen her photograph, her wide, dentally enhanced smile jumping out from the "Gotham" section of *New York* magazine. These photographs were the only place you'd ever actually see T smile. With her arm wrapped around someone more famous than herself—preferably an A-list client (the only kind she represented)—she flashed those porcelain veneers, but the rest of the time her face was as stony and cold as a slab of marble.

The day continued to limp along. Between the jackhammers in the background and the French pop music that played endlessly on the salon's fancy new stereo system, I felt alternately exhausted and wired—probably from the strong coffee I had been sipping all day, trying to stay alert. I saw some clients who felt like one-timers to me, not like people with whom I'd be building a lasting relationship. Like, for example, a slight woman with waist-length dark gray hair, whom I silently named Morticia the moment she was led to my station. During our consultation, she told me that she hadn't washed her hair in three weeks. And I'd thought my day couldn't get any worse. I had my assistant shampoo Morticia's hair three times before I could bear even to touch her.

"So is there some sort of . . . philosophy? In not washing your hair?" I finally asked her, striving for a delicate tone. What I really wanted to do was throw her out of the salon. I mean, *eeeew*. Who knew what she had crawling around in there?

"Um . . . well, the guy who cuts my hair says it's good for the follicle . . . the oil . . ." Morticia waved her hand in the air grandly. As I covered her gray, I also covered my surprise that there was someone she actually referred to as *the guy who cuts my hair,* given that, by my estimation, scissors hadn't touched her hair in, oh, a decade.

"And who's that?" I asked.

Morticia gave a name—a name I won't even mention here. Suffice it to say that it was one of the most famous names in the salon world, a British stylist whose multiple, very chic salons are scattered all over the globe. I wondered if Morticia was pulling my leg, but I let it go. There are some things you just can never know for sure.

By the time three o'clock rolled around, I had actually forgotten that I had agreed to squeeze (okay, it wasn't much of a squeeze) T into my schedule. I felt her enter the salon before I saw her. She was the kind of person who shifted the molecules in the air, changed the whole feeling of a room. Then I heard her voice rising above the salon's steady hum of blow-dryers.

"I *know* I'm not on the schedule, darling," she said, making the word *darling* sound like *asshole*. And then she appeared behind me, carrying two dozen perfect, pale cream roses in her arms.

She thrust them at me. "For you."

I was genuinely surprised, though I shouldn't have been. There was a reason T was one of the most successful publicists in the movie and television business. And music business. And book business. She knew—at all times, even while sleeping—

which side her bread was buttered on. And if she always wanted to be squeezed in for highlights, well, then she had to make a big impression.

"Thank you." I kissed her on both cheeks. We always kissed the clients on both cheeks. It was the French way, after all.

Then she leaned over, closer to me, and I was momentarily engulfed in a sweet cloud of Fracas—a heavy though rather beautiful scent that many of the clients of a certain age wore.

"Congratulations," she whispered in my ear.

I looked at her blankly. She was so close to my face that I could see tiny black-and-blue marks where the crease between her eyebrows ought to be. She must have just been Botoxed.

"The new salon," she whispered.

I felt the floor buckle beneath my feet, a seismic shift. *Holy shit.* How the hell had T found out? If T knew, it was as good as on the front page of the *Post*.

"T, listen, this is still a secret, and—"

"Don't worry," she interrupted. She made a motion like a zipper across her mouth. "It's in the vault."

"How did you—"

"Claudia G," she said.

"Wait a minute. How did Claudia—"

"Mrs. K," said T. She seemed to be enjoying this. Of course she was enjoying this. Publicists lived for this kind of thing—knowing what's happening before anybody else. But there was one thing she obviously didn't know. Somehow it had eluded her gossip radar that Massimo and I had broken up and that I was no longer a partner in the new salon.

She sat in my chair as I sent my assistant to put the roses in a vase. (We kept an entire shelf of extra vases in the staff room for the flowers the clients brought us.) Should I tell her? I wasn't sure what to do. Doreen had taught me, many years earlier, that when I wasn't sure what to say, I shouldn't say anything. So I started to work on T's hair, which, truth be told, was suffering from a lifetime of too much color. It was only with the help of styling products and an expert blow-dry that it looked sleek and healthy. It was, in fact, a strawlike mess.

"Are you all right, darling?" T asked. She sounded ever so slightly annoyed. I was being quieter than usual, not full of the day's gossip.

"Of course. What do you mean?"

"Your hands, darling. They're shaking."

I looked down at my hands, which were, indeed, trembling slightly.

"I'm a little hung over," I lied. "Too much champagne last night."

"I have just the thing for you," T said. She bent and picked up her bag—Hermès ostrich, encased in Jean-Luc's signature plastic (which, since our move to WXYZ, was embossed with small JLs, just like everything else in the salon that wasn't nailed down)—and pulled a silver pill case from an inside compartment.

"Try this." She offered me a tiny seaweed-colored pill.

"What is it?" I asked, examining it in the palm of my hand. No way in hell was I taking that thing. I was trying to figure out how to fake it.

"An herbal remedy," T said in that conspiratorial whisper of hers. If a whisper could carry across a room, it was T's. "I get it from Doctor Zee."

I stuck the pill under my tongue. Dr. Zee was a Chinese nutritionist/herbalist/acupuncturist so famous with the Upper East Side set that they actually ventured, in their chauffeur-driven cars, to Queens, a borough none of them ever set foot in except when they flew commercial out of JFK or La Guardia. Dr. Zee, whose injections and potions and little pills were legend.

I surreptitiously spat out the pill into a tissue when T bent to put her bag back on the lower shelf. Call me paranoid, but I don't like taking pills from strange unknown doctors.

All the while, I was thinking, *What the fuck am I going to do?* I needed to warn Patrick and Massimo, and I needed to do it fast. I didn't know exactly what would happen if Jean-Luc caught wind of their new salon before they were ready—but I knew it would be a disaster.

I worked as fast as I could on T's *baliage*. I had a couple of clients after her, but I figured I could probably call in some favors with one of the other colorists. I was always filling in for one or another. I needed to get out of there—to get downtown. It was the least I could do.

I finished T's *baliage* and led her over to the heat lamps. I had never done this before, and I would never do it again, but I had to leave while she was still processing.

"Twenty minutes," I told my assistant. I looked around to see who looked least stressed out. Who was the calmest, most centered, most likely to help me out colorist at the Salon Jean-Luc that afternoon? Of course. It was Faith Honeycomb.

She was standing by the window, looking out over the city. Her snow white hair was so razor straight in back that it looked as if it could slice right through something. From where I stood, I could see the angle of her jaw and cheekbone. Faith was untouched by plastic surgeons, dermatologists, even colorists. She was purely who she was.

I walked up to the window and stood next to her, surveying the view. The afternoon shoppers on Fifth Avenue looked as small as ants from our perch way up in the sky.

"Excuse me, Faith?"

She looked at me, her eyes clear and blue, bright with her own inner spark.

"Yes, dear?" Her voice was gentle.

"I have an emergency," I said. "Is there any way you could possibly—"

"Not a problem." She didn't even let me finish the sentence. She put a cool hand on my bare forearm, resting it there for a moment. I felt inexplicably calmed. "I hope everything turns out all right."

Impulsively, I kissed her on the cheek.

"Thank you, thank you."

So I LEFT T under the heat lamps and at least one client waiting on the banquette and took the elevators down to the massive lobby of the WXYZ building. Midafternoon on a summer Monday, hailing a cab was easy. Traffic, however, was another story. Park Avenue was a massive snarl, and Lexington was worse.

"What's going on?" I asked the driver.

He shook his head back and forth. "The president is at the Waldorf," he said in a lilting accent. "Traffic's no good."

Chaos and cacophony. Horns blared. Drivers cut their air-conditioning and opened their car windows to avoid overheating. In the cramped backseat of the taxi, separated from the driver by a scratched plastic partition, I was sweating as if I had just run five miles. I piled my hair up into a clip, to at least get it off my neck. Great. I was going to see Massimo looking like a complete and total slob.

But of course that wasn't what was important. What was important was letting Massimo and Patrick know that there had been a leak. The news had gotten out. I didn't trust T as far as I could throw her. I just knew she was going to plant a small item somewhere. "Page Six"? *Women's Wear Daily*? It didn't matter. Jean-Luc had a clipping service tracking any and all mentions of the salon in the press. It could be in the fucking *Chattanooga Times* and Jean-Luc would still see it.

Well then. You might ask why, if time was of the essence, did I not just pick up the phone and call Massimo down at the new salon. A reasonable question. And there are two different answers. One, the phone system had not, to the best of my knowledge, been connected. And two, even if it had been, I guess, if I'm being honest, I wanted to see Massimo. Maybe if I could really show him that I still cared . . . if I could save the day . . . maybe . . . what? He'd stop hating me so much? He'd open himself up to me again? Well, anything was worth a try.

By the time the taxi deposited me in front of the building on Mott Street, I was the one who looked as though she needed saving. Without even looking in a mirror, I knew that my cheeks were red and splotchy, my hair damp and limp, and whatever makeup I had started the day with was smeared under my eyes. I looked like a sweaty pink raccoon.

The front door of the salon was locked, and when I peered through the glass, I saw the lower half of a man on a ladder. I knocked, then watched as the man slowly climbed down and came to unlock the door. He was wearing work pants, a T-shirt, and a tool belt. A blast of cool air greeted me. Thank goodness they had gotten the air-conditioning to work.

"Are Massimo and Patrick here?" I asked.

"Upstairs, in the office," said the man.

I started for the stairs.

"Wait a minute—they expecting you?" he asked.

"It's okay, I'm . . ." I faltered. I'm . . . what? Massimo's ex-girlfriend? Patrick's ex–old friend? Their nonpartner? "It's okay," I said more firmly. The guy got out of the way when he saw the look on my face.

As I WALKED quickly up the stairs, I couldn't help but notice how totally beautiful the salon looked. To tell the truth, it looked a little *too* beautiful. As though Massimo and Patrick had been hemorrhaging cash. It was flooded with natural light, and every detail was perfectly chic, from the Jonathan Adler white vases at each station to the vintage photographs of downtown New York, framed in slightly distressed wood.

Massimo's dark head poked out of a door at the top of the stairs. His recent impassivity toward me was replaced, at that moment, by a combination of genuine surprise and annoyance. I had caught him off guard. But wait, I thought hopefully. Was there maybe just a tiny bit of gladness to see me?

"Georgia!" he exclaimed.

I heard Patrick in the background, saying, *"What?"*

"What are you doing?" Massimo asked. "I mean, here? What are you doing here?"

"They know," I said breathlessly.

"Who knows? Knows what?" Patrick was now standing next to Massimo at the top of the stairs.

"They— Can I come in?"

They moved out of the way, and I walked into their office. It was just as I'd pictured it during the nights and nights of poring over our architectural plans: a bright, airy, private space. A sanctuary. Tacked to the corkboard over the single desk were postcards, clippings from magazines—images of art, nature, and beautiful women, ranging from Isabella Rossellini to Louise

Nevelson, that were inspirational. A brand-new cappuccino maker gleamed on a small table set up in the corner. I remembered the china cups lined up next to it from Massimo's apartment and felt a pang. I had drunk my morning coffee out of those cups every morning, and I had been so happy. So blindly happy, with no sense of there being a limit to my happiness—a dead end to the road I was on.

"What's going on?" asked Patrick. He straddled a swivel chair and waited for me to answer. Massimo was perched by the door, ready to flee.

"They . . . um . . . T was . . . ," I stumbled. Why was this so hard? "T had an appointment today, and she . . . she congratulated me on the new salon."

They looked at me blankly.

"Which means . . . she knows about it," I said, gaining strength. "She heard about it from Claudia G, who heard about it from—"

"Mrs. K," Massimo finished my sentence.

I was stunned.

"How did you know that?" I asked Massimo.

He leaned against the door frame. His physical presence, being so near to him, was almost more than I could take.

"Because I told Mrs. K to tell Claudia G," he said matter-of-factly. "And I knew that of course Claudia G would tell T."

I looked from Massimo to Patrick, then back to Massimo. Patrick didn't even blink. Obviously this was some sort of master plan.

"So you knew . . ."

"We are opening later this week," said Massimo. "We're ready."

"So let the rumors begin!" Patrick laughed.

I burst into tears. Actually burst, as in exploded. The two of them just looked at me, a little surprised, I'm sure. I don't think either of them had ever seen me in quite such a state.

"I thought . . . but I thought . . . ," I managed to stutter.

They just kept staring at me. They weren't going to help me out of this.

"We're telling Jean-Luc tomorrow," Massimo finally said. "So it's time for some free publicity. Obviously, we couldn't tell T directly—it was much better for her to hear it as gossip. There will be an item on 'Page Six' on Wednesday. And a mention in *New York* magazine's 'Intelligencer' column next Monday."

As usual, Massimo had thought through every angle. The whole thing suddenly felt so real. Not that it hadn't been real before, but this was different. This was *now*. The idea that they were going to be gone, that I wouldn't see them every single day as I had for years, was something I had known, of course. But knowing something is going to happen down the road is way different from having it happen in front of you, one painful minute at a time.

"I'm sorry—" I gulped. I couldn't get a grip on myself. I had turned into a regular Miss Waterworks. "I'm going now."

My eyes met Massimo's for a split second as I sidled past him, moving in the direction of the stairs. There was so much anger and disappointment between us, it seemed impossible. We loved each other. That hadn't changed for me, and I had to believe that it hadn't changed for him, either. Why couldn't we be together? This released a whole fresh torrent of tears. I ran down the stairs, past the guy painting the ceiling, and out the door onto sweltering Mott Street.

THE NEXT MORNING, showing up at work was the last thing I wanted to do. I walked all the way to the salon from my apartment, moving slowly through the rush-hour crowds. As I always did, I stopped on the corner of Fifty-ninth and Lexington and scanned the front pages of the papers. I was half expecting to see a huge headline in the *Post*: SALON JEAN-LUC DEFECTION! UPPER EAST SIDE HAIR STARS HEAD DOWNTOWN! I went into a deli and bought myself an iced coffee, then sipped it as I walked. Finally, I couldn't dawdle any longer. My first client was at ten o'clock.

I couldn't imagine what the day would bring. The wrath of Jean-Luc had already scared the shit out of me more than once. And I had a feeling that I hadn't even seen the tip of that particular iceberg. Why was I so nervous? It wasn't me going in there to quickly and efficiently announce my departure. It wasn't me who was going to have to duck when Jean-Luc threw a chair in his rage. I couldn't imagine how I'd feel if I had actually been planning to go in there with Patrick and Massimo. I wished I had asked them what time they planned to do the dirty deed.

Every single thing I did felt like the last time I'd be doing it alongside Massimo and Patrick. The elevator rose to the top floor, the numbers whizzing by. The doors *swooshed* open, and the cool, scented air of the salon engulfed me immediately, as it always did. But it all felt different. And not in a good way. I was sad, bereft. A chapter in my life was ending, and the new chapter already felt lonely and scary. I scanned the floor and saw Massimo and Patrick, both at their usual stations. The salon was already very busy, even this early in the day.

My first client was the wife of the editorial director of one of the hot women's magazines, herself a former model. I wove two colors of blond—ice white and a reddish strawberry—onto her wavy hair.

"Are you coming out east this weekend?" she asked. *Out east.* I knew that her house—one of those rambling, shingled cottages—was perfectly situated on Georgica Pond in East Hampton.

"I didn't get a place this year," I said. Even if Massimo and I had been together, we had planned to spend the whole summer, and every last penny, on the new salon.

I looked over at Massimo's station. He was trimming the bangs of the socialite wife of a plastic surgeon. He seemed completely focused on her, not remotely nervous. As if this were a day like any other day. Not a care in the world, that Massimo.

Faith Honeycomb was at her station by the window, doing a single-process. When she had finished and had a free moment, she came over to me.

"Did everything go okay yesterday?" she asked.

"Yes—thank you," I said. She was being so kind to me. "Was everybody okay here?" I asked Faith. "The clients?"

"Your files were perfect," said Faith. "But more importantly, I'm glad you're all right. Feel free to ask, anytime."

Faith headed back to her station and began to work on an actress who looked familiar but whom I couldn't quite place. And I went back to the line of clients who were already piling up on the banquette. I was afraid even to look at my schedule, I had such a crazy day. Which, I guess, was a godsend. At least I couldn't focus too hard on Massimo and Patrick. I had caught only a glimpse of Patrick when I'd first walked in. He was doing an elaborate updo on a women's talk show host.

I did a quick single-process, and then Mrs. H was next. Her corrected formula was already waiting for me, ready to go. Chestnut and golden auburn. An elegant combination, I must say, which took more years off her face than cosmetic surgery. I wove the colors onto her hair, trying to stay centered. I was having trouble concentrating—not on my work, but on the usual gossipy conversation. The clients expected this. They expected you to be up on all the current events, movies, restaurants, fashion, and, most of all, scandals. They seemed to know who else had recently been in my chair. If I did highlights for the wife of the leading contender for the Democratic nomination, they knew that—and asked me what I thought his chances were. As if I would know. And if I did a single-process on the new chef of a trendy brownstone restaurant in the West Village, they thought that meant I could get them a table. But today I just didn't have it in me.

"Did you hear about Mitzi P?" Mrs. H asked, one eyebrow raised ironically, as if to imply that she didn't actually care about that week's social tragedy: a middle-aged heiress whose husband had run off with . . . the au pair? a flight attendant? his secretary? I couldn't remember. I didn't care. I made a few noises, but the conversation sort of sputtered out. I could tell that Mrs. H was disappointed.

"Fifteen minutes under the lamps," I said, finishing her up in record time. I made sure she was settled and content, with a British *Vogue* and a café au lait balanced precariously on her lap.

It was then that I heard a crash and a sickening thud behind me. The sound of a person falling to the ground with no resistance is horrifying, jarring. It is at once muffled and loud. It cuts through everything else.

For a split second, the salon became dead quiet. Blow-dryers were turned off. Conversation stopped. Someone screamed. I spun around, and there was Faith, collapsed on the tile floor, her hair fanning around her head like a halo. Her eyes were closed, and the corners of her lips were turned up, as if whatever thought she'd had before falling had been a happy one.

"Somebody do something!" I heard shouting and realized it was my own voice. "Call 911!" I looked around wildly. Everyone was moving too slowly. No. There was Massimo, a phone pressed to his ear. He was speaking fiercely, urgently, into the receiver, relaying all the pertinent information. Of course it was Massimo. Who else but Massimo?

A few assistants and one client were bent over Faith.

"Give her air." Patrick moved toward the group. "She needs air."

Sweetie was wailing in the background, which wasn't helping matters. His voice was so high-pitched, it sounded almost like an ambulance's siren.

"Does anyone here know CPR?" Patrick asked. "Is there a doctor here? Or a nurse?" The clients, stylists, and assistants were all frozen. This wasn't supposed to happen in a beauty salon on a beautiful summer Tuesday. And this wasn't supposed to happen to Faith Honeycomb.

"Faith!" Sweetie wailed. "Wake up!"

"The ambulance, it is on its way," said Massimo. He bent over Faith and gently lifted her head and placed a small pillow beneath it. Patrick and Massimo each tried to find a pulse.

"You know, this happened to my daughter-in-law," said one of the clients, who stood off to the side, bare arms crossed over her burgundy robe. "She just fainted one day—turned out that it was an anaphylactic reaction to a perfume she had just tried at the counter at Barneys."

"She has a pulse," said Massimo. I must say, he was being amazing.

"Thank God," somebody breathed.

A commotion at the door, the sound of metal clanging, of

squeaking wheels against the uneven tiles, moving around the fountain. The paramedics had arrived—big men in uniforms who looked completely incongruous amid the potions and mirrors and vases of flowers.

"Move out of the way!" one of them shouted. "Coming through!" They loosened the top of Faith's smock and attached sticky heart monitors to her paper white chest.

"What happened here? Did she fall?" one of them asked the group of us.

"She seemed to just pass out," I said.

An oxygen mask was clamped, almost immediately, over the lower half of Faith's face. They hoisted her onto the stretcher and checked her vitals at the same time, then carried her out on a stretcher.

"Where are you taking her?" Massimo called after them.

"Lenox Hill," one of the paramedics said.

Patrick had moved next to me without my even sensing his presence. "Looks like a heart attack to me," he said.

Tears sprang to my eyes. "Don't say that!" I cried.

Patrick grabbed my hand and held it. "Honey, it won't make it any less true."

As Faith's stretcher disappeared into the elevator, everyone still seemed to be rooted to the same spot. Massimo stood near the door, his head bowed. I saw his lips moving, and I realized, with a start, that he was praying. When he had finished, he opened his eyes and looked at me. We just stood there, Massimo and me, looking at each other, as slowly the salon around us started to sputter back to life. I didn't want to look away. I'll tell you, all I wanted was to be with that man—to see him and be seen by him, to love him and be loved by him—for the rest of my life.

"I am going to the hospital," said Massimo.

I nodded. Of course he was going. Someone had to be there for Faith.

He looked at his waiting clients on the banquette.

"I am sorry," he said. "She has no one." His voice caught in his throat, but then he got hold of himself. "We . . . we are her family."

WHAT IS THERE that can be said about the hours that followed? A day doesn't recover from events such as these. Clients came, clients went. Jean-Luc asked me to take over Faith's waiting clients along with my own. Somehow time slowly ticked by. My fingers ached, and I had a throbbing pain in my head. For a few of us, Faith's condition was the only thing on our minds. But for most everybody else, it might as well have happened on daytime television.

Finally, it got to me. What can I say? I needed—as in required, craved, couldn't live without—a cigarette. I probably smoked five cigarettes a year, but this was one of those moments. Massimo still wasn't back from the hospital. There was no word on Faith's condition. Patrick and I kept looking at each other over the clients' heads, trying to connect, to steady ourselves. If nothing else, the events of the day had cut through a lot of bullshit.

I went to the stairwell—expressly forbidden, but what choice did I have?—with a cigarette I had bummed from one of the assistants, and I lit up. I tried to slow my breathing, get a grip. I exhaled a thin stream of smoke through my nostrils. And then, as my mind slowed down, it occurred to me: It had been a while since I'd seen Jean-Luc. Where the hell had he gone in the middle of this crisis? I noticed that the door at the top of the service stairs was open. These doors were never to be opened, and they were to be used by staff only in the event of fire—so quickly, quietly, doing nothing more than following a hunch, I walked upstairs. The door to the Jean-Luc conference room at the top of the stairs was open as well.

"So there are no loopholes in the coverage?" I heard Jean-Luc's voice.

"Of course not—we're covered. Absolutely. I'll have the papers brought up from Business Affairs just to make you comfortable, but believe me, in terms of liability, we have no problem—"

I was pretty sure I recognized the voice of Ms. WXYZ.

"This stupid woman . . ." Jean-Luc's voice got a little louder. "What if she says she slipped on the tiles? Or developed a sudden toxic reaction?"

I backed away slowly, the way you move away from a dangerous animal likely to pounce. I felt nauseated. Really, I know people say that, but I thought I was going to puke. How many years had Faith worked for Jean-Luc? And before that, how many years had they known each other?

I stubbed out my cigarette in the stairwell. Doreen had taught me many lessons in life, and one of them came roaring into my head: *God's talking to you all the time,* she used to say. *All you have to do is listen.* And by *God* she didn't mean that big, all-knowing man in the sky. She was a little too cynical and beaten up for that. No, she meant that only a fool would look right at a sign and not be able to read it.

AT SIX THAT evening, Massimo walked in the door of Salon Jean-Luc. He looked weary and enormously burdened. I knew how much he admired Faith. We all saw her as the best of the best.

She was such an idol, it seemed impossible that she could be so sick. Or worse.

"The doctors are hopeful," he said simply. "But they are keeping her in intensive care. They think . . . maybe she passed out from stress. They are waiting for test results."

We stood huddled together, Massimo, Patrick, and me. And while I was very worried about Faith, the words running through my mind, right at that moment, were *We are together.* I was never letting them go. Not for anything in the world, including my own stupid fear.

"So, my friend . . ." Massimo turned to Patrick with a deep sigh. "The timing is not good, but we have no choice. It will be in the newspaper tomorrow. So shall we go see Jean-Luc?"

Patrick nodded, a small, resigned nod. It wasn't supposed to be like this. This was their moment of glory. The two of them began to walk to the elevator, where they would go one flight up to Jean-Luc's office. They were almost at the door of the salon when I sprinted across the floor, toward them.

"Wait!" I called.

They turned back to me, my two men.

"I want to come with you," I said.

Massimo looked at me.

"Can I come with you?" I repeated. "Please?"

They both stood by the door. My God. What if they didn't want me anymore? What if it was too late?

But then Massimo reached out a hand.

"Let's go, partner," he said.

Color War

Doreen's Salon on Mott Street in the then little-known New York City neighborhood of NoLIta threw open its doors on a beautiful, warm summer morning. Our first appointments were scheduled for ten o'clock. The night before, we had called all of the clients who had upcoming appointments with the three of us at Jean-Luc. In fact, we called all of our clients, period. Everyone who had ever seen us at Jean-Luc was now going to be coming down to Doreen's.

"Hello, Mrs. L? This is Massimo from Jean-Luc, here. Well, actually—I'm no longer from Jean-Luc. Wait—don't worry. I'm calling to tell you that we've opened a brand-new salon on Mott Street. . . . No, let me spell it for you . . . M-o-t-t . . . That's right. In NoLIta. That's downtown. Yes, downtown Manhattan. You'll see it in the newspaper tomorrow. I just want to confirm that we are holding your eleven-thirty appointment for you . . . Oh, very good. We'll see you tomorrow, then. *Ciao!*"

We made call after call from the lists that Patrick and Massimo had carefully been compiling over the past months. Everyone said they'd be coming. Everyone! We were overcaffeinated from our morning cappuccinos and so full of energy that we could have run around the island of Manhattan.

To top it off, early that first morning, the phones began to ring with calls from assistants who worked at the Salon Jean-Luc.

"Doreen's Salon, can I help you?" I answered the phone that first morning. It was ringing even as we unlocked the front door. *Doreen's, can I help you?* It was a phrase as familiar to me as my own face in the mirror—and one I never thought would be a part of my life, ever again.

"Georgia?"

"Yes?"

"This is Tiffany."

My heart skipped a beat. I was afraid it was all about to start: the anger, the betrayal, the recriminations.

"What's up, Tiff?" I asked, striving for a casual tone.

"I saw it in the *Post* this morning," she said. "That's why I'm calling."

"Listen," I said, "I'm sorry, I—"

"Can I come work for you guys?" she blurted out.

I felt the warm, safe sensation that I'd had since the moment I had made the decision to go with Patrick and Massimo.

"Of course," I said. I was a little choked up.

"Emilio and Sue want to come as well," she went on. "Have you guys hired assistants yet?"

We hadn't. Massimo had foreseen this happening, I suddenly realized. And of course he couldn't have asked any of the Jean-Luc staff to join us. But, as it turned out, he didn't have to.

"Tell them to come on down," I said.

I hung up the phone and turned cheerfully to Massimo,

who was arranging a huge spray of orchids and freesia in a simple, square vase.

"Tiffany, Emilio, and Sue," I said.

"And Lori and Geoffrey as well," he said.

"God. Jean-Luc is going to freak out," I groaned.

"*Going* to?"

I thought back to the previous night. Jean-Luc had been calm—scarily calm—when we walked into his office and told him we were leaving. The only telltale sign of whatever must have been boiling inside him was a whiteness around his lips that appeared almost instantly, like an overnight frost. He listened quietly from behind his desk as Massimo said the words, simply, economically: *We are leaving and will be opening our own salon.* And then Jean-Luc rose, glided across his office, and held the door open for us. He motioned us, with a sweep of his arm, to leave. As I walked by him, I felt the force field of his rage.

"He's losing, like, half of the good assistants," I said to Massimo, who had arranged the flowers so beautifully, they looked as if they had just been delivered by a florist.

"We will hear from him," Massimo said. "I'm sure of that. He'll probably make voodoo dolls of each of us and stick them with pins."

"Don't say that!"

"Come on, *bella.* I'm only joking."

Massimo didn't sound worried. Not at all. And something had happened to me. I didn't understand it and couldn't possibly have explained it, but all my fear had drained away, and I was left with the contented feeling that it would all, somehow, be fine.

"Come here, Georgia," Massimo said, his arms spread wide. He engulfed me in a bear hug, squeezing me so tightly that the breath was knocked out of me. We had come so close to losing each other, though now, being held by him, it seemed inevitable that we were together. "I am so very, very glad that you are here."

"Me too," I said softly. "I'm so, so sorry that I—"

"Let's move on," Massimo interrupted, pressing a finger to my lips. "When something is right, it takes its own time, yes?"

AT TEN O'CLOCK, the music in the salon was playing—Massimo's favorite jazz classics—and the flowers were arranged perfectly at each station. The scissors and combs were spread on spanking white towels, and my station was ready, with rolling tables, packets of foils, hairpins, long strips of cotton. The first assistants from Jean-Luc had arrived—the ones who'd quit the minute they'd heard the news.

The clock ticked past ten. The clients were late. Then it was ten-fifteen. Then ten-thirty. I was beginning to get a sick feeling in the pit of my stomach. We should have had half a dozen clients coming in by now, and no one had shown up. Could they *all* just be running late? Perhaps it was a coincidence.

"Maybe they are having trouble finding Mott Street," said Massimo. "Many of them have never been in this neighborhood."

"Or maybe they misunderstood," said Patrick. "They might have thought we were opening next week, not this week."

They seemed to be grasping at straws.

"Well, let's use the time, since I'm sure it's going to get busy later in the day," I said. "There's still a lot that needs doing around here."

And this was true. There were a thousand kinks to work out. The lighting in the color station was not as bright as it needed to be, so we called the lighting designer. The front door made a squeaking sound as it closed, so Patrick ran down to the hardware store and picked up some oil. The CD player got jammed, but Massimo managed to unjam it.

It was noon. Then two. Then three-thirty. And not a single client who had promised to come had walked through the open door of the salon.

"Um . . . Georgia?" Tiffany came up to me as I stood near the back doors that led to the perfect cobblestone garden, where we imagined that clients would sit in the sunlight as their highlights processed.

"Yeah, Tiff?"

"Don't take this the wrong way, but . . . is this going to be okay? I mean, I thought the clients would all be here."

"So did we," I said. "So did we."

"So this is going to be harder than we thought," Patrick said from behind us. "That shouldn't really be surprising. I mean, we're asking them to change their whole way of thinking. Uptown to downtown. It's a completely different vibe."

"Yeah, but is it a vibe they're going to get?" Tiffany asked nervously. I couldn't blame her for being nervous. At least at Jean-Luc she had made some kind of living from her tips. Here, if there were no clients, she'd have nothing. We'd all have nothing. I swallowed hard against the fear. I wasn't going to allow it to creep back in.

"That's right," I said brightly. "It's going to take some work. But look at this place!" I spread my arms wide. "Isn't it the most beautiful salon you've ever seen?"

And it was. It truly was.

Just at that moment, a girl walked through the front door. It was all we could do not to jump. She walked over to the reception desk. I didn't recognize her as one of the Jean-Luc clients. She had bright red hair, *definitely* not Upper East Side. She was wearing faded jeans and an orange-and-green tank top. A small diamond stud glimmered on the side of her nose.

"Can we help you?" asked Massimo, who was the first to reach her.

"Is this place new?" she asked, looking around.

"We opened today," said Massimo.

She did a full circle, checking the place out. "Nice," she said.

"Thank you," Massimo said a little stiffly. *Nice.* She couldn't do better than that? The poor girl. We were hanging a whole day's worth of disappointment on her shoulders.

"How much for a haircut?" she asked. She ran a hand through her bright red mop top.

"Ninety for a junior stylist, and one fifty for a senior stylist," said Massimo.

She cocked her head. "One hundred and fifty dollars?" she asked. Her whole body was practically exploding with disbelief.

"Yes," said Massimo. "We are from—"

She shook her head, as if she were truly sorry.

"Shit. One hundred and fifty dollars. What kind of moron would pay one fifty for a haircut?"

She turned around and walked out the door, her hips swaying in her faded jeans. She let out a chuckle just as the door was closing behind her. *One hundred and fifty dollars for a haircut,* I heard her say, laughing.

THINGS DIDN'T IMPROVE much over the next few days. Oh, there were a couple of intrepid clients who found their way down to Mott Street. The magazine editor came. And one particularly brave client from Short Hills, who said that actually we were closer now that she could drive through the Holland Tunnel. Some clients had their secretaries call to cancel. Others simply didn't show up. In the meantime, we found out that Jean-Luc had sent out a massive mailing.

Dear Loyal Jean-Luc Client, it began. *We would like to extend to you an offer for a complimentary haircut with any of our senior stylists, along with an electrical current facial with Violet, our newest aesthetician. And while you relax in the comfortable environs of Salon Jean-Luc, we have the world-renowned plastic surgeon Dr. Derick Dermis on hand to perform complimentary Botox to clients of Jean-Luc during the summer months.*

Jesus H. Christ. How were we supposed to compete with that? Jean-Luc was offering literally hundreds of dollars of free services.

"We need to think about how long we can go on this way," I said to Massimo on the fourth afternoon.

"I know exactly how long we can go on," said Massimo. "Three months. We have thirty thousand dollars to float us— ten thousand a month. If we haven't turned things around by then . . ." He trailed off. I wasn't sure which he felt worse about: his miscalculation about the clients following us downtown or dragging me along with him. I was doing everything I could not to make him feel bad, but it was impossible. We were all on this sinking ship together.

So IT WAS a Wednesday afternoon, at the beginning of the second week of business. Massimo and I had opened the shop at nine in the morning—way too early for the sleepy, Bohemian neighborhood, where people started to tumble out of bed at ten or eleven, and most stores—with the exception of the twenty-four-hour bodega—didn't open until noon. But what the hell else were we going to do? Sit around and be depressed at home?

No. Instead, Massimo, Patrick, and I sat around, depressed, sipping our take-out cappuccinos in the back garden.

"Who's that guy?" Massimo looked through the glass doors.

I looked into the salon and saw a man standing in the reception area, shifting his weight from one foot to the other. He didn't look like a client, much less one of the downtown hipsters who kept wandering in to tell us that we were overcharging. Anyway, this guy—how can I put this without sounding like a horrible snob? Oh well. I probably can't, so here goes: He was wearing a tan suit, and not a nice tan suit. Like, a suit from Sears. And his shoes were black—a dull, scuffed black, with rubber soles. I took all this in as I paused for a moment and watched. He seemed to be asking the receptionist a question. I saw her hesitate for a moment, then point her finger into the garden, at us.

I started feeling a little anxious, though I had no idea why. My palms were sweating. The three of us didn't move. We just sat still on the custom-made wrought-iron lawn chairs that we'd had designed for the salon by an artist in TriBeCa.

"Georgia Watkins?"

I stood up, a little dizzy from the blood rushing to my head. "Yes?"

"Ladies first," he said, handing me a large, official-looking manila envelope. And at that moment, I realized why he seemed familiar. He looked like a detective on a television show or a plainclothes cop.

"What's this?"

"A subpoena," he said, a flicker of pleasure in his eye. Then he turned and handed a similar envelope to Massimo. Then to Patrick.

"Did you just say subpoena?" Patrick asked.

"Jean-Luc is suing us," Massimo said flatly.

There was no question.

"But he can't do that!" I cried.

The man in the bad suit had already turned and walked out. I'm sure he had somebody else's day to ruin.

"Let's go," said Massimo.

We all filed upstairs. The assistants in the salon looked at us, worried, but we didn't try to reassure them this time. This time, we were scared to death.

Massimo dialed the number. Patrick reached over and held my hand.

"Hello, I need to speak with Mr. K," said Massimo. "I don't care if he's in a meeting. This is an emergency."

IT IS A measure of a successful partnership to be able to navigate through a crisis with a clear head and a strong heart. On the clear-head front, it was seven at night and we were waiting for Mr. K at one of those fancy midtown steak restaurants where the martinis are served in bathtub-size glasses.

And we were drinking them. A doctor would have prescribed them, really. We were all just a little bit in shock. I mean, Jean-Luc had threatened to sue Richard when Richard had opened his own salon—but Jean-Luc had not actually served him with papers.

"He's out of his fucking mind," Patrick muttered.

"Well, we knew that already," said Massimo.

The papers were spread in front of us on the cocktail table.

It seemed—no, it didn't seem, it was a fact—that Jean-Luc was suing each of us, Massimo, Patrick, and me, for a million dollars a piece. A million dollars! The words and numbers floated before my eyes, forming, then dissolving, then forming again. It was impossible to believe. We had *stolen trade secrets*. We had created *unfair competition*. The lawsuit went on to explain that every client benefited from *a secret formula*.

"Secret formula!" Patrick exploded. "Tell that to Edna Bosco!"

"Who is Edna Bosco?" Massimo asked.

"Our teacher in beauty school, back in Weekeepeemie," I answered. Thinking of Mrs. Bosco almost made me smile. Almost. She had taught me one of the greatest lessons a colorist can learn: In a pinch, a jar of Jolen will do.

"This is insane." Patrick downed the rest of his martini. "I mean, everybody does what we're doing. Everybody."

"What are you talking about?" I asked.

"Every single salon owner has had this done to them—from Kenneth to Vidal Sassoon. People leave. They go out on their own. He should just be grateful that we didn't do it right around the corner."

"Jean-Luc himself left Hiroshi to go out on his own," Massimo said with a small smile.

"You would think he'd understand," said Patrick. "I mean, I don't expect his blessing or anything, but this"—he slapped a hand down on the pile of papers—"this is a terrible thing to do."

"Hello, folks."

Mr. K plopped himself down in the empty chair that was waiting for him. He pulled a handkerchief from the breast pocket of his suit and patted beads of perspiration off his bald head.

"How are you all holding up?" he asked.

"Not so good," said Patrick.

"Full of questions," said Massimo.

And me, I was mute. What happens when the thing you fear most is in danger of coming true? All I kept thinking was, *We were so close. So close to having it all.*

"He has no case," said Mr. K, who had read the papers we'd faxed over to his office a few hours earlier. "None. This is a frivolous lawsuit. There's no precedent for it. It's meant to scare the shit out of you."

"Well, that part's working," I said.

Mr. K ordered a martini, then pulled a business card from his briefcase and handed it to Massimo. "This is the guy you need to call," he said.

"Who is he?" Massimo asked.

"He's an attorney friend of mine who specializes in this kind of thing," said Mr. K. "He's the best."

Of course he was the best. Everyone Mr. K had sent us to— from the real estate lawyer to the contractor to the book-keeper—had been excellent. And excellently expensive.

"How much is this going to cost?" I asked.

"I spoke with him this afternoon," said Mr. K, avoiding my question. "He's sure he can get the judge to throw this out. But it may take some time."

"How much?" Patrick nudged.

"You can't afford not to do it," said Mr. K.

"How much?" Massimo repeated.

Mr. K sighed. "He wants a retainer. All these guys do. I'm figuring thirty thousand should do it."

THAT NIGHT, I don't think Massimo or I slept a wink. We both tossed and turned, holding on to each other, then letting go, the sheets twisted and damp with sweat. We took our usual solace and comfort in each other's body, the ceiling fan revolving slowly over our heads, circulating the humid air in Massimo's bedroom. What we didn't do was talk.

What, after all, was the point in talking? Thirty thousand dollars. It was eerie, uncanny. It was our only cushion, our precise financial comfort zone, the only way we could possibly get Doreen's Salon off the ground.

In the morning, I guess I had finally fallen asleep, because when I woke up, Massimo was gone. On the bedside table, beneath a ceramic ashtray from a restaurant in Rome, was a note. *I have gone to the salon,* it said. *Meet me there. I love you, M.* I wondered why he had wanted to get to the salon so early. What was the point? What was there to do? I imagined Massimo sitting in the upstairs office, looking at columns of numbers, and trying to get them to add up differently.

I HEADED OVER to Doreen's at a civilized hour. I didn't want to get there too early. The last thing I wanted was to sit in an empty salon with Massimo, the two of us staring miserably at each other. I made my way over to Mott Street from the West Village, walking through Washington Square Park. A few New York University summer students were throwing around a Frisbee. A guy with a long beard sat on a bench, where he looked like he had been all night long. He was talking to himself softly, murmuring gently, as if he were comforting himself.

The shops in NoLIta were all closed, of course. Ever since we'd first begun construction on Doreen's, a few new businesses had opened up. One store sold French children's clothes and was so small that only a few customers could shop there at a time. Another sold outrageous lingerie. The window display was simply a translucent mannequin wearing a pink-and-black conical bra. Who would ever wear that thing? It looked like something Madonna would have worn on tour in the 1980s.

As I rounded the corner onto Mott Street, town cars and limousines clogged the block, double-parked on the narrow side street. There must have been eight or ten of them. What the hell was going on? Had the president stopped at the café for a croissant? Was the prime minister of England picking up a pair of funky shoes for his wife?

A chauffeur popped out of a black Mercedes that was double-parked directly in front of Doreen's. He opened the back door, and I saw one long silky leg extend, its pedicured foot wrapped in a pale lavender Jimmy Choo sandal.

It was an Upper East Side leg, right down to its François Nars cotton candy toes. I recognized it instantly.

"Yoo-hoo!" a honey-toned voice sang out.

Roxanne Middlebury. She saw me standing, frozen, in the middle of the sidewalk and came over and planted a gigantic, bougainvillea pink Chanel kiss on my cheek.

"Roxanne! What are you doing—"

"Hello!" I heard another voice as a limo door clicked quietly closed behind me. I spun around, and there were Muffie Von Hoven and Tamara Stein-Hertz heading toward me, arm in arm.

"Tamara! Muffie!"

A taxi pulled up next to the line of limousines and its battered door opened. I stood, transfixed, to see what was going to happen next. My heart was beginning to pound. Two trousered legs swung to the street, and slowly, very slowly, a sleek, snow white, razor-sharp-bobbed head made its way out of the cab.

"Faith!" I started to cry. "Oh, my God, Faith!"

"Let's all get going. There's a lot to be done," she said crisply.

INSIDE THE SALON, music was playing. Betty Carter's throaty wail filled the salon, the thrumming of a bass. I quickly climbed the stairs, followed by the ladies. I heard voices in the office before I walked inside, and I took a deep breath. I needed to be strong—if not for myself, then for Massimo. I mean, it was nice of the clients (and Faith!) to come, but really, what could anyone do? It was over. I was certain of that.

Massimo was sitting on a swivel chair, and T and Claudia G were perched next to each other on the long wooden desk, their bare, shiny legs swinging in their Lambertson Truex mules.

T was on the phone. She fluttered her fingers at me as I walked into the room. I looked at Massimo. I know I must have appeared completely befuddled, because . . . well, I was. What the hell were all these clients doing in the office? It was rule number one of salon etiquette: Never let the clients see the unsexy, behind-the-scenes inner workings of the salon. No good could ever come of it. It erased the magic.

But here they were nonetheless.

"Richard Johnson, please. T here," T said crisply into the receiver. Her voice affected the slightest hint of a British accent. She thrummed her shiny red nails on the desk.

"Richard! Darling, how are you?" She didn't pause for an answer, just said, "Good, good. And how's your son? Wonderful. Listen, darling—I have a scoop for you. But you've got to promise me the top of 'Page Six' tomorrow. The whole thing."

She paused, winking at Massimo. Then she laughed uproariously, as if Richard Johnson had just said the most hilarious thing. As soon as she stopped laughing, her face became impassive and her brow furrowed (time for Botox!) in determination.

"Jean-Luc, darling. You ready for this? That horrible Frenchman is suing these three delightful, gorgeous, talented young people who just left him and went out on their own. For . . . you'll never believe this . . . a million bucks apiece."

In the meantime, Claudia G had gotten busy working the phones. I handed Massimo his cappuccino and sat on his lap. Claudia peered into the screen of her BlackBerry and dialed a number.

"Kate? It's Claudia G. What are you doing answering your own phone, honey-pie?" A pause. "Oh, I hadn't realized." She clamped a hand over the receiver and whispered, *"Her father's in the hospital,"* rolling her eyes at us. "So are you working? Do you want to hear an amazing story?"

And so it went. By midday, the office on the second floor of Doreen's Salon on Mott Street had so many publicists and so-cialites, movers and shakers who were moving and shaking, that the office smelled like a garden of the world's most expensive perfumes, and the floor was littered with so many handbags that it resembled the accessories department at Barneys. It was a moving, beautiful thing to see, let me tell you. I was overwhelmed by the sight of all these—let's face it—not always so nice women putting aside their work, their hair appointments, and even their petty differences to come to our rescue.

L and M, notorious rivals, teamed up to call Anna Wintour, queen bee of all magazine editors, and secured a feature in *Vogue*. T, in the span of just a few hours, had extracted promises from all the tabloids, *Women's Wear Daily*, and even the business section of the *Times*.

"Don't you guys get it?" she asked, finally taking a break

and sipping one of the endless cups of coffee that the assistants kept bringing in. "Jean-Luc gave you guys a huge gift."

"How's that?" Massimo asked, although in truth he already understood.

"Everybody in the world is going to want to know what makes the three of you so fucking valuable. Why is he suing you for millions? Everybody's going to have to know who you are now."

"These talented, hardworking kids," L said excitedly. "Pursuing their little piece of the American dream."

All the women nodded. "We love an underdog story," one of them said.

"But all that is the truth," I blurted out.

There was a moment of silence in the room as they all pondered the word *truth*, as if it were a seldom seen delicacy, a rare and exotic thing.

"We know that, darling," said T as she picked up the phone once again. "Why do you think we're here?"

Happily Ever After

Somebody famous once said that you can't go home again, but I think you can. And there is nothing sweeter than going home after you've built a life that you love far, far away from that home. Going back is a touchstone, a comforting reminder of all that you've accomplished. But the most important thing is to never, ever forget what got you there in the first place.

When I walk down Main Street in Weekeepeemie, I am Doreen Watkins's daughter, and that's who I always will be. People in Weekeepeemie don't tend to read *Vogue* or *Bazaar,* and even if they did, they'd skip right over an article about a celebrity hair colorist, because, after all, what does that have to do with their lives? They don't know the story behind the lawsuit and the storm of publicity that followed, and how Jean-Luc dropped the lawsuit, but not before making us the most-talked-about salon in New York.

Funny, the way things work.

Every year on Christmas Eve day, Massimo, Patrick, and I close the salon early and head north to Weekeepeemie. And we always arrive just as Doreen and Melodie are putting the finishing touches on the Christmas tree—leaving it to the last possible minute, as happens in so many busy, happy families.

But this year—the fifth year since we opened (and very nearly closed)—instead of our coming to Weekeepeemie, my mother and sister are coming to us. This year, it's been harder for us to get away.

The salon is decorated for Christmas. A wreath hangs on the front door, and tiny white twinkling lights shine on the trees in the garden out back. Reindeer cut like snowflakes from crisp white paper prance across the tops of the mirrors—Massimo's whimsical addition to the decor. And (what can I say?) a jazz version of "Jingle Bells" is playing on the stereo.

We're planning to have the salon's Christmas party tonight—we now have sixty-three employees, including the reservationists and front desk staff—and a light snow has begun to fall just as Doreen pushes open the door to Doreen's and is immediately swept up, engulfed in hug after hug, kiss after kiss, by everyone in the salon. It's a while before I can even get to her—my own mother!—because everyone who works for me, and the clients who have been around since the beginning, love her so much.

"Hi, Mom." I brush her long, wavy hair off her face and we kiss hello. The way she smells, of pinecones and baby powder, never fails to bring tears to my eyes.

Massimo comes up behind her and gives her a squeeze. "Hello, my beautiful mother-in-law."

"Where's my girl?" Doreen asks. Her eyes dart around the salon.

"What do you mean? I'm right here," I tease. I know exactly what she's talking about.

Then she spots what she's looking for. In the reception area, on the floor (newly carpeted for just such a purpose), sits a little girl with wild, wavy blond hair—the kind of hair that no colorist could ever dream up.

"There she is! There's my baby!" Doreen rushes over to her.

She's not playing with blocks, my daughter. She's not even playing with dolls. No. In the last rays of afternoon winter light streaming through the glass front of Doreen's Salon, she is slowly turning the pages of a fashion magazine, pointing to the models, and using her Crayolas to change the color of their hair.